Women
of
Granite

Also by Dana Andrew Jennings

Mosquito Games

Dana Andrew Jennings

Women
of
Granite

Harcourt Brace Jovanovich, Publishers

New York   San Diego   London

HBJ

Library of Congress Cataloging-in-Publication Data
Jennings, Dana Andrew.
Women of granite/Dana Andrew Jennings.—1st ed.
p.   cm.
ISBN 0-15-198367-4
I. Title.
PS3560.E5175W66   1992
813'.54—dc20   91-48174

Designed by Trina Stahl

Printed in the United States of America

First edition
A B C D E

For Deborah, Woman of Granite

FAMILY TREE FOR *Women of Granite*

Nanna Page marries Elgar Felch (he changes his name to Page)

Henry marries
Fat Dot Mott
(they have many
children)
(their daughter Jenny
is the child of
Elgar Felch and
Fat Dot Mott)

Ella marries
Chaney Huckins

Sarah Huckins marries
Russ Britton

Hannah Britton
Wayne Britton
Page Britton

Wayne Britton marries
Charlotte West

Jessie Britton (sold)

Charlotte West marries
Russ Britton

Winona Britton
Nan Britton

William
(Uncle Dead)

Leah marries
Howie DesMarais
(no children)

Robena marries
Allen Swett
(one miscarriage)
(no children)

Prologue

Nanna Page: 1957

ALL THE CHILDREN, but especially the girl children, were warned away from Uncle Billy's shed; warned the same way you tell a child not to fool with matches, or flirt with November ice. But Sarah wanted her bicycle back. Uncle Billy'd already spent three weeks fixing on it. Enough was enough.

As weather-whipped as Billy Page himself, the shed squatted on a knoll above Page's Village, that wild nest of shacks, sheds, and marshland wedged between Route 49 and the piney backside of Cedar Swamp; Uncle Billy, not yet called Uncle Dead, lived in—some say, haunted—those dark woods, keeping his shed as a way station between his Page past and his swampy present.

Sarah slipped up the muddy path, the red-brown muck sucking at her bare feet. Past Auntie Fat Dot's—her aunt's brood, prisoners to the squall that'd just punched through, pressed to the windows—the path skinnied to a one-man rut and Sarah slowed. Knobby granite knuckles poked through the dirt; toothy weeds, tall as brooms, bowed deeply; thorns, thistles and prickaburrs snapped at her ankles. Sarah wasn't so sure she wanted her bicycle anymore, but she refused to go back.

As she crested the hill the late sun, blood-blister red, broke through, kindling the shed windows to bronze fire. A mud wasp—Uncle Billy's sentry?—materialized above a flaming puddle; Sarah jumped. Rainwater dripped from the roof, each quivering droplet shot through with sunlight before it plopped into the rain barrel.

Squaring her narrow shoulders, Sarah gathered a deep breath and, sneak-eying the hovering wasp, marched to the shed door and rapped so hard she skun her knuckles:

"Uncle Billy! . . . Uncle Billy! . . . It's me, Sarah!"

She closed her eyes, cocked her head, listened; be just like him not to answer just to spite her. At first, she didn't hear anything. But after a few seconds, she could make out what sounded like animal stirrings: whimpers, grunts, straw rustlings. She'd never known her uncle to keep stock, and she shivered at the low, fierce noises; goose pimples stippled her arms and legs. Her fear shamed her, mainly because she didn't know what it was she was scared of. She would have liked nothing better than to skitter down the hill and pretend she hadn't wanted her bicycle. But Nanna Page, her grandmother, hadn't taught her that way. Though Sarah Huckins was but nine years old and shaking with fear, she would grit her teeth and make herself open that shed door.

One finger at a time, she wrapped her hand around the rust-pitted door handle, burred steel biting soft palms. She creaked open the door the way you do the door to a place that hasn't been lived in for a long time.

On all fours, Uncle Billy tore at Sarah's eleven-year-old cousin, Jenny, the way a stringy barn cat sets upon a field mouse in winter. He drove at her, grinding her into the bloodstained dirt, as if he meant to snap her in two.

Sarah had no illusions about people. Even at her age, she knew that most folks were mean, ignorant and stupid, and would take advantage when they could. It'd been an early lesson: Her mother, Ella, had tried to sell her when she was four; the next year she was simply abandoned by Ella one winter's morning and, to be honest, it had been a relief. But when Sarah saw Uncle Billy mauling cousin Jenny, she realized she didn't know nothing.

Sarah's scream rattled windows, made dogs bark and set babies and small children to crying. It was a scream, a beseechment, meant to rend the heavens and summon avenging angels. A scream that drew throat blood and would steal her voice for a week.

Panting, sweating, Uncle Billy slithered off Jenny, a twitching fetal ball, and grinned at Sarah like a boy who's just killed a small animal—a squirrel, say, or a bullfrog. Blood dripped from his wet penis.

"Old enough to pee, old enough for me," he rasped, laughing as Sarah fled. "That's it, girlie, run to Nanna and tattle on Uncle Billy. Go ahead, tell the old bitch. Go right ahead."

Billy dropped a grease-stained blanket over Jenny, wriggled into his dungarees, and vanished into the woods.

Arms windmilling, Sarah freewheeled down the hill; weeds lashed, thorns nipped and gnawed, half-buried rocks nicked and gnashed. She paid them no mind. How could she? In this new world where uncles devoured nieces, how could she admit to pain? Ever confess it again?

Accelerating downhill, she hit the rain-smoothed flat by Auntie Fat Dot's at a dead run and her knee buckled, a transmission slipping gears. She stumbled and pitched forward, sucking down mud and bloodying her chin as she skidded, splatted and spluttered a good five yards before scrambling to her feet and once again bearing down on her grandmother's house.

She took Nanna Page's back steps two at a time, whung open the screen door, and slammed headfirst into her grandmother—Nanna didn't budge or make a sound—who'd been standing at the door as if waiting on her.

"Nanna!" shrieked Sarah, blood flooding her throat. "Uncle Billy! . . . Jenny!"

Nanna was out the door and down the hill before Sarah finished. From the back steps, Sarah saw her grandmother, like a judgment, close in on Uncle Billy's shed. As she watched, throat throbbing, Sarah quarried her earliest memory of Nanna, conjured the woman who'd carved so much of her life.

⚜

Stirred by midnight's blue-black silence, Nanna Page is stalking the stars.

She paces the roof peak, not so much daring gravity as shrugging it off. The peak is no more than four or five inches wide, but Nanna steps strong, purposeful—a no-nonsense, Sunday-morning-and-off-to-church stride —as if she's walking out to the cedar-post clothesline to take in the wash. First to wake and last to sleep, Nanna walks, sloughing the dead day's rough skin; she'll be damned if she'll give in to the weight of days. This walking, this relentless back-and-forth rhythm, is as close to prayer as she gets.

She stops, finally, at roof's edge, her dress billowing witchy and black before the cold-eyed March moon. She sucks in the crisp night air, which is tempered by the promise of spring; she feeds on the stillness, the razor stars, the moonlight like watered-down milk. The old stuff, that's what Nanna Page is made of. Dense, powerful stuff forged in fires kindled at the Beginning. She has always taken care of her own, whether she — or they — liked it or not. And in that caring, she has sometimes diminished those who depend on her. Oh, and they do depend on her, this granite matriarch planted landmark-proud and landmark-tall upon the roof of her house, they depend on her: friends, relations, supplicants.

So she stands on her roof, Nanna Page, taking in the night, regarding her shacks — Page's Village, the townspeople call it — seeming impossibly tall, tall enough maybe to pluck a star or two from out the sky and stick them in her apron pocket.

This is what Ella Huckins, Nanna's oldest daughter, sees as she looks out the window of her shack and up the hill to the house. And, seeing her like that, Ella is even more afraid of her mother than usual; there hasn't been a time when she hasn't feared Nanna Page. Like most Pages, Nanna is tight with her love, hair-trigger with her anger.

As if hearing Ella's thoughts, a rustling in the night-quiet, Nanna turns her head owl-slow and trains raptor eyes on the window where Ella stands. Even though Nanna Page is up the hill some hundred yards away, and even though Ella Huckins has been married, divorced, nearly done in by childbirth, and holds down two jobs, her cheeks flush, her fingers tingle, and there's a ringing in her ears.

Ella Huckins faints.

Ella's three-year-old, Sarah, weasels out of bed, creeps through the chilly shack, pauses at her unconscious mother, then steps out into the silver night.

She wears one of her father's old tee shirts as a nightgown; he's long gone, but his cigarette-and-Brylcreem smell still clings to the shirt. She stares up the hill to where her moon-drenched grandmother sits perched on the peak of the house. And Sarah is gripped by such an ache and longing that she trembles. Tears burn her eyes, sobs swell in her throat.

"Nanna, uppy!" Sarah cries out, her skinny arms outstretched and desperate. "Uppy!"

But Nanna Page doesn't move.

❧

Jenny's head nested between her grandmother's jaw and shoulder as Nanna Page hugged her, almost jealously, to her chest and carried her from the shed, through Page's Village, and up the hill to the house.

Nanna looked neither left nor right, walked neither fast nor slow. She simply moved as Nanna Page. The head woman. The woman whose people had been on this land before there was a United States of America, before there was a New Hampshire, before there was a Granite even.

As Nanna's shadow marked each shack, women and children, like the mosquito squalls that rise after a summer's rain, swarmed outside to watch her ascend the hill. No one, not even the tiniest bare-bottomed baby, called out or ran to her. Nanna'd taken charge, cradled Jenny in her strong arms. For them, that was enough.

Enough even for Fat Dot, Jenny's mother. Fat Dot had a damned good idea as to what'd gone on in that shed, and she knew in her gut that her no-good-son-uvabitching husband, Henry Page, had something to do with it. But she would keep her own counsel until summoned by Nanna, who would take care of everything. And, with six or seven other kids helling around, Fat Dot was grateful that Nanna had taken the burden.

Nanna Page climbed the hill erect, spurning her back's attempts to hunch her, to bring her nearer to earth. It seemed to Sarah that Nanna—black hem flapping, sleeves snapping—might any second take wing, turn into some great grandmother raven who would gather them all to her broad inky breast and lead them to an even better Page's Village: a place where mothers didn't abandon daughters, where hearts didn't bear thorns, and where rageful men didn't eye the girls and women in greasy hunger.

Sarah held the door for Nanna, who clumped up the steps. Jenny, bundled in a blanket that smelled of bacon fat, sawdust and sweat, shuddered, burrowed deeper toward Nanna; brown, wilted hair was all Sarah could see of her cousin.

Nanna paused at the threshold and spoke to Sarah without looking—"Hot water, girl!"—and took Jenny upstairs.

———

Nanna's night walk had, as she figured it might, doubled
her back to Billy's shed, a shed she'd helped her son
build. She had no desire to go inside. The next time she
did would be to seal it up permanent. No good had come
of that shed, and Billy, no one, would use it again. So
she waited outside, resting on Billy's chopping block,
an ax-scarred circle of blood-seasoned oak as big around
as a washtub. She expected Henry, her oldest, her
dumbest. Wouldn't be Billy, who, like most Page men,
bared an alligator mouth but showed a hummingbird
ass. Besides, Henry would do anything Billy asked. No
question. Henry.

Eyes closed, pleasuring in the night cool, she traced
the chopping block's scored wood with callused fingertips; a smile caught her by surprise as she remembered
the knife-carved back of an old lover. As her fingers
read that scar-ified hank of oak, its fierce tales told in
the blunt tongue of remorseless steel, she couldn't help
but think of it as the story of her life. Told in the language of ax and hunting knife and sickle and, most important, the echoing silences in between.

She heard Henry—stumbling, tripping and swear-
ing as he clomped along the logging road from Cedar
Swamp—before she saw him. She shook her head with
a mother's devout disgust. Born without the cunning of
a true Page, Henry stamped into the clearing as if nobody in Page's Village could hear him, as if no one could
possibly be looking for him.

"Come sit next to your mother, Henry," she said.
"Room right here."

"Huh? What?" said Henry, squinting. "Ma? That you, Ma?"

She sighed. Her son'd grown up to be a scarecrow of a man, the kind of laughingstock scarecrow that crows take pains to shit on before they pilfer the corn and pillage the field. There'd been no overcoming her husband's, Elgar's, blood in Henry.

"Yes, it's me, Henry," she said.

"What you doing here, Ma?"

Not answering, she let his question sink into the darkness, waited for it to turn on him, make him feel as if it had been put to him even though he'd asked it. The corners of Nanna's mouth creaked toward a small smile as she imagined him blushing at his own question.

"Henry."

"Ma. I . . ." said Henry, retreating.

The air thickened, as in a closet on a hot day, and Henry started to sweat. His legs trembled, his voice withered.

"Come here," snapped Nanna, sniffing his fear. "Now."

Henry ducked his head, did as he was told.

"Look at me," she said. "Look. At. Me."

Nanna hard-stared his face, waited, knowing he'd speak first. No one out-quieted Nanna Page. Certainly not Henry, who fidgeted, fussed with the buttons of his flannel shirt, thumped his foot back and forth against the chopping block.

She saw no resolve in Henry's putty face — not that she'd expected it — only the mask of Billy's threats, wheedling and extorted promises. Those would give way to her will the same as Jenny'd been forced to give in to Billy.

Grinding his teeth, Henry had to make himself look at his mother. The same way you have to make yourself look at your foot when the ax slips, or how you have to look at your dog after he's been nailed by a car out to the highway. Once, Henry moved to turn away, but Nanna raised her left hand, her hitting hand, ever so slightly, and he stayed put.

When Henry's eyelid twitched, and twitched again—a moth trapped on the wrong side of the window—she knew she had him. Next would come the trickle of crocodile tears, the bull, and then the foot-dragging truth.

"Billy just wanted me to come and get some of his riggin'," Henry said. "That's all. That's why I come by."

"Can't he come and get it himself?" Nanna said. "He ain't cripple."

"You know how busy he gets out there in that swamp of his. Doing him a favor."

She bore down with her eyes; she smelled his sweat: "What else, Henry?"

"Huh?"

"What else, goddammit?"

"What?"

Left fingers opening and closing, Nanna hissed at him in a voice all razors and snakes: "You want to see her, Henry? You want to see your little girl all ripped open and tore apart? Do you? 'Cause we can go right

now, mister man. And you can see where your brother
bit her and pawed at her and shoved his way up inside
her. . . ."

She stopped, caught her breath, went on: "Quite a
brother you got there, Henry. Quite the brother.

"Look at me, Henry. I ain't there on the ground.
Look at me. That sonuvabitch raped your daughter,
Henry. What're you going to do about it? Huh? What're
you going to do?"

"What'm I supposed to do?"

"Jesus H. Christ!"

Killing Henry with her eyes, she called forth her
rage and disgust, let it sculpt her face into a look that
said, You ain't no son of mine.

Henry whimpered, a small boy about to get spanked:
"I didn't think he was going to hurt her so bad. . . . And
I really needed that truck."

"Truck?"

"He made me do it, Ma. Honest, he made me."

"What truck?"

"He said he'd give me that old truck of his if I made
it so he could . . . be with Jenny. I really need that
truck, Ma. Besides, it ain't like she's really my daughter
or nothing. You know Jenny ain't mine. Know she ain't
no Page. I'm sorry, Ma. I really am."

He let her slap him in the face till her hand ached.

Thus, Nanna Page banished Henry from Page's
Village.

———

Nanna had never quite known what to do about Ella's shack. In the years since her oldest daughter'd forsaken Sarah and, in doing so, spurned Page's Village, Nanna had just put up with the shack's mocking presence — cursing soft whenever her eyes happened upon it. To Nanna, who'd never dared lay claim to infallibility, but who'd considered the possibilities, the deserted shack embodied her failings when it came to her family; she didn't like being reminded. And, too, there was the part of her that expected to wake early one morning to see smoke snaking once more from the shack's chimney, to see Ella returned. But Nanna knew what to do with the shack now — Ella's sin would be redeemed — and she went to work.

She nailed shut the windows and the back door, inside and outside, with tenpenny nails, then boarded the windows; she back-crawled under the shack, spiders and snakes giving her a wide berth as she sucked in web, dust and mildew, and braced the floorboards with two-by-fours; sank three dead bolts into the front door; choked the rooms with bricks of yellowed newspaper as brittle as December leaves, bales of old straw, and more than fifty bottles sloshing with kerosene; and, finally, she soaked the floors, walls and roof with gasoline.

Done, she let it be known that she wanted to talk with Billy.

"I want Ella's place burned down," Nanna told Billy. "I'm getting sick of looking at it."

"We even . . . after . . . Right?" asked Billy, taking his mother's silence to mean yes.

Nanna sat stiff at the top of the back steps, while her son slouched against the railing at the bottom. Billy had arrived with dusk's shadows, creeping up out of the swamp with the mosquitoes, frog bleats and other night beasts. He pulled wet, like an old man, on his cigarette; its tip glowed orange and feral in the fresh darkness.

"Don't have to be so quiet, Ma," said Billy, the cocky bad boy sure of his mother's love. "That bull might play with Henry and all, but don't pull it with me."

Every mother has that one child, the one against whom all the others are measured, the one who makes her laugh hardest, who makes her cry hardest. The one who thinks he can get away with murder. For Nanna, Billy had been that one.

"Your brother was any kind of man," Nanna said, "you'd be dead and buried already."

Billy laughed—a harsh pig snort.

"Don't you laugh at me."

"Now why would Henry want to kill me, Ma?"

"You know damn well why."

Billy took one last, long drag on his Camel, flung it down and heeled it out. He looked up at his mother and said:

"Ain't like that girl was no Page or nothing. Elgar ain't no Page—how you ever got my old man to give up his manful name, I'll never know—and Fat Dot sure ain't no Page. Last I knew, Daddy put the meat to Fat

Dot once upon a time and they made Jenny. Whether you like it or not."

"Was a time I would've done anything for you, son," whispered Nanna. "Anything."

Billy laughed again, shook his head, said: "So, when do you want it torched, Ma? Tonight? Tonight good? After midnight, say? I'm always up for a good burning."

Nanna nodded.

"See ya later, Ma," said Billy, dissolving down the hill. "Much later."

Nanna unlocked the front door to Ella's shack, the lock's action reminding her of a rifle's, and let Billy in.

"Jesus, Ma," he said. "Think you laid down enough gasoline? Place smells like the inside of a gas can."

"Billy," Nanna said. "I want you to remember one last thing. Jenny might not be a Page, but she belongs to me. All of you belong to me."

"Ma, listen to me. I don't have to hear this fucking shit. Okay? Okay? . . ."

She struck a wooden match, a blue-tip, and, savoring the sulfur smell, said: "Good-bye, son."

She flicked the burning match onto the floor, saw it catch, slammed the door shut, threw the three dead bolts, and walked away to the hymn of Billy Page's screams.

She heard him banging around inside the shack — a rat in the rafters — before it went "whooom!!!" and was swallowed in flames. All Nanna could hear then was the slow, crackling hunger of fire as it fed.

The women and children of Page's Village flowed from their shacks, drawn by the fire, and stood before Nanna as if she were giving a sermon. But words weren't needed. They could tell from the sharp set to her chin, from the way she clutched Jenny to her chest, that she had taken care of Billy — Uncle Dead, the children were already calling him.

Retribution's hot fire tempered Sarah that night. Seared her imagination as surely as it seared her cheeks. It was the night she learned her grandmother could kill and, in that knowing, gave Nanna her unconditional love. Nanna had taken her fear and rage, and Jenny's, and everyone else's, and made it her own. Not only that; she'd acted upon it.

Sarah glanced up the hill to Nanna's house, and saw the shadow of Grandpa Elgar at an upstairs window, where reflected flames capered on the glass. She blinked. He was gone.

Part I

Chapter One

June 1985

THE BABY CRIED—one jagged half-note—testing the night.

Sarah, who'd spent her life swimming through the night-darkness to banish her babies' demons, had already jerked up in bed and planted one foot on the splintery floor before remembering the baby wasn't hers; her son and his wife had moved in after Jessie'd been born. Still, her granddaughter's lone yelp had knotted Sarah's stomach. Partly for self-preservation, she had never let her babies cry; she'd made herself sick over their tears, as if she'd cried them herself.

She slid back into bed, listening, the loose, warm muscles of sleep stiffening. She might be a grandmother, but she was only thirty-six. It hadn't been that long since she'd kept the mother's watch—who knew, she might keep it again one day—and instinct hadn't deserted her.

The baby cried again, stop-and-start this time, like the first fat raindrops that splatter before a downpour.

If Jessie'd been Sarah's, she would have gone to her right then, dispelled her night fears; no good ever came of a child crying in the dark. She couldn't say why, but Sarah knew when a baby was winding up for a long, hard cry. It was, she supposed, something a mother, a grandmother, was obliged to know.

Low, urgent, the real crying started. The kind of steady, almost reasonable crying that seems it could last through till morning; there'd been times when Sarah herself, drowning in black seas, had cried like that for days on end.

Why are Wayne and Charlotte letting that poor baby cry, Sarah wondered. She was my baby, she'd already be nesting in my arms.

Then the squalling: raw, ragged gusts that made Sarah sick to her stomach as she pictured the baby red-faced and rigid in her cradle. And still no other sound from upstairs. She poked her husband, knowing she wouldn't be able to wake him. Far as Russ Britton knew, his wife and his kids hadn't spent a sleepless night in the past twenty years. Sarah may as well have been jabbing leftover meat loaf.

Her granddaughter's cries got louder, and Sarah allowed anger — that homemade venom — to seep into her blood, swell in her chest and stick in her throat. Her ears and cheeks prickled with it as she kicked back her sheet and stormed from the bedroom, nicking her thigh on the night table, to the foot of the stairs.

Ain't somebody going to pick that baby up??!!

That's what she wanted to yell. She wanted to shake the house, shudder the timbers, shatter the windows and make shingles fly off the roof. But when she opened her mouth, the words, stunted and twisted in childhood, abandoned her.

Sarah stood there, working her jaw up and down, up and down. A ventriloquist's dummy.

When Russ woke, it being the sole right of the man of the house to steal an extra fifteen minutes of sleep, he was surprised to find his wife still in bed. For the twenty years Russ and Sarah'd been married, she'd always been first up. The one who, after knuckling the sleepy-seeds from her eyes and rubbing her bare arms against daybreak's chill, put water on for coffee, fixed lunches, listened for the children. Even after she started working with Russ over to the chenille shop, she still rose first, still jump-started the Brittons' day.

"Sarah?" said Russ, not quite touching her shoulder. "Sarah?"

She rustled, curling tighter, boring her face into the pillow; then a muffled: "Don't feel good."

Russ knew the tone of voice — remindful, even on a

clear summer's morning, of heavy November rains and trees raped of their crabbed leaves—and stopped talking.

After Russ crept from the bedroom, snicking the door closed behind him, Sarah wriggled to his side of the bed and, like a garter snake sunning on a granite ledge, soaked up the warmth her husband had left behind.

Sarah seesawed in and out of sleep, seeking its solace, its healing. It was one of those mornings, which sometimes stretched into weeks, when Sarah couldn't bear even the thought of facing anyone or anything beyond her cool, dark room. She'd learned not to fight them, these to-the-marrow blues. Instead, she retreated into sleep, daring them to follow. She'd never been able to explain it to Russ, never been able to explain nothing to Russ, though he could finger the signs. He accepted it the way he accepted most of his life—with a shrug and a six-pack. But Sarah had once told Hannah, her oldest, who'd fled to the state university, that on those certain mornings it was as if the quarry ice had come in black overnight, and that she'd awakened under that ice: trapped winter water.

Often, on such bleak mornings, Sarah, desperate to understand her relentless sadness, journeys back to Page's Village, its smells, its sounds . . . its ghosts. Giving in to the humid whispers of the past, her girlhood collapsing into minutes, seconds, instants, she obsesses over the women who haunt her, in whose shadow she took root: Nanna Page; her mother, Ella; Auntie Leah; Auntie Robena. Even on Sarah's best days, Page's Village is never far away.

✖

A smoky wet snake coiling through the night woods, fog had laid siege to Page's Village overnight, spilling into the hollow where the village slept. By midmorning the fog would wither, and daybreak's thick blanket would be barely remembered or forgotten altogether, a day-old dream. But the sun-tinged promise of midmorning is hours away as Page's Village stirs, yawns, shakes off the night.

The nervous light of kerosene lamps pulses in the creamy gray even as the sweet smell of woodsmoke roams from the shacks. Sounds are, at the same time, smothered and magnified: the clatter of silverware; an outhouse door's rusty-hinged rasp; a baby wailing in sweaty hunger; a back door screeked open, then slammed shut, the day's weather taken in, evaluated, and rejected; the scrape of a butter knife on toast; the halfhearted yips of a dog not quite awake. . . .

Nursing black coffee, Leah sits quiet at the kitchen table. The hot cup prickles her hands, the steam teases her nose. Out of habit, though she knows she can't see for the fog, she looks up the hill toward Nanna Page's, toward her mother's. It seems to Leah that she, like all of them who scrabble down below, has spent her life looking up the hill to Nanna's house in fear and anticipation. Even without seeing, Leah knows the kitchen light is on, Nanna sitting in the rocker next to the woodstove, sipping Lipton tea, rocking, thinking on them even as they think on her. . . .

Ella washes her hair at the kitchen sink. She'd gotten up even earlier than usual—at deep night's morning edge—filled the four teakettles and heated them. (She's the only one of them who has running water. Cold as spring runoff, but goddammit she doesn't have to lug it from the well like all the rest.) She plunges her head into the hot water, scalp tingling, hair seaweeding out till it fills the chipped enamel basin. She lathers up with a sharp, new bar of Ivory, rubbing the soap up and down her head like erasing a blackboard. Then, in a closed-eye grimace, Ella lights into her hair with the fury of a revival preacher cleansing souls, elbows flying, bony fingers scrubbing and scratching, gnawing and kneading. She stops quick as she started, pauses (listening to the low crackle the soap makes as it clings to her hair), then rinses.

Drying her hair, Ella looks in on Sarah, who sleeps with her right thumb resting on her chin. Sarah had been a mistake, born of passion and stupidity, and Ella'd actually found the nerve to ask her mother to raise Sarah as her own. But Nanna, her black, snapping-turtle eyes afire, had spit one half-sentence: "You made your bed . . ."

Leah would take Sarah in a minute, Ella knows. But Ella won't give her sister the satisfaction. . . .

Misting out. Leah lifts her face to the powder-fine rain. Taking a deep breath, she sucks in the loam-smelling fog, starts on the path to Ella's. . . .

Allen Swett, boy-skittish though a married man, fumbles in the dark for pregnant Robena, cupping a warm, pink breast in his cold, trembling hand. Robena yelps and elbows him a good one in the ribs. Allen, the fire between his legs damped, shrinks to the far edge of the bed. . . .

Leah scratches at Ella's door.

"Can't you knock like normal people?" snaps Ella, letting Leah in. "You'd think you was a g.d. cat or something."

"Didn't want to wake Sarah up," Leah says.

"She's got to get up anyways. I swear, if I let you, you'd spoil that kid something fierce."

"Let me go get her. I'll carry her over to Bena's."

"Jesus Christ, Lee, she can walk, you know. She ain't cripple."

"El . . . the poor thing's asleep."

Ella shoots Leah a curdled-milk scowl, waving her hands in surrender and disgust. Ignoring Ella, Leah tiptoes into her niece's room and gentles the sleeping Sarah over her shoulder.

At Robena's, Ella waits while Leah carries Sarah in; like most mornings, Robena and Allen are still in bed, so Leah tucks Sarah in on the couch. She has other nieces and nephews, but there's something about Sarah that touches Leah in a way that surprises her. She's three years old, but Sarah still carries a newborn's sweet helplessness, and that helplessness has breached Leah's steep walls. She can't understand why Ella, the girl's very mother, doesn't feel the same, and she begrudges her sister Sarah's motherhood.

Pages don't much touch — unless it's to hit, or worse. But, as awkward and stiff as it feels, Leah bends down and kisses Sarah on the cheek.

"What took so damn long?" Ella asks even before Leah's out the door. "Hurry up, or we'll miss our ride."

The fog closing behind them, the two sisters trudge up the hill in prickly Page silence.

The fog burns off by nine. The day's work begins — for these women whose lives are lived in a relentless present tense — the day passes:

Swollen knuckles, red and raw, grate against washboards; brooms rasp; an ax bites into a log, chunk . . . chunk; windows squeak open; the children, skinny and barefoot and half-naked, swarm, chanting "Momma had a baby and its head popped off!" — the dirty yellow heads of dandelions decapitated at the flick of a thumbnail; the water pump creaks; sun-shocked sheets, baptism white, snap in the wind; shifty-eyed chickens squawk, peck at the ground . . . plot; wet hands are dried on aprons; screen doors slam open and whang shut, sounding like .22 rifles; beet-faced and sweaty, the children dart in, under and around the shacks, chasing each other with stickaburrs, pussy willows, milkweed, cat-o'-nine-tails and rubbery, reddish-green rhubarb whips; spatulas rattle in skillets; hands reek of babies, chopped onions, and fresh-picked zucchini; the dogs, tongues lolling, loaf the same as the beer-pregnant men who kill time over to Brandy Brow's junkyard: scratching, farting, belching and barking for no good reason; pebbled knees are stained green and smell of weed juice; a rock, flung in a child's animal rage, cracks off of a skull and blood sieves, hushing the children even as the bloodstained shrieks bring the women running; kneading the small of their backs, sighing, the women squint into the late afternoon sun; and Billy Page, already dead to Nanna Page though he doesn't know it, paces the hill that overlooks the village — a premonition.

✖

By noon Sarah, blinking, managed to leave her safe-bed, leave Page's Village, and plant herself in Nanna Page's old rocking chair, which she kept in the kitchen as Nanna had. Nanna had made that oak rocker, and its virtues were those of its maker: blunt lines, broad back, built for the long haul. Whether knitting a sweater or building an outhouse, Nanna had always said: "A thing needs to be well-made so that it can be hard-used." Sitting in the rocker, Sarah — still shedding that morning's suffocating skin — felt as if she were somehow being held by her long-dead grandmother. The thought painted the faintest ripple of a smile at the corners of her mouth. Everything Nanna Page had touched in her life had become an extension of her and of her will, and Sarah and Sarah's rocking chair were no different.

She peered out the window, pulled back quick, stunned by the sun-drenched brilliance: Hard summer sunlight suffused the grass-stubbled gravel that made up her backyard, glinted like a dewy spiderweb on the shattered windshield of Wayne's gutted Pinto wagon, bleached Russ's white shirts waltzing on the clothesline, and made the frog pond down below blink and sparkle as if it were heaped full of stars.

A fresh breeze, smelling of mown hay, summer greenness and the ocean some fifty miles away, blew in through the screen and made the curtains curtsy. Sarah took a greedy breath, shut her eyes, and let the breeze clear her head the way, on the first day of spring, she banished winter's stale fried-food-and-cigarette reek by joyfully—even maniacally—ramming open every window in her house so that the panes rattled and bits of dried caulking rained down.

The ceiling creaked; Sarah opened her eyes. A bureau drawer got yanked open—squealing—slammed shut.

Sarah frowned, sighed. She supposed that Charlotte and Baby Jessie were home; the house'd been so still that she had dared believe she was alone.

Charlotte clumped down the stairs—Sarah could tell from the weight of her steps that she wasn't carrying the baby—slow and angry, her usual gait. For a beanpole, she sure made a lot of noise.

Charlotte West—she'd refused to become a Britton even though, homeless and pregnant, she'd shrugged and married Wayne—was one of those skinny, sullen,

flat-chested girls who smoked like an oil-burning 1960
Ford Fairlane and tended toward crotch-snug jeans and
white tee shirts to show off to best advantage what she
didn't have. It made Sarah shake her head and sigh that
Wayne'd jumped Charlotte's illusion.

"She's homely. She's mean. And she's stupid," Russ
liked to say. "But I'll be good and goddamned if she
ain't turned that into a virtue."

Charlotte edged into the kitchen as if she were wading into the lake in January. "I've got to go walk to
the store," she said without looking at Sarah. "Can you
watch Jessie?"

Sarah sighed: "I . . . guess."

She gave Charlotte her back, pretended to look out
the window; she thought of her grandpa Elgar, who,
afraid of what he might see, had spent his life staring out
the closest window handy rather than look at his family.

"Uh-huh," said Charlotte, who fumbled her pack of
cigarettes and dropped it on the floor. The cigarettes,
stark white against the grimy, threadbare carpet, rolled
toward the door like runaway logs.

Sarah watched Charlotte, motor-oil hair lank in her
eyes, as she snatched up the cigarettes; she looked down
the neck of Charlotte's tee shirt, saw her daughter-in-
law's pale, schoolboy chest—Christ! Russ's tits were
bigger than Charlotte's—and wondered how in hell she
had ever nursed Jessie. Though she didn't realize it,
Sarah's face twitched and constricted into the sour-milk
look of disgust she'd learned from her mother (who'd
inherited it from Nanna Page) and passed on to Hannah.

A look that bore the weight of generations of unarticulated rage and loathing.

When Charlotte glanced up, Sarah's look smacked her square between the eyes. Charlotte ran outdoors, the screen door clapping shut behind her, before Sarah could see her cry.

Sarah picked up the two cigarettes still on the floor and flung them out the door after her daughter-in-law.

Sarah I

She sits hunter-still in her grandmother's rocking chair, stalking the night as it gives in to day. Her husband and children are asleep; he chain-saw snores, the kids rustle and whimper. Her eyes burn, and there's the slightest ringing in her ears: church bells two towns away overheard on a Sunday morning. Seduced by the past, she sighs into the ghost light that suffuses the house at this hour. When she takes to her grandmother's rocker, its seat worn smooth by generations of women rocking away their blues, she sometimes imagines that she's once again snug on the dead woman's knobby lap. But not this morning. This morning she props an elbow on one arm of the chair, and her chin slumps into an open hand.

Chapter Two

1953

IT WAS, OH ... SOME
three miles from the summer-green heart of the Plains
(Protestant-white colonials drowsing in the close night)
to the packed khaki dirt of Page's Village.

A short drive.

But not one Constance Woods'd ever imagined making. Not since she'd married to the Plains, anyway.
Nowadays, whenever she drove past Page's Village,
she'd look away sharp, as if ambushed by something
shameful, and stomp on the gas. Growing up, she'd had
her fill of tar-paper shacks, outhouses and bare-ass kids.
She didn't need no reminders.

Oh, she remembered the Page girls, Ella and Leah, all right, because she'd been just like them: predator quiet, bound in homemade dresses as stiff and coarse as scrub brushes, as high-strung as fighting dogs. It hadn't surprised her when they'd quit school after eighth grade; their older brothers, Billy and Henry, hadn't even staggered that far, having given up the ghosts of readin', 'ritin' and 'rithmetic in fourth and in sixth grade. But Constance had grit her teeth and clung to her schooling (the way other women in her family clung to their good-for-nothing men) to become the first Gonyer ever to graduate from high school.

What *did* surprise Constance Woods was that she found herself jerking her husband's pickup (no sense risking the new Buick) left off Route 49 and bumping down the mumpy dirt road, the Ford's high beams jitterbugging, to Page's Village. To Ella Huckins' shack.

Hand in hand, small-town women wade subterranean currents, seining for the small truths that men don't (won't? can't?) see: the flotsam of adultery and abortion, of battered wives and hidden bastards, of cancers and alcoholism—of unwanted children. Those currents, strong, black and angry, bore Constance Woods from the Plains to Ella's door.

Looking at that weather-warped door, the screen patched, repatched, and patched again, Constance trembled, believing that there was no good reason, really, why she was the one snug in the womb of the Plains, while Page's Village sucked at Ella's life the way bog sucks at your shoes. No good reason at all.

A hunched shadow peered out, flowed away. Constance fingered her keys, fearing for a moment that there might be no getting back to the Plains once she stepped foot outside the truck. But, finally, she cleared her throat, forced down a deep breath, and walked into the past.

"Door's open."

She cracked the door just enough to slip inside, where it was as hot and stuffy as a July attic and smelled of kerosene and bacon grease. (She thought of her dead mother.)

Ella, weaving the silence to her own ends, waited at the kitchen table. Constance hovered by the door, jittery, blinking—a night insect flown inside by accident.

(All Constance could see was her mother; or, more accurately, her mother's broad stooped back. It seemed to Constance that her mother, shoving back gray-streaked hair, had always been bent over: cooking, washing dishes, elbow-greasing floors, wiping phlegmy snouts—crying.)

"Is . . . is that you, Ella?" Constance managed, her voice, dry bones, screeking, breaking. "Been so long." She cleared her throat again, tried a smile that wilted.

Ella nodded: "Has been."

The two women, seller and buyer, stared. Each, at once, trying hard to understand, while understanding too well.

"Sit down, Connie Gonyer," Ella said. "You don't have to act like no stranger around me."

Connie Gonyer—Gon-ya. It angered Constance

that the name still shamed her. It *is* who she *was*, god-damn-it-all, until Davis Woods'd been fool enough to fall for a Gonyer girl, then have the guts to marry her. To most people in town, the Gonyers were, at best, an infestation of retards and thieves who scraped supper up off the highway and shopped at the dump. (*Oh, but that Connie Gonyer. She's different, that one. She's smaht.*) If you wanted to start a fistfight in Granite—school-yard, the VFW, town hall ... anywhere—all you had to do was accuse someone of Gonyer blood; Gran-ite's children spat the word *Gonyer* at each other the way children in other towns called each other cooties. Hell, even a Gonyer'd take a poke at you if you called him one.

Constance Woods settled across from Ella.

"We know lots of things, don't we, Connie? How to use a washboard without skinning our knuckles. How to wring a chicken's neck. How to make one skinny dime last six months." Ella paused, stringing a barbwire smile: "How to run away from brothers and uncles"—a broken-glass giggle—"there's just things, no matter how hard you try, you can't forget, Connie girl."

It wasn't Ella's words so much as her tone of voice, familiar and nettling, that made Constance bristle. The ignorant, knowing tone Constance's family had used—still used—to "knock her off her high horse."

Never a Gonyer swilled air or beer who saw any good in one of their own bettering the rest of the tribe. Ever since she'd married Davis Woods, it seemed, Constance had spent her days justifying herself to those who thought she was a snob, and to those who thought she wasn't enough of one.

Drawing the Plains about her, as her husband had taught her, Constance snared Ella's hateful, animal eyes in her own and said: "I heard about . . . your little girl, Ellie."

Ella's cheeks reddened; she picked at a fingernail. "Ellie?"

She wouldn't look at Constance. She mumbled to the table: "You know what I'm asking, right?"

"Yes, Ellie . . . Word . . . gets around."

"I'll bring her by tomorrow morning."

After Constance left, Ella blew out the lamp, shrank into the musty overstuffed armchair, and nursed the darkness.

Early light, clear, watery, seeped at the window shades' frayed edges, trickled into the shack. Ella woke in the chair, neck stiff, back aching; sleeping in that chair was like sleeping on the ground.

Sleeping on the ground. Ella shook her head memory slow, cultivating a thorned smile. That'd been one of Nanna's best punishments. All of them, one time or another, had been made to caterpillar up to the foot of the back steps and cower in the dark. "Now you'll never want for a place to sleep," Nanna'd say by way of good night, her voice neither harsh nor gentle. You'd wake the next morning—bone-sore, night-damp, dirt-streaked and mosquito-chawed—more tired than when you went to sleep and smelling like an earthworm.

Denying the new day, Ella squinched shut her eyes and squirmed back toward sleep, remembering, dreaming:

✄

The new sun a mere rumor lollygagging below the tree-tops, Nanna and Ella walk Mill Road. This particular summer, Nanna has taken to sharing her daybreak rambles with twelve-year-old Ella, who laments the lost sleep, but prizes this small entry into her mother's mysteries. It is understood that Ella is expected, as in most things, to keep up and shut up.

Nanna swerves from the road and expertly slithers through a barbwire fence without once catching her ankle-dusting dress. She stalks into the field—dew-smitten bramble-berries, firm and ripe, strain toward the ground—and, scorning the prickers, scoops the berries (the red and the black) into apron pockets. She looks back at Ella, stopped at the fence, holds the look for a beat, and then lights into the berries.

Nanna's look is, at once, a challenge, an order and a rebuke. With that one, sharp backwards glance she has questioned Ella's courage, told her she damn well better pick some berries, and asked: Are you going to let that barbwire fence, of all things, keep you from giving your mother a hand?

Ella knows, no matter what she does next, this is her last morning walk with her mother.

Keeping one strand of wire at bay with her foot, Ella bows another strand upward with the heel of her hand

and, shutting her eyes, tries to duck through. A barb snares her back. Slowing her movements, she takes a deep breath and turns to free herself. As she tugs at her back, a sleeve snags, her knee catches. She tries to ease backwards, but gets her hair tangled. She becomes aware that Nanna is watching, sees the disgust smeared on her face; Ella breathes some harder, starts to sweat. Trying to shake a leg loose, she stumbles and arcs forward. Throwing her arms out to break her fall, she ends up squeezing two fistsful of barbwire. Feet off the ground now, hung up in the gnawing wire, she quits, goes limp. She is hurt and bleeding, but she won't cry; Pages, real Pages anyway, don't cry.

Almost smiling, Nanna looks down at her—waiting; she wants Ella to ask for her help, to submit. But Ella won't. If her own mother can't help her without being asked . . .

"I don't want these berries getting spoilt," says Nanna, slipping through the fence and out onto Mill Road. "No sense letting them go bad."

So she leaves her daughter drowning in barbwire, knowing that she'll figure a way out, and that the two of them will be the better for it. If, by some odd chance, Ella isn't home by noon, she'll send Billy and Henry to fetch her.

Hung up on barbwire. That's how Ella'd come to see herself: trapped and useless, the years performing the slow carving that stops only at the bone. And, thinking that, she nearly cried for the girl she no longer was (and the woman she could never be), as if her adult tears could somehow flow down the years and soothe that pained child. But even as she summoned those tears, a fierce fire smoldering behind her eyes, she ground her teeth, sunk her nails into her palms and stanched them.

Nanna Page might've been proud.

✕

The swaybacked Mahoney saltbox smooching a lame two-cow barn was the first thing you saw after Nanna Page's place as you headed toward town. Both stricken structures seemed to be gulping in terror and glancing backwards at the pushy fence-busting, field-devouring woods, all the while clinging to a glacier-raked hillside whose best crop looked to be boulders the size of Studebakers.

Across from the Mahoneys' slouched Dickie West's deserted shack. Dickie West'd died of a heart attack years ago while putting up curtains — same curtains that still hung slantways in the front window. When she'd been younger, Ella'd been tempted to sneak inside the dead man's shack and finish hanging those curtains; they spoke to her of unfinished business and, though she didn't understand why, they had made her angry. But she'd come to realize that if someone'd ripped the curtains down or finished hanging them, townspeople would've more easily forgotten Dickie West. That window's slanting slash of curtain was a reminder that Dickie West had once lived, that he'd died clutching imitation lace; better those curtains fronting Route 49 than a chiseled chunk of rock planted in some cemetery where no one ever went.

Sarah, as always, peered into the shack's dust-fogged window, drawn by the pull any death, even the hint of death, brings to bear on a child's imagination. She couldn't see anything, really, as she squinted through the window. But the slow waltz of light and shadow in a barren room was enough for her at that age. She turned and looked at her grandmother's brooding house, the back windows blazing with the copper fire of a new sun.

"For Christ's sakes, Sarah, come on," Ella said. "We ain't got all day, you know."

Nanna Page's crude castle of thorns and silence, her mother's shadow-wracked shack, Auntie Leah's house of kindness. Those were places Sarah could not set apart from herself. They were as much a part of her as the timbre of her voice, the driving-rain slant of her handwriting. She had lived in those houses; those houses had lived in her. Dark, sawdust-smelling rooms where the years had worn the floors smooth and concave; the peeling tar-paper skins; the blueing windows started on their hundred-year melt to opacity: those things, they were the architecture of memory.

Davis and Constance Woods' house, though, Sarah always would remember as if from a storybook: light-drenched, high-ceilinged rooms (vast enough, it seemed, to swallow a Page's Village shanty or two); broad, sweeping stairways cascading from the upper floors;

wood polished to the glow of a low fire. A house of dreams.

Some fifty yards off of Main Street the Woods colonial held court, its lawn a soft, green tongue curling from the fieldstone foundation. The house was painted an unforgiving white that hurt your eyes when the sun hit it; its shutters were silo red. There was no nod toward decoration; generations of Woods had decided that a green lawn, a white house, and blue sky were enough.

Grandfather oaks at least as old as the town picketed the crushed-rock driveway. Head down, Ella stood at the top of the drive, toeing the candy-sized stones like a child cowed by some scold's wagging finger. She looked up at the house, then back down again quick as if there were a town ordinance that forbid a Page's Villager from taking too long a look at a center-of-town colonial.

"What are we waiting for, Mommy?" Sarah asked.

Ella wanted to smack her, but feared Connie might be watching. No sense damaging the goods in front of the customer.

"Shut up," Ella answered.

What made Ella stall wasn't the business she was about to conduct with Connie Woods—she had no qualms about that; she'd learned from her mother that second thoughts did nobody any good—but the house itself. Its bulk, physical and historical (built in 1694), weighed on her. Until she had stood before it, Ella hadn't realized how oppressive the house was in its size and perfection. Though she would have denied it, the Woods colonial made Ella feel insignificant, made her desperate Page's Village life seem worthless. She was of half a mind to turn around and walk back home, Connie Woods and her money be damned. And though that particular flavor of spite would have tasted fine in its bitterness, it wouldn't have solved Ella's problem.

"Come on, girl," said Ella, snatching Sarah's wrist and dragging her along, making the child do a hop-skip stutter-step to keep from falling.

In Granite, as in many small New Hampshire towns, a house's front door was for show only; some willful creatures even went so far as to nail them shut, reasoning that they wanted no truck with someone ignorant enough to paw at the front door. Front doors, as thick and uncompromising as ten-term selectmen, were meant for salesmen and strangers; company, expected or not, used side or back doors, which generally opened into the kitchen.

So Ella knew exactly what she was doing when she slashed across the lawn—tugging Sarah as if she were a balky mutt—stalked up the front steps and, shunning the brass knocker, walloped the front door with her fists . . . boom, boom, boom, one after another.

It tickled Ella to picture Connie Gonyer, *Connie Davis*, drying her hands from some kitchen chore, defrosting the 'frigerator maybe or wrestling the guts out of a chicken, and having to trudge all the way to the front of the house to let in whoever was hammering on her front door.

She heard the light thud of Connie walking down the hall, envying her this house where a body's footfalls didn't rattle the windows or jar the door.

"Who we seeing, Mommy?" Sarah asked.

Ella turned, looked at her, and Sarah scuttled for the quiets quick; it was a look that usually prefaced a cold, bony backhand across the face.

The door hushed open (Ella had never heard a door so mute) but before Constance could speak, Ella jumped her silence: "I brung her like I said."

Constance peered around Ella and down the steps at a scabby-kneed little girl clutching a burlap potato sack; she wore a once-red dress faded to a watery pink.

Constance looked down the steps . . . and saw herself. Tears nipped at the corners of her eyes.

Gotten soft, Connie girl, Ella thought, seeing the tears; inside, she smiled.

"Have you told her about this?" Constance asked Ella.

"That's your business," Ella said. "You said to bring her. I brung her." Ella stepped back, abandoned Sarah and Connie to each other.

Cheeks prickling, like crowding the woodstove after tramping in out of the cold, Sarah felt her gaze, but couldn't bring herself to look up at Constance Woods. She wasn't used to such strict attention from an adult, from someone acting as if she mattered. She'd grown up in the shadows of an indifference sometimes pierced by a casual cruelty or, rarer, an accidental kindness. Like some small animal, a field mouse, say, or a shrew, she'd learned to dart for cover at the least hint of trouble. Only four years old, she already favored silence, twilight, the crooked look. Those things had served her well in Page's Village. Had, perhaps, saved her.

Taking in Sarah, Constance saw everything that she had fled years before; it was if she'd found a long-lost little sister. She tasted the demons that haunted the child—Constance wasn't *that* far removed from her Gonyer self—ached in self-recognition at the hungers that lit her eyes. Sarah provoked in her a tenderness she hadn't felt since her two boys were babies, since the court had decided that they belonged to their father and not to Constance.

"Sarah!"

Both Constance and Sarah jumped at Ella's bark.

"You listen to me, Sarah. You're going to be staying here with Auntie Connie for a while," Ella said. "You understand that?"

"Huh?" Sarah said. "What?"

"You're going to live with Auntie Connie here."

In almost the same moment, Sarah's face blanched then reddened, and then the tears exploded, flooding her face. She fought for air as if her mother were drowning her.

Face hard, Ella grabbed ahold of Sarah's arm and shook her: "Stop it! You stop it right now!"

Sarah jangled in Ella's talons—a broken marionette; it seemed she meant to shake her daughter till she started coming apart.

"I want to go home, Mommy," Sarah howled—

hoarse, desperate. "I don't want to live here. I want to see Nanna and Auntie Robena and Auntie Leah."

"Let go of her, Ella!" Constance warned. "Let go!"

"She ain't yours yet."

It never changes, Constance thought. You can hide on the Plains, but there's no escaping. How many times in her life had she seen this scene played out in one way or another? How many times had she been the little girl on the business end of some grown-up's rage? She was sick of it. *Sick of it.*

Constance Woods hauled off and smacked Ella Huckins in the face so hard that she knocked her down.

"Give me my money, Connie Gonyer," Ella shrieked as Constance carried Sarah inside. "Give me my money, you Gonyer whore."

Constance, with the quick, capable movements of a longtime mother, dried Sarah's tears, washed her face, and gave her two Fig Newtons and a glass of milk.

When they walked outside, Ella was gone. Constance drove Sarah back to Page's Village in the new Buick.

Ella came home three days later.

Sarah II

She fixes lunches at the kitchen table, peering into the winter dark beyond her kitchen—snow bankings hulk in the dooryard—as she rattles the knife in an almost empty jar of mustard. A naked light bulb glares down from the ceiling, mean, useful. Her fingers dimple the slice of bread in her hand. The pink-and-green slab of olive loaf—its processed-meat smell almost makes her gag—the peanut butter and jam, three brown-spotted apples, chocolate cake frosted white: these are the tools of domesticity. A white Sylvania radio (the *S* in Sylvania hangs upside down) squats on the windowsill, spitting out the news and weather; the orange glow of its guts reflects in the window. She will remind the children (and her husband), as she does each day, to save their lunch bags, hang on to their Baggies.

Chapter Three

June 1985

HEAD DOWN, HAIR sweat-glued to his forehead, fists rammed into his dungaree pockets, Wayne Britton—scuffing, scowling—trudged home from his ex-job under a dirty-dishwater sky; third time in six months he'd been canned. At a distance, he wavered heat-watery, a rippling Route 49 phantom. Even with plenty room, oncoming traffic veered as if he were a car-gutted woodchuck plastered to the center line.

It was the kind of still, hot day where the air smelled of trailer-truck exhaust, where leaves hung as stiff as passed-out drunks, where mothers smacked their kids for no good reason. A day to get fired. When he got to town, Wayne stopped at Buzzell's Variety to buy a tonic.

His prices were a few pennies higher than the other stores', but Wayne always gave his business to Buzzell's when he had the chance—not that his business amounted to much. But it was the loyalty of people like Wayne that earned Buzzie Buzzell a living. Oh, Buzzell's sold the freezingest tonic and beer in town—the serious, almost professional, hot-weather beer guzzlers drove from all over Sanborn County to buy their cold ones at Buzzell's—and Buzzie was one hell of a nice guy, but that wasn't what drew Wayne to the store.

Buzzell's, reeking of sawdust and tobacco, as dim-lit as a root cellar, had once been Wayne's church, the purveyor of childhood icons: Nutty Buddy ice-cream cones, Table Talk chocolate-cream pies, Topps baseball cards, black and red licorice whips, cat's-eye marbles (which his mother would fry in a skillet to give them a cool cracked-glaze look), Fudgsicles, *Incredible Hulk* comic books, candy cigarettes, balsa-wood airplanes. But it wasn't mere nostalgia that drove Wayne to Buzzell's; he couldn't afford the luxury of nostalgia and, really, he had no stomach for stalking the past. No, on Buzzell's bowed and dusty shelves Wayne sought solace, however brief.

The genial jangle of the door's bell tingled Wayne's skin as he walked in . . . pausing to let his eyes adjust to the store's dusky innards.

"Buzzie." Wayne nodded to the man behind the counter, who wore a Boston Braves baseball cap; he admired Buzzie's stubbornness: The Braves'd fled Boston after the '52 season.

"Wayne," Buzzie said in a gargly growl—throat cancer.

"Come off hot," Wayne said.

"Yut," Buzzie. "Sure hell did."

"Supposed to be like this all week."

"Boil shit right out ya."

Wayne shunned the refrigerator that chilled the Coke, the Pepsi and all of their caffeine-free, sugar-free, calory-free and taste-free cousins; that was tourist tonic, flatlander fizz. He craved a real tonic, something so cold, sweet and syrupy he'd be tasting it next week. He tugged open what he thought of as the town refrigerator—a squat, round-topped Frigidaire decades old— the only place in Granite where you still could find such local institutions as Old Kerry's ginger ale and Mr. Frostie root beer and all of those great Piscataway Beverage Co. flavors: Ripplin' Razz-Berry, Granite Grape, Chugalug Cherry and Flossie's Famous Fruit Bowl. Piscataway Beverage, situated north of town in Banks, had even fired Wayne once. But he still drank the company's tonic; no hard feelings.

He settled finally on a Moxie, bittersweet and thick as fresh-laid tar, a slushy iceberg floating in the bottle. Just the way he liked it.

Setting down his Moxie to pay, Wayne saw a display of balsa-wood airplanes—what they'd called gliders when he was a kid. Seeing those gliders brought out in him a certain little-kid glee and a certain little-kid selfishness. He thought of the times when he'd wanted something as simple as a pack of baseball cards or a Nutty Buddy and there hadn't even been one nickel or a dime to spare, and he'd had to blink hard to stanch the tears.

He studied the finger-worn ten-dollar bill in his hand, his last ten bucks, and looked back at the gliders. (Buzzie waited quietly, used to his customers worrying over their money; there were even still a few that he let cuff a loaf of bread or a gallon of milk till payday.) Wayne couldn't say why, but he just had to have those gliders, all of them; he felt, somehow, as if he were owed.

"Screw it," he muttered as he pocketed his seventeen cents change and banged out the door.

No one home. Charlotte and the baby gone, his parents at work.

"Good," Wayne said.

Sitting on the back steps, he shucked his work boots and whung them—wounded crows—across the dooryard, one dinging the dead Pinto, the other tangling in the empty clothesline. His black tee shirt, washed one time too many, shredded as he yanked it off.

"Fuck it," he said.

He gnawed open one of the glider packs, spitting out the tongue-sticking scrap of plastic, and put the plane together: threading the wings through the fuselage, slipping on the tail assembly, sliding on the metal nose clip and, finally, snugging the half-bubble of the red cockpit. He did the nineteen others the same way, same as when he was a kid. Lining the gliders along the house's back wall, he hummed "Off we go into the wild, blue yonder."

Once he had them set just so—half with their wings thrust forward for loop-the-loops, half with wings slid back for distance—he picked one up and flicked it into the air, where it flitted through a couple of lazy loops before stuttering to a stop at his feet. He gentled it back into line.

Taking in his perfect row of twenty gliders made Wayne smile, reminded him of how, as a kid, he'd line up his toy cars by year and make, or how he kept his baseball cards in four even cardboard bricks—one for each Major League division—on his bureau, the teams stacked in order of that morning's standings and the players alphabetical within the teams. His mother once told him that he had cried at night when his window shades weren't tucked flush to the sills.

He launched the first glider, dipping and fluttering like a good knuckleball, toward the pond; heaved the second hard, making it turn tight, fierce loop-the-loops; when that one crashed nose first in a puff of dust, Wayne almost grinned; inspired, he scuttled down the row now, whipping the gliders into the air as quick as he could, conjuring a balsa-wood squall, a flock of gliders looping and swirling, climbing and diving, marking parabolic arcs, then skidding to earth as Wayne, red-faced-heaving, galloped around the yard, launching, re-launching, never letting them touch down for more than a few seconds, through sheer physical will trying to get them all aloft at the same time, trying, somehow, to balance his circumscribed world on the wings of balsa-wood airplanes. He flopped backwards into the dirt, the grit sticking to his sweat-slick back. The gliders flurried above him, seeming to hang suspended like the first tentative snowflakes of a new winter; he watched the gliders descend as a baby in a crib stares at a mobile swinging round and round, round and round. He was asleep before the last glider came home.

The desk, splinter-bristled, scarred, massive, hunkered scorned in the back office at Granite Chenille Co. Seemed the chenille shop'd sprung full-built from that desk, which'd been carved out of a wall. There was no question of its enduring. Anyone who'd ever knelt in its brute shadow knew it'd never give in — to sledge, fire, ax — even after the shop itself'd crumbled to dust and longing. Sarah, who worked in spitting distance of that primal stick of furniture, often lost herself for days at a time in its lacquered labyrinth of drawers, slots and dead ends; obsessed over it as if it were memory itself. Some days, it seemed that only the lure and mystery of that desk stood between her and quitting.

Granite Chenille kept Sarah's traitorous hands busy, strangled the minutes hours and days, brought a little extra to the household. Her thoughts gorged on themselves no matter what, so she figured she may as well get paid for the devouring as mope around the house. No clock-watcher, she knew it was lunch or quitting time only when Russ walked toward her, jabbing at his watch.

While his wife daydreamed amid the "slap, slap" of the belts and pulleys that drove the shop's nineteenth-century machines of oak and steel, Russ snuffed out one small crisis after another: a rat's-nest skein, a gap-toothed gear, a blunt blade. The chenille shop played to his skills; inflated them, even. Russ Britton could look at a machine and, in less than a minute, tell why it was broke and how to fix it. Tools sang in his coarse hands, motors thrummed; and he babied those cranky old machines.

Russ didn't much care about the product. Chenille, after all, was just dyed rayon twisted around cotton strands; Granite Chenille sold most of its stock to companies that used it to tie trout flies. It always gave Sarah the willies to think about her chenille catching in the gullet of some spasming fish.

No, Russ didn't worry over the chenille, one way or another, so long as it didn't snarl his machines. Screwdrivers (Phillips head and slot) jammed in one back pocket and a can of WD-40 lubricant in the other, he liked nothing better than to stroll among them: hands nuzzling work-aged oak varnished with finger oils; sucking in the smells of grease and oil, sawdust and cotton thread; listening to the metallic squeak, sigh and rustle of the ancient, women-coaxed machines spinning out skein after skein—seventy-two yards to the skein—of chenille; scrutinizing the ten or so women, their spools and scissors hanging from gargoyle nails

driven into the oak decades before, cotton strands playing through their callused, work-skinny fingers as they
fed thread into his hungry machines.

Russ slouched against the back wall (his boss and
the shop's owner, Bud Moss, wasn't in) and started a
piece of gum. Where Sarah, given half a chance, turned
inward, Russ pleasured in his surroundings. He noted
with satisfaction the plank shelves bowing under the
weight of new crates of thread, the just-checked-last-
week fire extinguishers, the pale flashes of straining
breast as the women sweated over their machines. He
supposed it was a good thing that he worked with his
wife.

At day's end, Russ and Sarah were the last to leave,
Russ being responsible for opening in the morning, closing at night. Stepping into the bright late afternoon, they
blinked, savored the barest hint of a breeze after being
cooped up all day in the stuffy shop.

"Bud coming in tomorrow?" Sarah asked.

"Hope so," said Russ, starting the car. "I need to
talk to him about that raise."

"Uh-huh."

"Cock-knocker best not give me any shit, neither.
I've been practically running the joint the last six
months."

Sarah sighed. "Wonder when I'll get a raise."

"Christ, it was hot today. My poison ivory was
enough to drive ya to drink. 'Specially where I got that
patch on the crack of my ass."

"It's good Bud trusts you so much."

"Trust don't feed the fuckin' kitten."

Sarah sighed again, stared out the window. "You know that old desk Bud's got in the back?" she said. "One that's all beat up and stuff?"

"Yeah . . ."

"Reminds me of Nanna's old place, before they tore it down and everything for that highway. Looking at it got me to thinking about Nanna all day long."

"Remember that time we come in early and caught Bud screwing that new girl on the desk?"

"Figures you'd remember that."

"She must've been picking slivers out her aching ass for a good month."

"Can't believe Nanna's been dead twenty years."

Russ and Sarah lapsed into their usual coming-home-from-work silence. A comfortable quiet earned only after long, twining years of marriage, when the days, even the fraying months and years, finally grow indistinguishable; a silence, if not of satisfaction, then at least of consolation. Weaned on marriages of subjugation and despair, Sarah gladly settled for consolation.

The car rattled over fresh-laid tar as thick and black as hornpout eggs.

"Mmm! There's a summer smell for ya," Russ said. "Hot tar; ranks right up there with cow flops. When we was kids we used to eat it—tar, I mean. Bittersweet and chewy's hell. Christ, we were dumb."

"Tar?" Sarah said.

"We'd eat anything when we was kids. One time someone told my brother Tommy that if he ate poison ivory he'd never catch it again, and the stupid bastard went ahead and ate a peck of it. His throat closed up tighter'n a constipated a-hole and his face puffed out all pink and watery. He was sicker'n a dog for a week."

She'd heard the story dozens of times, sometimes longer, sometimes shorter, but Sarah still gave her head a laughing shake; it was a good story, and Russ's brother *was* one stupid bastard.

Russ swung by Buzzell's to pick up a six-pack; Sarah forced herself not to say anything. Russ, cradling his six in one arm, brought her out a Fudgsicle.

"Buzzie says Wayne was by this afternoon," said Russ, cracking a brew. "Wonder what he's doing home so early?"

Sarah snorted in disgust. "You got to have a talk with him, Russ," she said. "I don't like the way he's been treating that baby. And I ain't going to put up with it in my house. It's bad enough having that Charlotte bitch around."

Whenever Sarah said more than one sentence at a time, Russ knew she was mad. "I know, I know," he said. "I try talking to him and talking to him. But it's like it goes in one ear and comes out the other."

"Well, you better talk to him again. I ain't going to let him treat that baby like that."

"Okay."

"Jessie's my granddaughter, for chrissakes. I saw enough of that shit when I was growing up."

"I'll take care of it, hon."

"Love that baby."

Wayne spread-eagled on the gravel was the first thing
Sarah and Russ saw as their car crunched into the driveway. And in that split second between seeing Wayne
and his lurching awake, Sarah dizzied as her breath
caught and the blood boiled to her cheeks; he's dead,
she thought even as Wayne woke, and that whore killed
him. The fierceness of her reaction, so swift, so strong,
staggered Sarah—shaking, sick to her stomach. Seeing
her son sprawled like that had, somehow, ruptured an
emotional fault. It was as if, when it came to Wayne,
Sarah expected the worst. But she could see now,
though her cheeks still prickled, that he was alive, was
his usual bellyaching self.

"Hey, watch out! Watch out!" he yelled as the car
toothpicked one of his gliders. "Aw shit!"

"What're you pissing and moaning about?" Russ
asked. "What's the matter with you?"

"You run over one of my gliders."

One hand resting on the steering wheel, the other
coddling his bottle of beer, Russ took in his glider-
glutted dooryard: "Where'n hell did all these gliders
come from?"

Wayne shrugged.

"And what do you think you were you doing laying
on the ground like that? Like some fucking retard. You
about give me and your mother a heart attack."

Another shrug.

"You numb or something?"

Wayne worked his lips, meaning to speak. Russ cut

him off: "I swear, you and that wife of yours are enough to drive anyone to drink. How come you ain't at work, anyways?"

Wayne wouldn't—couldn't—look at his father. At his own bare dirty feet, the Pinto, his mother (red-faced, about set to cry), anywhere but at his old man.

"I don't goddamn believe it," Russ said. "You got shit-canned, didn't you? You got fired again, you dink. Then you go and blow your money on friggin' gliders. Well, you better not come crying poverty to us this time. You best better get your ass in gear and find another job.

"Tomorrow."

Staring at Wayne, Sarah ached for Hannah. Her daughter soothed her, understood her; Wayne only glared. Sarah was ashamed she'd thought he was dead. Even so, she wished that Hannah lived at home, that Wayne'd been the one smart enough to go away to college. Not that she'd ever admit that to anybody, not even Russ; especially not to Russ.

After his parents went inside, Russ slamming the door so the house shook, Wayne lined up his gliders again.

Most summers, the serious heat—the muggy, merciless, mosquito-ragged heat—took up residence at the Brittons' come late June and didn't head south till the first Canada-crisp days after Labor Day. Serious heat: sleep-stealing, nerve-gnawing, beer-killing heat. Fans couldn't suck it, open windows couldn't coax it. Heat that hunkered down. Siege heat.

"Sure wish we could get an air conditioner," Wayne said to no one in particular.

"Look like I'm made of money?" Russ said.

Slumped in the living room, Wayne and Russ were watching the Red Sox. Nibbling her fingernails, Sarah sweated at the kitchen table. Charlotte had escaped upstairs with the baby.

"Want to hear why I got fired?" Wayne said.

Russ, barechested and dog-comfortable on the couch, glanced over at Wayne, called to Sarah: "Honey, you want to make me some ice coffee?"

Sighing a sigh of habit, Sarah scraped away from the table. Satisfied, Russ turned back to the ball game.

"You want to hear?" Wayne asked.

No answer.

"Do you?"

"Huh?" Russ said. "What?"

"Want to know why I got canned?"

"Sure," said Russ, not looking up. "It's a free country."

"They said I was a know-it-all. That's why they fired me. You believe that shit? A know-it-all."

"Uh-huh."

"How can you get rid of someone for being a know-it-all?"

"Boy, this kid can hit. Look at that sweet swing."

"Tell you one thing. I've been getting more than my share of the short end of the stick lately."

"Did you see that? You see that? Bastard tried to bean him."

Russ sipped his ice coffee, eyes on the TV.

Wayne looked at the TV, too, and made a face like he'd just slurped cod-liver oil: "Look at nem assholes, getting millions of bucks to play baseball. Play a frigging game. I don't even got the money to put my goddamned car back on the road. Felt real good today. Get the royal heave-ho, then I got to walk five miles to get home."

"Sure was hot," Russ said.

"Tell me about it. Figures I'd get canned on a day like today."

"Hey, you know who I saw up to the store tonight? Johnny Temple. Ain't seen him in a coon's age. Me and Johnny go way back."

Wayne was all set for Russ to launch into one of his Johnny Temple stories; he could use a long, funny story. Maybe the one about the time Russ and Johnny slept out in Cedar Swamp. Or the one about when they shot the skunk and nobody'd talk to them for a week because it stunk so bad. His old man sure could tell a good story. Wayne'd give him that much.

But Russ's eyes lit for just a second at the thought of Johnny Temple. Lit, flickered and died, as if trying to tell a story was too much, as if the joy he usually took in shaping the past (like shaving dice in your favor) had become a chore.

"Jesus, the Red Sox suck this year," Russ said.

Upstairs, Jessie started in crying.

"Aw, man," Wayne said. "Not tonight."

Russ, overcoming his gut's gravity, grunted himself up off the couch and turned up the TV. Sarah, still sitting at the kitchen table, sighed, said: "I wish we had something good to eat." (If Charlotte would only ask, she thought, I'd hold Jessie for her, shush the poor thing.)

Seemed to Wayne that the summer so far had been one endless bout of scorch-your-bones heat and *that* baby's crying. He'd never known a thing to wail so, an hours-on-end caterwauling that made him think of Jessie as no more than a cry in the dark, a hoarse, unwanted burden. His mother and Charlotte said the baby had the colic (what the fuck did Charlotte know, anyway?), that she'd outgrow it soon. Sometimes they'd rock her in their arms, whispering and nuzzling in secret women ways. But other times, they'd let her squowl, cocking their heads to one side, as if listening to a favorite old song on the radio, as they interpreted the pitch and intensity of her cries. In those moments, the two women didn't seem so different, after all.

Closing his eyes, all Wayne wanted was to sift through the wreckage of his day in peace. Was that too much for a fired man to ask? But all he could bring into focus was the baby, spasming with the purple shrieks.

"Charlotte!" Wayne yelled up the stairs, startling Russ and Sarah. "Get that baby to shut the fuck up!"

Charlotte laughed at him, laughed in his face though he was downstairs.

"Don't you laugh at me. Don't you ever laugh at me."

Charlotte quickstepped down the stairs and thrust the baby at Wayne as if she were punishing him.

"Here," she said, "you can at least hold her while I go to the bathroom."

Sweaty, still bawling, the baby stuck to Wayne's bare chest. He'd gone stiff when Charlotte handed him the baby; it was as if Jessie were made of razor blades and he was afraid of getting cut.

He tried a couple of bounces on his knee; the baby cried louder.

"Sshh, Jessie," he tried. "Sshh." The baby cried louder.

He patted her rump, rubbed her back, tickled her stomach; the baby cried louder.

He pried her from his chest, let her writhe on his lap: fists clenched, tears flowing, upper lip quivering, snot oozing. He looked hard at her for some seconds, trying to connect, trying to really see this thing called his daughter. But all he could see was a squirming, squealing, ball of raw meat.

And before he could stop himself—he had wanted to stop—he roared: "I'm going to hang this fucking baby if she doesn't shut up!"

Jessie suddenly stopped crying—the silence after a vicious storm—and Wayne saw that his wife, mother and father were all looking at him.

"What's everyone staring at?"

Sarah couldn't sleep. When she shut her eyes, all she heard was Wayne bellowing at Baby Jessie, threatening to hang her. She thought about Page's Village, so many babies loved and unloved, wanted and unwanted. How she, one of those unloved and unwanted (by her mother, anyway), had spent her childhood seeking refuge, sniffing the air for the barest scent of love:

✕

Plumped down on her front steps, Auntie Robena sops up the late afternoon's whiskey-gold sunlight. Page's Village has quieted: the women retreating indoors to fix suppers (the air thick with the smell of potatoes frying) and the children, spent after the day's chase, lazing in the long itchy grass, deciphering the clouds, dozing.

Sarah, whom Robena calls Susie (because it ticks off Ella), plays at the foot of the steps, building scrap-lumber towers and houses. Sarah isn't yet allowed to run with the older children, so pregnant Robena, on Nanna's orders, looks after her. Not that she minds. Robena, so far spurning her Page-hood, is a talker, the village soliloquist, gossip and seer, owner of a wicked, blood-drawing tongue. Sarah gives her someone to gab at.

"I'll tell you one sure thing, Susie girl," Robena says. "Men are sons-ta-bitches. Mean little snakey sons-ta-bitches."

Sarah glances up at her aunt. Even at three, Sarah knows she isn't meant to say much, just nod, listen and forget. A sponge to be wrung out at the end of each day.

"Your uncle Allen knows I ain't been feeling good, but off he goes anyways, gallivanting to the dump with Grandpa Elgar and them. What's it say about a man who'd rather be out picking the dump and shooting at stinky old rats than home with his sick and pregnant wife?"

"Don't know, Auntie 'Bena," Sarah says.

Most Pages are pickerel-bodied, all bone, scale and gristle. But Robena's an overripe apple: round, soft and fleshy, breasts like fresh-fluffed pillows; you can't even tell she's pregnant. Sarah loves her aunt for that body, prefers her to Ella. Robena's a special hiding place; Sarah can crawl onto her aunt's lap, burrow into her softness and vanish. Touching Ella's like hugging barbwire.

"I know I should've known better," Robena goes on, "the way he come sneaking around, hiding behind Daddy, wouldn't even look me in the eye, and then trying to squeeze my poor titties the first time we went for a walk down to the frog pond."

So much talk. So much that Sarah wishes she could save some for home, for the shadow hours when Ella sits mute at the kitchen table, gnawing on her own guts. It seems to Sarah that Robena says more to her in one hour than her mother does in a month. Robena dizzies Sarah with her talk; Ella starves her with silence.

"Oh, I don't mind having this baby—and I hope it's a girl just like you, Susie sweetie—I guess I got what was coming to me. But why did Nanna punish me? Make me marry dumb old Allen Swett?

" 'But he's so stupid, Nanna,' I says to her. And she says: 'Not as stupid as you thought, was he?'

" 'But I don't want to get married,' I says. 'I know you don't like him no more'n I do.' She says: 'You stop your whining. That baby's got to have a name.'

" 'What's wrong with Page?' I asks her. Then she stops talking, stares me down with those sharp black eyes of hers, and I clam up, too. When we was kids we knew what her hush meant. A smack in the puss or a switching. When she stops talking, I know right then and there that I'm going to end up being Mrs. Allen Swett, whether I like it or not."

"Were you bad, Auntie?" Sarah asks. "That why Nanna got so mad?"

Swept away by her story, Robena doesn't hear Sarah: "Us kids are all grown, but sometimes I wish that she still hit us. I'd rather feel her bony hand grab at us, hear it crack us, than be gobbled up by her wicked looks and her black quiets."

Robena squints up the hill at the house, which looms over her the way Nanna had when she was a child, and whispers: "Why did she make me marry him?"

The whisper draws Sarah to her aunt the way the jingle of change draws her to Grandpa Elgar. But, about to settle into Robena's lap, Sarah looks down and says: "Auntie, you're bleeding."

When Robena sees the bloody delta of her white shorts, she looks to her mother's house and sighs before saying: "Go get Nanna."

❦

Smoking a cigarette, Russ sat in the dark on the back steps, comforted by the song of the peepers down to the pond. It was after midnight, but he couldn't sleep. He wasn't sure whether it was the heat, or because Wayne hadn't come home yet from running off. Seemed Wayne was always running from something or doing the wrong thing. He was smart enough, strong enough. But his head wasn't screwed on quite right; a couple of threads'd been stripped somewhere along the way, and Russ wasn't sure whose fault that was; and he sure wasn't going to discuss *that* with Sarah. There'd been that time the winter before when Wayne couldn't get his car started. Instead of lugging the battery into the house or draining the crankcase oil to heat it or waiting for the day to warm, Wayne'd stoked a fire under the car. They were still finding bits and pieces of that Olds buried in the gravel.

Shaking his head, as if trying to shoo such thoughts, Russ took a long, hard pull on his Lucky Strike, forcing the smoke deep into his lungs; a harsh warmth billowed in his chest. Eyes closed, Russ gave himself up to the chorus of peepers. He'd had enough of Wayne for one day.

Sarah III

She cries at the kitchen table, shivering in the chill that each day settles on her house after the children leave for school. Hers are silent tears, tapping ancient black springs of sadness as deep and dark as the water-filled quarries that lay in the backwoods. The tears burn; she tries to swallow the grief caught in her throat, but can't.

Chapter Four

1959

THE SUMMER SARAH
turned ten, her auntie Leah fell in love.

Yes, Leah'd been shacked up, disowned, married, separated, undisowned and divorced, all by the time she got a handhold on twenty, courtesy of Howie Des-Marais—"duh-maris." She still even wore Howie's name (hocked the ring, though) as both penance and re-minder: "I went through enough g.d. trouble to get that name," she'd say. "May as well get some use out of it."

All Howie DesMarais had turned out to be was a mangy mutt blessed with a little spending money and a big Dodge. Leah, unschooled about men (purposely) by her mother and fighting her pull, had known that she was confusing ninety-mile-an-hour drives to Manor Beach, new sweaters, drive-in movies, sips of beer and backseat lessons with . . . something. They got married anyway. And within three months, Leah—a prisoner to fierce, forty-watt, whiskey nights—fled back home to Page's Village, where the satisfaction of a hard lesson taught played on Nanna Page's scar-thin lips.

Later, after months spent whittling her ex-husband down to his hands' leather smell, the crinkle of crumpled dollar bills, the coffee-brandy-and-milk breakfasts, Leah could laugh and say of her marriage that she'd been "DesMaraised."

But love? *Love?* The women of Page's Village tended prickly gardens of silence and spite, lust and submission. Making do was a virtue. Love was a foreign language spoken by people who didn't have to break their backs to make ends meet. Love was a frill, like spending money you didn't have.

Wrapped around a broom that looked to be sweeping her—instead of the other way around—Sarah flailed at the shack grit (the dirt and dust transformed into flecks of gold as it paperweight-swirled in the early-morning sun) while Leah, up to her elbows in vegetables, worked at the kitchen table: quartering tomatoes, scraping carrots, slicing cucumbers, chopping celery, dicing green peppers, gutting heads of Boston lettuce.

Shaming the sun, they'd been up since five: boiling water; scrubbing and bleaching sheets, towels and pillowcases, then hanging them out to dry; banging rugs against the shack; drowning the outhouse hole in Lysol disinfectant and leaving behind fists of bog laurel—violet bomb-bursts; mending screens; plucking crisp flies from dangly fly-strips; dusting windowsills; and washing windows, inside and out, till they squeaked. So caught up were they in their frenzy of cleaning and preparation that if they'd been at church, they would've been speaking in tongues.

Sarah shooed the last of the dirt out the back door and, red-cheeked and sweaty, slouched against the doorjamb: "Ain't we been working like Pages, Auntie?" She grinned at Leah, who grinned back. Conspirators.

Coltish legs pyramiding out of the steamy water, Sarah took a bath in the cast-iron tub. She shut her eyes and slithered low as she could, the lip of the tub gouging her neck. She smiled and imagined just sitting there till noon—soaking.

"Wake up there, you lazybones," Leah said. "Auntie's friend'll be coming before you know it. Here, let me wash your hair."

Leah knelt behind Sarah and nudged her niece's head forward, chin flushing to her chest. Leah stroked the blond down that feathered Sarah's neck, rubbed her smooth, narrow back, trying, for a few seconds anyway, to fill the empty places Ella had left behind. And Leah, without realizing, gave her head an ain't-that-a-shame shake, knowing even then that whatever ended up happening to Sarah would be a shame, same as it was for all of them born to Page's Village.

"Close your eyes," said Leah, slowly pouring the lukewarm teakettle water.

Leah used bar soap on her own hair, but splurged on baby shampoo for Sarah, who shivered at the dollop of coldness. Leah worked the shampoo in with her fingertips, kneading Sarah's scalp.

"I like it when you wash my hair, Auntie," said Sarah, pressing her head to Leah's palms the way a cat nuzzles the leg that feeds it.

"Me too," Leah said.

"I make believe like I'm sitting in one of those beauty shops, like Mr. Steve's over in Lamprey. Sally Wilson said she went there Easter to get her hair done up."

"Uh-huh."

"Nanna ever used to wash your hair, Auntie?"

"No. We always had to do our own riggin' when we was kids."

"Like me when I lived with Momma. Right, Auntie?"

"Keep those eyes shut now. I'm going to rinse."

Sarah was turned out in her company's-coming best: the white cotton dress with leg-o'-mutton sleeves, white plastic hair band, white ankle socks embroidered with purple lilacs, and patent-leather Mary Janes (pinching her toes) as shiny and black as Nanna Page's eyes. When she'd first dressed, Sarah had squirmed, nettled by the hold-your-breath self-consciousness of wearing her "good" clothes. But after some minutes, she calmed, stopped fidgeting, grew into her clothes by not thinking about them.

She stood tiptoe on the front steps, squinting up the hill to Route 49, where the sun flashed off the glass, chrome and steel of the cars darting by.

Sarah liked to wait. It spooked her that time passed so quick; it was more than four years already since her mother had run away, but to Sarah it seemed it couldn't have been more than a few months since Ella left. Waiting lent time heft, texture; when Sarah waited, she felt time weigh on her, could almost touch it. She had lost childhood's impatience, like a bald, one-armed doll, early on; it was one of the reasons why grown-ups liked having her around. Waiting allowed Sarah both to meet obligations and to burrow into herself, her surroundings. (She wondered how long she would have to wait before her mother came back.) Her aunt had asked her to wait outdoors for Rachel Davidson, and she happily did so. But, still keeping an eye on Route 49, Sarah also gathered in the afternoon, Page's Village.

The day'd come off warm, smelling of dried straw, the clear sky the color of the threadbare knees of old dungarees; wasps sawed in the eaves; heat rippled from the shack's shiny black shingles; off toward Auntie Fat Dot's, hidden cousins whooped. Up the path, the charred circle where her mother's house had once stood held her spellbound for a few seconds. She'd spent her first five years in that cold, dark shack—that thorned

womb—and it had thrilled her to see it burn, have
Nanna use it to punish both her mother and Uncle
Dead, because she knew she would never have to live
in it again.

A droplet of sweat slid down her forehead as a dust
cloud suddenly billowed at the top of the dirt road and
boiled down the hill behind a nail-polish-red Thunder-
bird convertible.

"She's here, Auntie! She's here! She's really here!"

The T-bird coasted to a stop in front of Leah's shack,
Rachel smiling, waving. Sarah turned to her aunt and,
in a loud whisper, said: "She's beautiful!"

Leah and Rachel worked together at the furniture
factory. Though Rachel was a college girl and the factory owner's daughter, they'd become fast friends. They
sweated side by side over the relentless stitching machines, wolfed down brown-bagged sandwiches in the
half-hour they stole for lunch, griped to each other about
Dufour—that filthy, radish-faced, chinless weasel—
their foreman, covered for each other, trusted each
other. Talked to each other.

By the time Rachel had graduated that spring she
was fed up with college girls' brittle chatter; she craved
stronger medicine. Leah DesMarais—five years older,
high-cheekboned face already lining—spoke to her of
real life; Leah's stories, her words spent as carefully as
the faded dollar bill that stands between hunger and
payday, about Page's Village, her ex-husband, the furniture shop, Granite and the like revealed to Rachel an
unseen, unsuspected world. Like that first time peering

into a microscope and seeing a school of paramecia making its way in a world suspended in a drop of water. For Leah, raised on circumspection and punished with silence, Rachel was the first friend she'd ever had to whom she could tell anything—everything! Talking about Page's Village felt like betrayal (if Nanna Page had ever known . . .) but not talking was suffocation. She gratefully gave Page's Village to Rachel. In return, Rachel gave her Boston: the Pops, a Red Sox game at Fenway Park, the Museum of Fine Arts, Bloody Marys at the Ritz-Carlton.

"Hi, Leah," said Rachel, hugging her. "I thought I'd never get here."

Leah blushed and, arms stiff as two-by-fours, hugged Rachel back as best she could.

"You must be Sarah," said Rachel, looking her in the eye, hands lighting on her shoulders. "You look like you could be your aunt's sister." (She said "aunt" like "ant.")

"Hi," Sarah whispered.

"Hi," Rachel whispered back.

That year in fourth grade, Miss Walsh one morning had brought in a strip of silver-white metal, struck a match, and lit it. The magnesium sizzled with a dazzling white light that Sarah had obsessed over for weeks after. Eventually, she forgot about the magnesium. Until she met Rachel Davidson, who, she decided right away, burned with the same stark white light.

"You must be starving after that long drive, Rachel,"

Leah said. "I fixed us a big salad and I've got hamburgs frying on the stove. We even bought some tonic."

"I am hungry," Rachel admitted. "Do you need help with anything?"

"Nope. Nothing at all," said Leah as the two women went inside.

Sarah stood dazed in the dooryard. She still smelled Rachel's perfume; her shoulder blades still tingled where Rachel had touched her; her ears buzzed.

Sarah was used to the sweat-smelling women of Page's Village, who spent their days like cornered animals. Their eroded faces etched by a troubling mix of resignation and ferocity. She'd never met anyone like Rachel, whose presence—though she'd done her best to dull herself: red kerchief, white tee shirt, jeans—seemed to diminish the village, make it skulk off toward Cedar Swamp like a mortified dog or Uncle Allen when Auntie Robena threw him out of the house for the umpteenth time.

Sarah closed her eyes and imagined Rachel Davidson—hair a waterfall of tight dark curls, skin the color of the foot-worn stairs at school after they'd been varnished—until her aunt called her in to eat.

A small marsh oozed at the foot of the hill, hemmed in on one side by the path up to Nanna Page's and on the other by the dirt road. Every spring the marsh would exact a small measure of revenge for its imprisonment by overflowing, washing away both path and road until

Grandpa Elgar got one of his town buddies to bring in a couple loads of fill. Punky, gray boards crisscrossed the marsh, letting the villagers harvest it: blueberries, blackberries, rhubarb, bramble-berries, strawberries, grapes, pussy willows, cat-o'-nine-tails. Not that the picking was easy; nothing in Page's Village was ever easy. Over the years, the marsh had woven a thick, barbwire tangle of thorn and thistle. The berries grew plump and juicy; picking them required blood. There were snakes and snapping turtles, too, but nothing to fuss about compared to their brute brothers who ruled Cedar Swamp, which lay miles deep in the woods.

Once she'd quit school and started working, Leah had shunned the marsh. Growing up, it'd been one of her jobs to berry the marsh, and she'd had enough of getting thorn-whipped, bug-bit, leech-legged and snake-spooked. Nanna Page, of course, gloried in the whole business.

"I'll never forget it long as I live," Leah said as they ate. "And I ain't making it up. One day Momma goes berrying, and she's thrashing around in there for a good long while. And when she scutters out all scratched and scraped up, she's got one bucket of blueberries hanging round her neck, she's lugging another bucket in one hand, and in the other she's holding a friggin' water snake that must be six foot long. And if that ain't enough, I'll be good and goddamned if there ain't a baby snapping turtle muckled ahold of her boot, and Momma keeps trying to fling it off till, finally, her whole boot comes flying off, snapper and all, and does a cartwheel over our heads."

Rachel'd been trying to keep a straight face since the six-foot snake slithered into the story. But when Nanna Page's boot, snapper-ballasted, came whipping off, Rachel couldn't keep it in no more and she started laughing—just as she took a gulp of Moxie. Then, she started choking.

Leah pounded her on the back, factory girl thumps that about nailed Rachel to the floor; red-faced and teary, Rachel caught her breath. But when she looked at Leah—"That Moxie got bones in it?"—she started laughing again, doubled over, clutching at Leah's arms as if she were drowning, the sweet music of her laughter suffusing Sarah and Leah, making them smile.

When Rachel finally calmed, tears still winking, she said: "Well, let's go berrying."

That was how Leah found herself tramping through the "g.d. marsh" with Rachel on a sticky summer's afternoon. (Sarah had stayed behind. As much as she wanted to be with Leah and Rachel, she feared the marsh the way her relations feared Nanna Page; she knew it wasn't true, but it struck Sarah that the marsh was the kind of place where Nanna could've been born.)

The sun bore down, boiling the talk right out of the two women as they sloshed along, mosquitoes and horseflies getting acquainted and, no matter how careful they were, thorns nicking and nipping. Leah, a Page woman through and through, wouldn't complain; in fact, she was surprised to realize, she almost liked the situation—her leading, Rachel following. Rachel's family owned the factory and Boston was her city, but Page's Village belonged to Leah. Rachel needed her to negotiate it.

"Where are those goddamned blueberry bushes, Lee?" Rachel asked.

"Almost there. Wait here a minute. Let me check through there."

Rachel sighed, feeling stupid about trying to prove how tough she was, prove how Page's Village wasn't too much for a city girl. Then the snake hissed.

Snake wasn't that big, maybe a foot and a half, but it was mad, black and hissing. Rachel wasn't so much afraid, though the snake's rasp knotted her stomach, as ignorant. She didn't know what to do. She knew how to unravel Boston traffic, but a ticked-off snake? They stared at each other.

The boot smacked down on the snake's head—Rachel jumped—skull bones crunching as they were ground into the board, the body arching, coiling, then whipping in that frenzy that comes before death.

Rachel hadn't heard Leah return—Pages *are* good sneaks—and neither, apparently, had the snake.

Leah toed the dead snake, a coil of old clothesline, into the water. Rachel said: "I don't suppose that Nanna Page gives lessons, does she?"

Even as place defines a person, so, too, is that place defined by that person. Nanna Page's Granite *was* Page's

Village. She owned it, and drew from it what she needed. She rarely strayed far.

Leah's Granite took in much more of the town than Nanna's. And when Rachel said she wanted to see Granite, Leah was set on teaching her friend her town. Not the state park (crawling with out-of-state flatlanders) and not the Plains, picketed by white-skinned, black-eyed colonials. So with Rachel driving and Sarah sitting on her lap, Leah revealed the true Granite, the Granite that'd shaped Leah DesMarais the way wind and rain etch the face of a cliff.

The summer camps, which the out-of-staters who owned them insisted on calling cottages, girding the lake; Leah pointing to places where she'd weeded flower beds and mowed lawns, changed diapers and mopped floors, fended off the smooth hands of dark-tanned summer boys. The B. Houston School, the one-room schoolhouse where Leah and her brothers and sisters had taken their eight grades' worth; its once-red paint bleached white-pink, its belfry bell-less; the town fathers, all of them grudgingly schooled there, used it for storage. The Marrying Tree, a back-road Bible oak, a tree rough with Old Testament bark, a great-grandfather oak that made you want to bloody your knees and shout your sins, a tree with thousands of branches striving toward God and millions of leaves singing His hymns; Graniters had been getting married under that tree since the 1600s, and it was where Leah'd married Howie DesMarais. Cheney's Sawmill, where, as a girl, Leah'd worked as hard and as well as any boy.

The fire tower at the top of washboard Rockrimmon Road, where Leah, like many Granite girls, had first closed her eyes, gritted her teeth, and opened her bare legs.

Places and stories. Stories and places. Trying to distill for Rachel (and herself) some kind of truth about Granite, New Hampshire. Trying to articulate a life bordered by silences, digging into the compost of dead, buried and decaying memories. She couldn't say why, but this was what Leah wanted to give Rachel Davidson. It was important to her that this city girl, this college girl, taste these truths.

Listening, listening as hard she could, Sarah sat still on her aunt's lap, afraid she might miss a single word. She had learned to listen early on in Page's Village, learned that grown-ups, even wary Pages, would ignore a quiet kid trying to weasel her way toward understanding: scrounging for scraps of conversation, sifting through nighttime whispers, interpreting sighs and grunts. Pages dammed their words (even once-gabby Aunt Robena, obsessed with breaking Uncle Allen, had granited up over the years) and Sarah had to work hard to catch the mistaken trickles; in that listening, Sarah began to understand how Nanna Page knew what she knew and she began to understand, just a little, her grandmother. But here was Auntie Leah, gushing to a practical stranger. Sarah believed that she'd learned more about her aunt during that afternoon drive than she had in the previous ten years.

And Sarah, like a true Page, would hoard that knowledge in her own dark wells.

Leah and Rachel sat talking at the kitchen table. They drank Bloody Marys thick with fresh-ground Page's Village horseradish from tall, sweating glasses. After midnight, and Leah's was the only light flickering in the heat-restless village. Moths and millers hurled themselves at the screen door; the peepers' chorus—counterpointed by the buh-wonk! of a lone bullfrog—swelled as night deepened; a mosquito would buzz within earshot, fade. Sarah, spent the way only a child can be, had been asleep for hours, lulled by the women's low voices.

"We used to drive through here when I was a little girl," Rachel said, "on our way to the White Mountains and Lake Winnipesaukee."

"Just another car in the Mass-hole caravan," Leah said, and the two of them snickered.

"But, you know what's funny, I don't remember Granite's lake, or the Plains, or the Congregational church; it seemed that every town we drove through had those. But I do remember seeing Page's Village; I didn't realize it until today."

"Oh, come on, Rache."

"I do, Leah."

"You sure? You ain't making this up?"

"I remember asking my mother once, 'Mommy, why do people live like that in such a pretty town?' "

Nanna called the time between midnight and sunrise the crying hours, and given the hour and the drinks, Rachel's story almost got the two of them bawling.

"We never even thought about it when we was little," Leah said. "You know how kids are. We didn't know no better."

Rachel nodded. Leah went on: "We didn't know nothing except Page's Village. That's all Nanna expected us to know. Wasn't for her, we would've all ended up in the poorhouse. She kept us all together, and she never let us forget.

"I'll tell you, you didn't never want to cross her. She never never forgives. She never forgets. Long as my mother's alive, there ain't no way in hell that my brother Henry's ever going to set foot in Page's Village again. Course, he got off easy compared to Billy."

Right away, Leah knew she'd gone too far. There were still stories meant only for Page ears. Leah suddenly was afraid. Afraid of Nanna. Afraid of that old bitch up the hill like she had been her whole life. Leah's fear both shamed and angered her.

"Leah, what's the matter? You look ill."

Shaking her head, Leah took a gulp from her Bloody Mary.

"Leah, talk to me. What's wrong?"

Leah's voice smoldered low and fierce, fueled by an old rage, rage that had burned in her gut since she could remember: "You want to hear about this place? I'll tell you about Page's Village. My mother killed my big brother Billy two years ago. Burned him up in my sister's shack. Did it because Billy fucked Henry and Dot's little Jenny. Got the poor thing out to his shed—with Henry's help—and about split her open. Reason Henry did it is that Jenny ain't his. My father, Elgar, is Jenny's father. Fat Dot's the mother. There's Page's Village, for you. There's goddamned Page's Village."

Without taking her eyes off Leah, Rachel poured fresh drinks. "How'd you grow up like this?" she asked, her words soft knives.

Leah shrugged.

"How could anybody grow up like this?"

"It weren't that bad, Rachel. We had food on the table. We had clean clothes on our backs. Nanna . . ."

Rachel reached across the table, fingers lighting on Leah's cheek, and whispered: "How?"

Leah's breath caught, even as her skin tingled, her face flushed. The question, the one she'd been wanting to ask all day, was posed in Rachel's eyes.

"Leah . . ."

She pressed Rachel's hand to her lips. Kissed her fingers one at a time.

Through summer's verdant hush, fall's brief blaze of color, and into winter's black bones and drawn white skin, their affair flourished—sanding smooth Leah's rough edges even as it rasped at Rachel's softness—nourished by secrets, discretion and the numbing flush of infatuation.

Rachel's red T-bird, mud-spattered and salt-shocked, appeared in the middle of a snow shower one midmorning in March. Head down, shrinking against the snow, Rachel hurried into the shack.

"Leah, we have to talk," she said as she stamped her feet, brushed off her coat. "Alone."

Leah's life had been a thicket of one-word sentences; little good had ever come of them.

"Sarah, why don't you take those eggs on up to Nanna now," Leah said.

"Okay, Auntie," Sarah said, then: "Hi, Auntie Rachel."

Rachel bent down and gave her a hug of affection and apology. "Hi, Sarah sweetie," she said. "I'm sorry I rushed in like that. I'm just not myself today."

Sarah walked outside, the sky ripe with big, spring snowflakes as wet as adolescent kisses. Nanna called snow like that "the poor man's fertilizer." Sarah stopped at the T-bird; its wide chrome grill seemed to grin at her the way Rachel usually did. She pressed her cheek to the warm, wet hood, where snowflakes winked into tears, listened to the engine tick. She kissed the hood.

Snowflakes frosting her hair, she started for her grandmother's.

When Sarah got back, Leah sat red-eyed, Rachel gone. It felt to Sarah as if something had been stolen.

"Auntie, what's the matter?"

"Rachel's moving away. To Israel."

In the old days, the days before Rachel, that would've been enough for any Page to say. But Sarah expected more from her aunt now.

Leah sighed and went on: "Her whole family's going. They're selling the furniture shop and all moving to Israel. . . .

"Rachel wants me to go with her. . . .

"But, no matter how hard I try, I can't leave this goddamned place. I can't even imagine it. Can you believe that, Sarah? Auntie can't even imagine leaving."

Leah started crying again, stomach-churning sobs that made her quiver. And as much as she wanted to, Sarah couldn't bring herself to walk across the kitchen and soothe her; she was frozen in place by her aunt's tears.

Chapter Five

July 1985

WAYNE, CHARLOTTE and Jessie left late one Friday, the red moon a burning cradle in the night sky. Winding northward, Wayne kept the Dart to tree-choked back roads, shadow short-cuts perfected long ago. Jessie slept in Charlotte's arms, head snugged one last time between her mother's neck and shoulder; Charlotte held the baby tighter than she needed.

They drove without speaking, the radio turned to a murmur. Now and again one of them would glance at the other, look away. Their wounds pulsed purple, raw, deep.

"We can turn around," Wayne lied in a whisper.

"No!" Charlotte hissed back, the air trembling with words unsaid.

Eating their own guts . . . they drove on.

Wayne and Charlotte came home to the nervous gossip of predawn birds. They came home alone.

Chapter Six

1965

DROWSING IN HER deathbed, Nanna Page listened to the ice storm; silver storms, they'd called them as kids. Iced rain pecked at the windows, clattered on the roof. She imagined each rain particle as it ticked the shingles: a fat, lazy droplet, sent from the warmish heavens, freezing suddenly at ground level, fusing with its sisters to sheet the roof, the village, in a diamond skin.

She'd come into this world in such a storm, a last hard kiss of winter late one spring: ice-coated cows smothered in the fields; chickens, sudden weather vanes, froze in the trees; the midwife, Mertie Swett, slipped and broke her arm coming up the back steps to the kitchen (before the steps themselves gave way to the ice's weight) but delivered the Page baby anyway. When Nanna had heard the storm's first halting taps at her window, beckoning, late that afternoon, she decided she had seen her last morning. Damned if she was going to let the cancer dictate terms of surrender.

Dusk hardened into night; the storm waned; ice-strangled tree limbs gasped, fell. She sensed her husband standing in the doorway behind her; it seemed to her that he'd spent their marriage fidgeting in doorways, never knowing whether he was coming or going.

"Elgar?" she said, her voice cracked leather.

He crept into her dark room as if it were carpeted with copperheads, timber rattlers, and lighted on the bed, taking care not to even graze his wife. He kindled a kerosene lamp; she'd forbidden him to hook electricity up to her room when he'd done the rest of the house years before.

"Elgar," she whispered, her voice seeming to hiss from the flame. "It's time."

"Huh?"

A little louder: "It's time."

"For what?"

Looking at Elgar, Nanna saw a husk, a winter cornstalk. She hadn't set out to marry a man weaker than she was; she just hadn't found any man as strong. Never mind stronger. At the time, it had seemed Elgar Felch would do; and, she supposed, he had.

"Elgar, go tell Sarah and Leah and Robena, all of them, that it's time," she said.

He stared at her, his head cocked sideways. He still didn't understand.

"I'm dying, Elgar."

"Oh"—his raw, bony hands writhing in his lap.

"Tell Sarah first. Tell her to bring the baby to me. Then get the others."

"Okay." A pause. "Sure's slippery out."

"Now, Elgar." A taste of the old steel.

Gratefully, he stood to leave.

"Elgar?"

"Uh-huh."

"Open my window before you go."

A full moon, cold and unblinking, broke over Page's Village, which shimmered in its sheath of ice. Nanna Page loved Page's Village, had fed it her own breath and bones to sustain it, but she had never thought it beautiful, would have bristled at the idea; she loved it the way you love a homely child, loving her for the very fact of her homeliness and for the sturdy, hardheaded character born of that plain face, knowing she was made to last, to endure. But that night Page's Village, all flash and flicker, made Nanna Page's breath catch: the marsh, a wild jewel shining in the village's heart, its rowdy grasses and vines turned crystal; footpaths and roads silver, treacherous; glistening rooves like skating ponds; groaning trees turned into towering ice kings (and the rifle-crack of breaking branches). Even dead Billy's shed, the blister at the tip of an icicle, was almost bearable to look at.

Nanna sighed, slumped into her cocoon of quilts, blankets, afghans. She laughed at herself as she burrowed toward warmth: We're always looking for the womb, she thought, always; even at my age; even at the end.

The cancer, an enemy as silent and patient as Nanna herself, had manifested itself in the usual ways: the day's work, stealing her breath, taking longer for no good reason; sudden slivers of pain; a wind-through-the-husks hack; blood where it shouldn't be. Though she knew she would lose, Nanna sought a way to win. And she found it when Sarah became pregnant by the Britton boy. She swore to fight until Sarah's baby came; and Sarah's Hannah had been born the week before. Nanna would pass on to the baby what was necessary; then she could die.

Down below, in her village, a door slammed, followed by the broken-glass chatter of shattered ice; Nanna hitched herself up to look out the window.

Clutching the rail, Leah eased herself down the steps. She stopped at the bottom and stared at the marsh for some seconds. Then she lowered her head, curled into herself, and trudged into the teeth of the stiff wind snarling down out of the north. The stars glittered—ice-coated, too.

The women of Page's Village, hunched shadows, huddled at the foot of the hill up to Nanna's. Leah was the only one who dared try to walk up. Bent double, arms thrust forward for balance, she took a small step, planted her foot, another step, planted, each time bringing her weight to bear on the balls of her feet, grinding them into the ice.

"Lee, what in hell're you trying to prove?" asked Robena, her voice spiked with spite. "You know you ain't gonna get up that friggin' hill. You know we got to go the long way round."

Leah squatted lower, slide-stepping now, fingertips almost brushing the ice.

Robena glared at her older sister, wished that she'd fall and crack her fool head open, the too-big-for-her-britches bitch. In the years since her forced marriage to Allen Swett and the miscarriage after, the flesh had melted from Robena's bones so she'd become all barbs and knobs, planes and angles; she'd learned to hone her words to razors. Instructed by Nanna, she'd finally donned the habit of her Page-hood.

"Look at her, will you," Robena said. "She always was the one to show off, to prove she was more of a Page than any of us. Always was the stubborn one. Once she got something into that thick skull of hers, forget it. Just like Momma."

Eyes tearing, knuckles stiff, cheeks burning in the cold, the women wanted to get going—it would take a good half-hour to skirt around to Nanna's—but Leah's grit held them in place as she inched up the hill. None of them believed she would make it. But they had to watch. They were all connoisseurs of futility.

"Jesus H. Christ!" Robena spat. "What're we waiting around for? She's just going to end up flat on her beak."

Even as Robena spoke, Leah couldn't fix her left foot on the ice; the right began to wobble. Sweating, even in that wind-shrieking cold, she bore down on her foot, tried to plant it by force of will; the Nanna Page method.

She slipped (a screwdriver jumping the slot) and, for an instant, found herself free of the earth, suspended at a forty-five-degree angle to the hill. She crunched down on her elbows, those bone hammers jamming into the ice; if she lifted them, she would slide back down the hill, sprawl at the feet of her sisters.

"You coming, or what?" Robena barked at her. "Or're you gonna stretch out there like an ironing board all night?"

Leah studied the crystal web spun in the ice where her elbows had cracked down; her sister's voice whistled in her ears, a high wind.

"Leah?"

She was reminded of summer fields shimmering with daybreak's dew-soaked spiderwebs.

"If we're gonna go, we better get going," Robena said to the others. "Let the loony muckle ahold of her hillside."

Shutting her eyes, Leah listened to the women follow Robena, their tiny steps sounding like long-nailed dogs click-clacking on new linoelum.

Steadying herself on her elbows, Leah looked up the hill, a slick silver stair punctuated at its peak by Nanna's dark haven. She knew her mother was watching. As usual. Watching, even on her deathbed, ripe with the disgust that disfigured her face whenever one of her children failed her. Leah pressed her cheek to the ice, shivered at the needles of cold. She considered giving in, ottering backwards down the hill, and chasing Robena's smugness. But nothing's ever so easy or simple for a Page, especially a Page woman. And that night Leah wanted to show her mother something like love, though neither of them would have dared call it that.

Wriggling forward, Leah raised her right arm, rammed her elbow into the ice, hitched herself ahead, then drove her left elbow into the ice, secured it, and advanced. Thus, using her elbows as spikes, Leah creeped up the hill, beating Robena to their mother's deathbed.

Each time Leah jabbed an elbow into the hill ice, Nanna Page grimaced, her daughter's pain giving her an excuse to vent her own.

Nanna, for the most part, had handled the pain in those long, labyrinthine months of her dying. She'd met it head on, wrestled it, parceled it out, each day increasing her tolerance to it; she listened to it, learned its language, and talked back. She wouldn't let the pain, however dogged, defeat her. It was only a symptom. It wasn't the pain that was devouring her body cell by cell, grinding bones to dust. It was the cancer; and the cancer feasted, pain or no.

Sometimes, though, in the blackest pit of night came

the pain beyond articulation. Pain that yanked her by the hair, wrenched her awake, and slammed her face on the floor. The pain of grunts and whimpers, of her jaw working silently; pain that cramped her hands into crab claws, ratcheted her chest. No denying that pain. It breached your defenses, no matter how finely wrought, made you dance its wicked waltzes, then flung you down. In those minutes, when her black howls echoed, fluttered in the night house like bats, Nanna came to understand how it might be in the end; she was grateful for the knowledge.

When Leah reached the top of the hill, a wretched and wracked survivor washed up on familiar shores, Nanna Page almost smiled.

"I was Nanna Page even before any of my own babies was ever born. I swear that the day after my momma, your great-great-grandmother Page, died, my hair turned iron and these ditches got dug in my face. Like that. Overnight."

Sarah's newborn, Hannah, nested on Nanna's chest; the baby smelled of milk, cornstarch, stale spit-up. Nanna Page had never drunk, never smoked; still, she whispered to her granddaughter in a whiskey-and-cigarette wheeze—the rasp of the dying.

"Ain't no way you're remembering me, Hannah. But I've been waiting on you, little girl; been waiting somethin' fierce. Though I'll be dead, buried and almost forgot, I want you to feel me in your bones, because I'll be there. I'll always be there.

"My momma had this talk with me just before she passed away and, by rights, it's your grandmother Ella I should be jabbering at right now, or Sarah. But Ella run off years ago, baby girl, and your momma ain't never been strong enough. Ain't a one of them've ever been strong enough. But, Hannah, you're the one where the rivers meet, the one who runs strong and deep. And, when it's time, you'll be ready."

Sucking in the cold winter air, Nanna closed her eyes, remembered.

"One time, when I was a little girl, when it still was my momma was Nanna Page, one of our barn cats lugs a field mouse—mouse still squirming and squeaking, even in that cat's mouth—over to one of her kittens. She drops the mouse, whacks it a good one, and nudges the kitten toward it. But that kitten, she don't want no part of that mouse. The mother cat cuffs her and pushes her back toward the mouse. Still, the kitten flinches. And the mother cat bats her again a coupla more times. Finally, after some six or seven more smacks in the puss, the kitten sniffs at the mouse, touches it, even licks it, and sits there quiet while its mother eats it.

"My momma raised me same way that cat raised that kitten. And that's how I raised my girls; the boys were Elgar's problem till they become my problem."

Nanna stroked the baby's smooth cheek, touched her own gullied face. Shook her head at the collapsing years.

"Ain't nobody gives a Page nothing, Hannah girl; the sooner you learn that lesson the better off you'll be;

Pages don't even give *each other* nothing. My girls all learnt that—eventually.

"I've kept this goddamned family, this village, together for almost forty years. And I did it by doing what I thought was right. Even when they hated my guts, even when they ran and hid when I walked by. But I never give in. Not to them. Not to the town. Not to the county. I ain't never give in.

"And, Hannah, if anybody wants to know: I'd still burn that sonuvabitch to death."

She stopped short, stalled. Billy'd snuck up on her again. He'd had a way about him of doing that when he was alive, and the talent hadn't diminished in death. But Nanna hadn't meant to feed Hannah poison about Billy Page; the child would hear enough in her own good time.

"What I'm giving you, baby, is that pure Page cussedness. The strength and will to carry the world on your shoulders. 'cause your momma's going to need that wicked bad, Hannah. She's going to depend on you. Take good care of her."

The women of Page's Village, and the girl children who had made those first wobbly steps toward womanhood, circled Nanna's bed, stared down at their shrunken matriarch; Robena, making a big show of snubbing Leah, sat at her mother's right hand.

Eyelids flickering, Nanna drifted, her brief dreams leaching into her dying night, her daughters' murmurs fleshing the dreams. She perceived the women as one presence, a hive, rather than singly. She smelled winter on their coats, scarves and kerchiefs, a frigid freshness she associated with clothes hung to dry in sub-zero cold; there were other winter smells, too: Pond's cold cream, ChapStick, Vick's VapoRub.

Once they had arrived, tiptoeing up the stairs, slinking into her kerosene-smelling room, Nanna had allowed herself to slip, to leave months-old defenses unguarded. She'd always imagined herself dying as she had lived — alone. She'd married, yes. Had five children (and grandchildren beyond counting), yes. Still, hers had been a life spent alone. In the end, though, she had wanted them to keep the deathwatch; they should see the woman die who'd kept them alive all these years.

Once again she saw Leah paining herself up that impossible hill of ice, sacrificing herself to be in her dying mother's grace, and Nanna suddenly knew there was one thing she needed to do before the night ended.

Having all the village women clustered in her grandmother's house reminded Sarah of her eighth-grade graduation, when, led by Nanna, the women had spent the day before snipping old bed sheets into skinny, foot-long strips. Those strips were then used to bind twists of Sarah's hair. Set free graduation morning, Sarah's hair fell in long, loose corkscrews — rag curls.

"Sarah! . . . Sar-ah!"

Sarah jumped as if startled by a snarling dog; she bounced off Fat Dot, who, unmoved, seemed not to notice.

Robena screeched again: "Sarah, wake up! Nanna wants you! She wants to talk to you! You!"

The way Robena said it, Sarah could tell that her aunt wanted to know why Nanna'd decided to speak, maybe her last words ever, to her — Ella's child.

Trembling, Sarah lifted Hannah to Leah and made her way to the head of the bed. She bent close to Nanna, who clasped her cheeks in sandpaper hands, and listened:

"Sarah . . . take me sliding." Each careful word a burr sticking to Sarah's skin. "Please."

"What?"

"Down the hill.

"Uppy, Sarah, uppy."

Such a small request. A jewel of a favor. Sarah's eyes burned with tears as she gathered up her grandmother, lighter than Baby Hannah, quilts and all. The women flattened themselves against the walls to let Sarah and Nanna pass. All of them. Except Robena.

"What in hell do you think you're doing, Sarah Huckins?" she shrieked. "You put her back in that bed right now!"

Backside to her aunt, Sarah said: "You heard Nanna just as well as I did. She wants to go out."

"What's she know? She's dying. We about froze ourselves to death to come up here and see her die, and now you're gonna take the crazy old bitch down the hill? In this cold?"

The room hushed. Silent, as before a blizzard, save for the wick-hiss of the kerosene lamp.

"Robena."

One word, three syllables, shredding the silence. Ro-be-na. A summons, a threat, a rebuke. Robena couldn't resist. Just a dying stick woman cradled in Sarah's arms, and still Robena couldn't help but obey, give in to her mother one more time.

Nanna struck fierce and fast, the flat of her hand darting, slapping Robena so hard that the red print of her hand didn't fade from her daughter's cheek for two months; and it wasn't until Nanna was dead that anyone noticed (it was the undertaker) she'd fractured her left wrist, her smacking wrist.

Sarah sat at the top of the hill, Nanna, sucking on an icicle, spooned to her body. Down below, Robena's Allen and Grandpa Elgar sat smoking on Robena's doorsteps, the tips of their cigarettes winking orange. Allen lost his balance, slipped a step; Nanna laughed soundlessly.

"It's too beautiful tonight, Nanna," Sarah said. "Some kind of Page heaven."

Sarah hugged Nanna, buried her face in her Ivory soap–smelling hair; the tears froze on her cheeks. Nanna clutched Sarah's hand, squeezed, whispered: "I never meant to run your momma off."

As they sat there, suspended in the unflinching light of the winter moon, Sarah realized that Nanna meant to die in her arms, in the arms of the one person she knew loved her. In the house, Hannah cried — selfish, hungry, unrepentant.

"That's my baby," Nanna soughed.

She curled more tightly into Sarah, shrinking, fighting: "Go."

Cocooning herself around Nanna, Sarah skittered forward. As Sarah poled away with her arms, Nanna Page creaked:

"Go fast enough, Sarah girl, and maybe we'll never stop."

Chapter Seven

❦

July 1985

A SATURDAY MORN-
ing like most others: Secure in the easy silence of a
couple bound by twenty years of marriage, Russ sat
at the kitchen table, chain-drinking black instant and
reading the *Union Leader* sports, while Sarah worried
over the stove, frying eggs, bacon, slabs of Maine potatoes. When Sarah thought on her marriage, she would
conjure these still, sun-tipped mornings where simply
being in the same room together was enough; but she
knew, too, that there would be no such mornings without those raging, star-snuffed nights where being in the
same room together was too much.

The upstairs floorboards screeked. Sarah stopped working the spatula, cocked an ear, listened, shook her head, and went back to cooking.

" 's funny we ain't heard Jessie yet," she said.

"Don't knock it," Russ said. "That baby cries enough for ten kids."

"I guess," she said.

Sarah hefted the bacon skillet and poured the sputtering grease into an old coffee can; she set a brown paper lunch bag on one of her good plates (a wedding present from Auntie Leah) and spilled the bacon, crisp and glistening, onto it; she slid the eggs, fried over easy, onto another plate, and heaped the potatoes onto another.

Russ snuck a scrap of bacon and winked at Sarah, who almost laughed.

"Honey . . ." she scolded.

"Sure tastes good," he said.

"Let me see if Wayne and Charlotte are up," she said, wiping her hands on her apron.

Not wanting to wake Jessie, Sarah tiptoed up, wincing at each creak and squeak, stopping at the head of the stairs. Wayne and Charlotte were dead asleep, Wayne snoring the funeral dirge.

She glanced at the empty cradle, and figured Jessie was tucked in with her parents. Nothing'd made Sarah happier than having her babies sleep with her, their small, milk-smelling warmth flush to her needful flesh; it'd ticked Russ off something wicked, but she hadn't cared. That Wayne and Charlotte would let Baby Jessie into their bed softened Sarah's feelings toward them, nudged her toward the brink of a smile. She *had* to see.

Pudgy fist resting at her rooting mouth, Jessie nestled between Charlotte and Wayne in a loose fetal curl—that's what Sarah expected to see. The image had blossomed so fully it took her a couple of seconds to realize that all that lay between Charlotte and Wayne was a patch of grimy, gray sheet and the snarled fan of Charlotte's hair.

Her own childhood a spiky thicket of desertion, betrayal and longing, Sarah knew right away there was no good reason for Jessie's not being there. She stared at Jessie's absence, steeped herself in it, let the knowledge rupture the sutures of the past, inflame primal, but still raw, wounds:

⚹

Sarah wakes to a cold, quiet house.

Frost devils caper on the inside of the window, she can see her breath, and the tips of her ears feel brittle. She shuts her eyes, listens hard for the soft slap of slippered feet, the whisper of restless bed sheets, the woodstove's spit and crackle. Nothing. She is five years old and knows that, overnight, her life has somehow changed. Her mother's bed is made—blankets taut as new-strung barbwire—clothes draws jammed flush to the bureau; the dishes have been washed, dried, put away, the sour-smelling dish towel draped over a chair; the fire's dead, no wood stacked next to the stove; and four teakettles stand at attention, spouts pointing west.

Sarah creeps outdoors in her pajamas and stocking feet, finds her mother's faint footprints in the frozen snow. Hunched over, she follows them, Ella's tracks fading with each step away from the shack, down past Auntie Leah's place until, at last, they vanish. Sarah scrutinizes that final footprint, one last illegible note scrawled in the snow, memorizing it, understanding that this rubber-tread hieroglyph may be the last she ever sees of her mother. She scrapes her index finger the length of the footprint, licks the snow crystals from her fingertip.

"Sarah! What're you doing outdoors dressed like that?"

Sarah looks up at Auntie Leah, standing on her front step in a nightgown, and shivers. "Mommy run off, Auntie," she says, hugging herself. "She run away. . . ."

✍

Still looking down at Wayne and Charlotte, Sarah shivered as the insistent past thrust itself into the present the way prehistoric veins of granite will punch through the thin New Hampshire soil.

✍

Sarah, seventeen years old, has been up all night, the last three nights, with the new baby. She rocks it, jiggles it, paces the floor with it, nurses it, slings it over her right shoulder and slings it over her left shoulder, burps it, rubs its gums (maybe it's cutting teeth), strokes its cheeks, changes its diaper, and finally —*finally*— the wailing stops and he gives in to sleep.

She eases Wayne into the cardboard box (Hannah, a year older, uses the crib) sitting on her bureau, slips the sugar tit—a wet facecloth dipped in honey—into his sucking mouth, and flops into bed next to Russ, who's snorting away in a deep pig's-sleep.

Wayne wakes up crying five minutes later.

Sarah rips back her blankets and jumps out of bed—"Shut up! Shut up! Shut up!"—grabs the baby's cardboard cradle and shakes it like a box of Cracker Jack, the baby yowling even louder, bouncing up and down and from side to side. . . .

⚭

So Sarah stood there in Wayne's and Charlotte's attic room, straddling past and present. Nanna Page would've smacked their pusses and booted them out of the house. All Sarah could do was stare at the space between her son and his wife that wasn't her granddaughter, and wrap herself in their betrayal.

Startled by the slightest whiff of why family members kill each other, Sarah, for an instant, imagined slitting their pale, fish-belly throats. But she let Wayne and Charlotte sleep their traitors' sleep and walked downstairs to a cold breakfast. Plenty of time later for the shouting, the lies, the silence.

⚭

Heidi Meeks vanished.

One day, she and Sarah were playing together—hopscotch, jump rope, and foursquare, tramping from one end of the village to the other as if they were Nanna Page—the next, Heidi was gone. Disappeared.

Led by the girl's very mother, Rita, the grown-ups cloaked themselves in a conspiracy of silence. And the children, those who had noticed anyway, knew nothing. Not even Heidi's brothers and sisters, who probably were grateful for the elbow room and the extra fish sticks and macaroni.

Heidi's disappearance—sudden, inexplicable, like a winter thundershower—troubled Sarah. She understood that her own parents had run away, that Grandpa Elgar would take off for weeks at a time. But Heidi . . . Heidi . . . When Sarah didn't mind her, Auntie Leah sometimes threatened to "give her to the Indians." Sarah didn't doubt that such a thing could happen.

In time, Sarah's memory would diminish Heidi Meeks—a hank of standard-issue brown hair, a swatch of pale skin, maybe a sprinkling of freckles—except for the mystery of her leaving. Heidi became defined by her absence, a mental scab to pick at as the years quickened. Most often, Sarah would recall the last time she saw her.

The night before Heidi vanished, the two girls, as they did most summer nights, soaked up dusk down back to the frog pond, watching the lightning bugs pulse like baby stars above the stiff black water as twilight's deep purple splotches, fierce birthmarks, darkened and thickened until the girls could barely see each other, just hear the slow intensity of each other's breathing, as much a part of the newborn night as the wheedle of mosquitoes, the almost-visible song of the peepers.

Finally, satisfied that night had indeed fallen, the two girls abandoned their shadow womb of woods and water and giant-stepped up the hill, holding hands, as young girls will.

✖

"I don't see what the big deal is," Charlotte said. "It ain't like Jessie has a personality yet. All she does is lay there."

Eyes tear-swollen, face flushed, Sarah gutted Charlotte with a look. Sarah'd come of age in a world where children were treated no better than the junked cars rusting in the backwoods; she had the most to say, but could say nothing.

"Besides," Wayne said, "ain't no law says we can't give our baby up for adoption."

"Adoption, my ass," Russ said.

"What do you mean?"

"You heard me."

"Jessie got adopted. We got papers."

"You know what you can do with your papers."

"She was adopted."

"In the goddamned middle of the night? You think I'm stupid?"

Wayne willed himself to look at his father.

"You sold that baby, Wayne," Russ said. "Don't tell me no different. I hope you and your cunt choke on that money."

"You don't know nothing. You just like to hear your-self talk."

Russ slammed his fist on the table, slopping coffee, rattling silver: "You fucking look me in the eye and tell me you didn't sell that baby. Come on. You tell me."

Charlotte looked at Russ, Sarah at Wayne.

"Tell me, goddammit!"

Wayne stared at the floor.

"I figured as much." There was no satisfaction in Russ's voice.

For five minutes, ten minutes, no one moved. No one looked at anyone else. Each nurturing a singular sorrow as the silence, the first snow of a long winter, settled on them.

"Wayne," Russ said in the softest voice his son'd ever heard him use, "I want you and your wife out of the house by the end of the day."

The next morning, Sarah woke before sunrise and threw up. She'd been sick to her stomach since the day before, and it was a relief to scrape her knees and purge the poison. Dizzy, she shut her eyes, pressed her cheek to the toilet's damp porcelain cool. When Sarah'd been sick as a child, Auntie Leah had finger-combed her hair, rubbed her burning forehead with the heels of her palms. She dreaded having to tell Auntie Leah and Auntie Robena about Jessie. They would shake their heads—doughy double chins hula-ing—cluck their tongues, and somehow make the loss of the baby a judg-ment on her and Russ. Barren, ignorant in children's ways, Leah and Robena saw Hannah's and Wayne's successes as belonging to the children, while heaping their sins at their parents' step.

She sighed into Nanna Page's rocking chair, testing the bitter silence that insinuates itself into a house, like dry rot or carpenter ants, after a child has gone too soon. Jessie'd been meant, somehow, to make up for Sarah's hollow years of miscarriages, false alarms and tears cried over babies conceived yet never born. In the secret calendar of her heart she remembered those unborn children's birthdays, knew how old they would be, memorized their names. She'd wanted nothing more from her life than to fill the house, cellar to rafters, with babies: babies nesting in bureau draws; babies, like possums, clutching her back, legs and hips; babies, ankle deep, bawling and cooing, cutting teeth and spitting up, nursing and nuzzling, with eyes only for her as they squeaked "ma-ma" and smiled. Babies offered solace, redemption, and it was for her brood of unborn babies that Sarah ached as she rocked toward dawn, the imminent sun turning the eastern sky the color of gasoline and water. Her unborn babies—and Jessie.

Jessie, Sarah thought. Jessie.

A hummingbird sipped from the cosmos in Sarah's flower garden, its blood-red throat throbbing like a newborn's heart.

Sarah IV

Out behind the barn, she pumps water into a steel
bucket. Water gushes from the pump, some splashing
her feet, as she squeaks the handle back and forth. She's
washed by a pure early-morning light—angel light—
that sets her skin afire, makes it tingle. Watching the
water spill into the bucket, she remembers her water
breaking when her oldest was born: She's sitting with
her grandmother, who's bedded by cancer, hands
steepled on her swollen belly, watching the old woman
weave in and out of sleep—and then there's a warm,
wet rush between her legs; she says: "Oh!" and her
grandmother cracks her eyes, looks at her, and tears,
somehow wrenched free, crawl down her caved-in
cheeks. When her bucket is full, she'll lug it to the house
and pour it into the tub for her husband's bath. It will
take ten more trips to fill the tub.

Chapter Eight

1970

HANNAH AT FIVE years old, swaddled in a dream:

Dusk. (When the air takes on a fine brown grain like it does when you're looking out through a screen door.) Bats, inky sickles, swirl and swoop at the peak of Nanna's house. Sarah kneels in front of Hannah, her cool hands light on her daughter's shoulders as she tells her that she can't go with her and Russ, who's already in the car ... waiting; his cigarette winks orange in the side mirror. Sarah, wearing a white cotton summer dress, shimmers in the dying day. The car, some make from the forties (like the rusting husks Grandpa Elgar hoards down back), looks new: voluptuous curves painted the maroon of winter sunsets; see-yourself chrome; grinning whitewalls. Sarah bends to kiss Hannah on the cheek and they get all tangled, lips and elbows and cheekbones working at cross-purposes. Then Sarah's in the car, and Russ pulls out onto Route 49. Sarah cranes out the window, looks back at Hannah; she smiles, waves, and is gone. Hannah cries plump, cheek-scalding tears. . . .

Gripped by her dream, Hannah woke crying, gulping air, the pain and the fear beating against the inside of her chest like a light-frenzied moth flinging itself at the screen door. It's the moment in a nightmare that scares a child most, when, somehow, the dream-darkness has burst through to the familiar bedroom darkness. After a few seconds the dream evaporated, leaving Hannah flushed with relief. But then, even as the dream decayed, came the burning need to remember, the longing to retrieve the half-life of a thing that was and never was.

Her parents were up. She smelled the toast, heard her father's spoon plink in his coffee cup, saw the light from downstairs trickle up through the floorboard cracks. She drifted back to sleep, lulled by their hushed morning voices.

A chilly November morning of wind-rattled windows, and Hannah and Wayne burrowed toward their mother, craving her warmth, her smell. Curled on either side, they hugged her as hard as they could, all squirmy, nuzzling her breasts. (Some mornings Sarah unbuttons her nightgown and offers them her smooth, dry breasts—they suck and root, contented, careful with their teeth, while she strokes their hair—but not this morning.) Sarah hugged them back something fierce.

They ate Shredded Wheat for breakfast. Sarah, devoted to those bristling breakfast biscuits, was serious about Shredded Wheat: First, she centered hers in the bowl; then poured boiling water to soften it; after draining the water, she broke it in the middle, sprinkled one level teaspoon of brown sugar on the biscuit, and only then did she add milk. She made Hannah's and Wayne's that way, too; another Nanna Page recipe.

Sarah didn't say much as they ate; children didn't either. When it came to meals, the Brittons were more of an eating family than a talking family. After breakfast Hannah and Wayne went off to play; Sarah started the day's chores.

Russ'd left the small Lionel train set up from the night before, and the children built Lincoln Log forts around it; forts swarming with plastic cowboys and Indians. Sarah's dress rustled as she worked back and forth in the kitchen; WBZ out of Boston static-ed from the Sylvania radio.

Hannah and Wayne, their mother's children, were quiet, watchful; they weren't sullen, but they weren't in love with their own voices either. Their father, Russ, was the gabby one, the gossip, the storyteller. Sarah provided the deep silences in the poetry of her family. To Sarah, silence's economy was a virtue. It was from her that the children first learned the true weight of words, spoken and unspoken; they found out early that a thing left unsaid can mean everything.

It was one of those mornings that Hannah liked best, when the house seemed to draw the silence around itself like an old woman pulling her shawl tighter as she steps into a winter's night. It wasn't even the quiet, really, that Hannah liked so much as the chance to hear the sounds that embroidered the stillness, counterpointed it: squirrels skittering in the rafters; the saw grass out back riffling in the slap-you-in-the-face November wind; Sarah scraping carrots; the grumbling of the Boston & Maine Railroad out beyond Cedar Swamp.

So, the morning passed.

Sarah slipped into the living room so quiet that Hannah and Wayne didn't hear her for the hum of the electric train. "Time to go to Grandpa's," she said.

Hannah jumped, knocking over cowboys and Indians. Wayne shut the train—the locomotive, coal car, two freight cars and caboose sparking to a halt on the dull silver tracks—and the children followed their mother to the back door, which Sarah shouldered open against the wind. She said, "Wait right here," and stepped out into the dooryard, where, right away, she rubbed her arms against November—one of those cold, windy days where the trees never stop groaning and the wind bullies the clouds across the sky. The cedar clothesline, which swayed between the two houses, creaked, its bowed lines jump-rope swinging, clothespins bobbing. Sarah looked up at the sky, at the children, then back up at the sky as a big, black fist of a cloud scudded by, shadowing the dooryard, its ragged sun-shot edges pulsing like dying embers.

A grin broke on Sarah's face like ripples on a small, still pond.

"Come on, babies!" she cried. "Try and catch me!"

Giddy with the wind, she pivoted and ran toward Grandpa Elgar's, her dress belling, hair blown back, springing across the dooryard: a little girl again. She let Hannah and Wayne catch her, and they all stuttered to a stop on Grandpa's back steps, laughing, out of breath, cheeks as red as snow-stung apples.

"I love the wind!" Sarah panted. "It makes me feel . . . drunk!"

Wayne and Hannah looked at each other, laughing again. Sarah laughed, too.

"Hi, Grandpa," Sarah called out as they trooped into the kitchen gloom. " 's only us."

A newspaper rustled in the front room.

Sarah started water boiling and said: "Go on in and say hi to Grandpa. I'll be right there."

Standing in the gray-lit kitchen, Sarah could feel the house—the house she had been born in—gnaw at her small happiness. Even on such a wintry day, the air hung thick and heavy, redolent of bitter battles of wills, bleak hearts and bone-weary souls the way other people's houses smelled of fried peppers or the Listerine-reek of dying kin.

The children, as always, found Grandpa Elgar

buried in his newspaper at the table next to the front double windows.

"Hi, Grandpa," they said.

"Mm-hmm," he said, not looking up.

Elgar Page spent his days planted at the windows, reading his newspapers and magazines—*True, Saga, Grit, Reader's Digest*—and the stray paperback Western, passing judgment on his corner of the world: a stretch of Route 49 dotted by three houses—the Mahoneys', the Pitkins' and the Marcouxs'.

Going back months at a time he could tell you who visited the three families, on what day, at what time, how long they stayed and what kind of car they drove; he knew what times they all left for school and work, and what times they came home; he knew that the Mahoneys went grocery shopping Thursday nights, the Pitkins Friday nights and the Marcouxs Saturday mornings; that the Pitkins got their oil delivered on the third Tuesday of the month, that when they went visiting the Mahoneys left lights on in the front room, in the left upstairs bedroom and on the porch, that the Marcouxs got twice as much mail as the other two families put together. It wasn't that Elgar was nosy. He didn't want to know what all these comings and goings meant. Just knowing, without understanding, that was fine.

That was why, after his wife died, he'd set his table at the front of the house, as far away from Page's Village as he could get without moving out. Sure, there were the pantry windows, favored by his wife, that overlooked the village. But he wouldn't've been able to take

in the goings-on without wanting to know why. And
that desire meant asking questions, looking his family in
the eye, making decisions—sticking his nose where it
didn't belong. He'd had enough of that shit when his
wife'd been alive. He didn't want to know anymore.
Better to ignore his own family and study the folks
across the way.

"Grandpa," Hannah asked, "can we look at the
book?"

Elgar sighed, scraped his chair away from the table,
and shuffled to the broom closet, where he reached up
with a grunt and pulled down a finger-worn one-volume
encyclopedia he'd scavenged from the town dump back
when. The children always asked for the book, and he
always made them ask. Using the book to hide from
their great-grandfather, Hannah and Wayne turned
their backs to him, left him to his newspaper, his
windows.

The treasure that lay buried in the book, with its
squinty print no larger than summer's red ants, what
mattered to Hannah and Wayne, was its riot of glossy
color plates—Fish of the North Atlantic, Snakes of Af-
rica, Butterflies of the Rain Forest. Wayne still was at
an age where strange animals and bright colors were
enough. But those paintings made Hannah's breath
catch and opened her eyes, nudged her toward the real-
ization and, more important, the acceptance of a wider
world beyond Page's Village, beyond Route 49, beyond
Granite even. The one painting Hannah liked best, the
one that made her head spin, the one she sometimes

conjured against the darkness as she gave in to sleep, was of the solar system: the planets floating in a black pool, Jupiter's raging red blotch, Mars's mystery scars, Saturn's creamy rings, and Earth. Earth! That was the hard one to believe. Earth—Hannah's earth, Page's Village—somehow hung out there in the forever night like on a clothesline.

Sarah hurried in with her grandfather's lunch—elbow macaroni drowned in Campbell's tomato soup, a blob of butter melting in the middle—set it on the table. She shook her fingers as if flicking water at a baby. "Hot," she said.

Grandpa folded his newspaper just so, slid his glasses into his breast pocket, and hitched himself closer to the table. He looked at the plate of macaroni, at Sarah, then back at the macaroni. Sarah pushed it to him.

"I'll go get your beer, Grandpa," Sarah said.

Filling his face with macaroni, Elgar didn't even try to answer.

On her way to the kitchen Sarah paused in the light-starved hall to squint at the black-and-white photograph of Nanna Page that hung there; she never came to the house without paying her respects to that picture. Nanna Page's photograph sat in a wooden oval frame a good two feet in diameter. In it, Nanna has just come out of the house and is walking toward the camera like a storm brewing, fisher-cat eyes shooting sparks, cheekbones set high, proud and sharp. She might be dead, and Grandpa Elgar might have hid her picture in a dark hallway, but the house, Page's Village, still belonged to Nanna Page.

Hannah stared at her mother, who seemed to be caught up in prayer. But Hannah understood.

Nanna Page'd died a few days after Hannah's birth, but she felt as if she'd known Nanna forever. After Sarah, Nanna Page was the most important woman in Hannah's life. Partly it was the photograph's power, but mostly it was that her relations all acted as if Nanna were still alive. They hadn't buried her in the deep past of memory. Instead, they still spoke of her in the present tense, still led their lives fearful of what the woman who'd once held court in the house up the hill would think.

Grandpa glanced at Sarah, made a big show out of ceasing to chew, and said: "Jesus H. Christ, the old cunt's been dead a good five years. Ain't no one around here ever going to stop mooning over that cold bitch?"

Sarah's face flushed, tears winked like stars.

"Ev-er-y fuck-ing day it's the same old shit," Grandpa went on. "It's Nanna this and Nanna that. And ain't it a shame that Nanna's dead? If it ain't you, it's Dot. And if it ain't Dot, it's Robena. And if it ain't her, it's some other one of those freeloading twats that live down back, taking advantage of my good nature and leeching offa my land. I tell you, if your murdering whore of a grandmother hadn't gotten that land all tied up with her last will and goddamned testament I'd a had those bitches out on their fat asses a long time ago."

It was more words than the children had heard him say in their whole lives.

"Fucking Saint Nanna," he said, shoveling in a forkful of macaroni. "Saint fucking Nanna. Makes me puke."

Sarah yanked Hannah and Wayne out of the room. Rushed them out of the house as if it were on fire. It wasn't until they were in the dooryard, on their side of the clothesline, that she broke down. Clutching Nanna's picture, she dropped to her knees and sobbed the sobs of a little girl lost. Hannah, holding Grandpa's book, and Wayne looked at each other, but didn't go near Sarah; mothers weren't supposed to cry, especially not like that.

And that's how Elgar Page stole from his granddaughter the house she'd been born in.

Sarah retreated to her room with the children that afternoon and sought the healing of sleep, but it wouldn't come. She waited there in bed, Hannah and Wayne snugged to her, staring at the ceiling: rippling, orange-brown rings born of rain-creep; paint peeling in window-shade curls; thick tangles of cobwebs tucked in corners; she traced its scarred snarl of ridges, fissures and fault lines; they reminded her of the Geological Survey's map of Granite that hung in the town clerk's office. She'd been sleeping under that ceiling for five years, Sarah realized, and had never really looked at it. Even so, it had only become worth the looking as a way to blunt Grandpa Elgar's rage. Sarah felt sick with his jagged words, his ragged voice.

When Sarah'd been small, six, seven years old, Uncle Dead—in pure Page spite—one subzero January left his dog Butchy out overnight; Butchy froze (she remembered Uncle Henry picking him up like some furry cement block). But before he died, Butchy had rent the night with his animal rage: barking and yipping, whining and whimpering, growling and howling; in between, the night silence rattled with his chain snaking along on the hard-packed snow. Grandpa Elgar, back there in Nanna's house, had made Sarah think of Butchy on the night he died.

She couldn't believe that her grandfather had turned on her, the one least able to defend herself, the one whose wounds had never healed. Her! The sweet one, the family always said. The too-sweet one.

She shook with the hurt and the anger, knuckles mushroom-white, teeth grinding. Just a scream, she thought, all I need is one little scream and I'll feel better. But she couldn't, had never been able to. And she thought she would burst, simply fly apart, trembling there on the bed.

Finally, denied its rightful escape, Sarah's fury turned inward, began boring. Eyes jammed shut and fists doubled, she lay there, as stiff and frozen as Butchy must've been that night, and let it have its way with her.

Sarah left the children sleeping, went out to the barn—the barn door, wed to a rusted steel track, squealing open with a tug—and climbed into the stock car, Russ's chopped-down '37 Pontiac coupe. She grabbed the steel-cold steering wheel, sucked in the sweet stink of gasoline, oil and burnt rubber, floored the gas pedal, let off, floored it again. Her husband and a couple of his buddies raced the car summers over to Hudson Sunday afternoons and down to the Pines Speedway in Groveland Saturday nights.

Painted a shiny crow black, the Pontiac sported a big gold "Crown Seven" for a number—Russ and the boys being loyal swillers of Seagram's Seven, cut preferably with a splash of Seven-Up; Seven-and-Seven being the drink of choice those nights they stayed up till three in the morning working over the car. On the trunk a flame-headed, wise-guy woodpecker (having usurped the imperturbable Pontiac Indian) leered at the world, a half-smoked cigar clenched in his teeth.

Sitting there hemmed in by the roll cage, a womb of welded steel, Sarah felt as strong and secure as she had as a child playing in the food-warm kitchen while Nanna cooked. Sarah touched the Pontiac's steering wheel and the car seemed to tremble—or was it her?—hot to throw off a hibernation forced by the coming winter.

When the Pontiac shuddered to life, Sarah wasn't even convinced that she'd started the car. Did it start by itself, she wondered, stomping on the gas with two feet, the car roaring, shimmying the way Auntie Leah's shack did when she was a kid and one of those jets from Pease Air Force Base swooped through too fast and too low and touched off a sonic boom. She let off the gas too quick, and the Pontiac backfired—a shotgun blast to the heart—shattering the barn's two back windows. Flames tongued from the manifold.

Sarah jumped—"Oh!"—and started laughing. Laughing the way she had on her wedding night, already pregnant, but aching and desperate to make love with her husband. All that they could possibly lay claim to, each other and the baby, there in that one small room.

She shifted the stock into first and rumbled into the dooryard, stopping in front of the house, where Hannah's and Wayne's faces were pressed against the bedroom windows. Sarah waved them down.

"Mommy! Mommy! What are you doing with Daddy's race car?" Hannah shouted as she ran toward the Pontiac. "What are you doing?"

"Does Daddy know?" Wayne asked. "Does he?"

The children's faces were lit with the same awe and exhilaration as brought on by first snow or the Fourth of July fireworks and bonfire on the Plains.

"Come on, babies!" Sarah whooped. "Let's go!"

Draping herself out the window, she lifted the children in, where they flopped onto the gutted back seat, its innards spilling out like burst milkweed pods. Hannah and Wayne giggled, wrestling like good-natured pups.

The Pontiac bolted out onto Route 49, its smooth rear slicks spitting rocks and gravel, then veered left off the highway and onto the dirt road that flowed down the hill and straight through the heart of Page's Village—chickens bitching, kids gawking, resentful dogs skedaddling—and into Cedar Swamp.

Sarah ran the dark woods flat out. Wind tear-ing her eyes. Branches switching. Kids pinballing in the back seat.

Yes, barrel-assing: The stock roaring in Sarah's gut; stuttering through razor turns, braking and shifting and accelerating, fighting—mastering—the wheel to sling-shot out of a veil of gravel and onto the straightaway; treading air, jouncing down, car-steel groaning; the trees blurred pickets, the sky a Vaseline smear.

Sarah's jawline firmed as she attacked those derelict dirt roads, roads she knew better than she knew most of her relations. Roads she'd resorted to as a girl when-ever it'd seemed Page's Village would smother her. Roads never far away.

Stomachs fluttering, Wayne and Hannah laughed and shrieked in animal joy, but their mother couldn't hear them for the stock car's bellowing.

Dozens of dead quarries—deep, weeping scars—haunted Granite's backwoods. They tended to seduce the young (swimmers, skaters, lovers, suicides) and the old (cracker-barrel philosophers, nostalgists, amateur historians, suicides), and scare away everyone else. Rare was a year that passed in Granite without someone quarry-drowned.

Growing up, Sarah'd spent more days than she cared to remember staring into quarry water the color of Nanna Page's eyes. Wondering what it would be like to dive from granite cliffs into that slate stillness, straining to touch bottom, to drink the old water, water that thought it was stone.

Sarah'd bushwhacked the Pontiac to her quarry (that's how she'd always thought of it), north and east of the swamp and village, and told the children to stay put. Trying to purge Grandpa Elgar's poison, she needed to, for a few minutes anyway, lose herself in these still waters of girlhood.

She didn't hear Wayne scramble out of the car, dutiful Hannah scrabbling after. Only Hannah's wind-piercing "Mommy!" had made Sarah turn to see her children struggling at the quarry lip, Hannah tugging on Wayne's arm even as he tried to jerk away toward the water.

Sarah Britton, who'd spent her life on the ropes, covering up, saw it all ending. If the quarries could take her children, her anchors, what was to stop her from finally tasting the water of stone?

Wayne wrenched free, staggered toward the edge of the cliff. Too surprised to be afraid.

What was to stop her?

Falling, arms windmilling, one foot already given in to gravity, Wayne, for an instant, looking as if he could rupture the earth with one mighty Rumpelstiltskin stamp.

Sarah snatched him by an arm, flinging him over her head on the fly; he landed hard on his back, the wind knocked out of him.

"Don't you ever scare me like that again!"—her

nose nicking his—"Don't you ever!"—their tears and gasps mingling—"Don't ever!"

Stricken by sobs like electric shocks, she collapsed on top of Wayne, made him bear the full weight of her love and fear. Hannah, crying too, hugged her mother as hard as she could, flushing her cheek to Sarah's broad, peasant back.

Sarah V

The wash hangs frozen on the cedar-post clothesline. Bowed by the clothes' icy weight, the line strains toward the ground; a couple of pairs of dungarees have broken free of the clothespins' pinch and lie in tortured shapes on the snow. The wind rasps through skeleton woods washed in winter light as pale as a dying grandmother's skin. Eyes watering, she lugs in flannel shirts stacked like logs, her chin snug on top of the pile. Band-Aids, weeping blood, are wrapped around two fingers bitten in the washer's wringer.

Chapter Nine

July 1985

ABANDONING THE stations of grief, Sarah cleaned.

She started downstairs in the saltbox's cobwebby southwest shadows and finished upstairs in the loam-smelling northeast, sweeping and scrubbing, mopping and polishing, dusting and disinfecting. Hair shrieking, loose breasts slapping time, she whirled through the small rooms, cleansing them with her passion, as she wielded brooms and brushes, sponges and dirt-rags—a white-knuckled fury bent on purification.

In Wayne's room (she would always think of it as his, even if she never saw her son again) she stubbed her toe on a nail. Hammering it down, she split a small section of floorboard. Beneath the broken wood lay an envelope—addressed to her. In Charlotte's handwriting.

Still winded some from her bout of cleaning, Sarah kneeled, wary, and stared at the envelope the way she would at an out-of-state car turning around in the driveway. She was tempted to put the floorboard back, cracked and all, and forget she'd ever seen that envelope. But there was no true forgetting; she had at least learned that much in thirty-six years. The past, no matter how deep you buried it and no matter how scarred the surface, eventually leached to daylight.

Charlotte's envelope, she knew, meant decisions, action. Her hands shook as she turned from it, eyes settling on Jessie's empty cradle.

Sighing, Sarah picked the envelope up, opened it. The jagged paper scrap read:

> The O'Connells
> Rowe's Road
> Banks, New Hampshire

Flushing its ragged edges as best she could, Sarah folded the piece of paper twice and tucked it into the envelope as if putting a baby down for the night. She put the envelope back, wedged the two pieces of floorboard into place, and covered the damage with Jessie's cradle.

It couldn't have been any clearer to Sarah if Charlotte had written: "This is where you will find Jessie."

Chapter Ten

❧

1978

THEY SAT SHIVER-
ing in the Ford Falcon. Waiting. Sarah in front—hands
nesting on her swollen belly—Hannah and Wayne,
teeth clacking, in back. The New Year had broken
brittle and cold, whipped by the barbarian arctic winds
that'd swept down out of Canada the week after Christmas: Chimney fires blossomed; lake ice groaned by
night; snow squeaked underfoot; cars died.

Conjuring her husband, Sarah hard-stared Chet and
Ginger's front door. She wore that disgusted look where
it seemed she couldn't decide whether to gag or cry. She
hadn't wanted to go to the party in the first place. But

Russ, who'd quit the barrel factory again, worked for Chet doing drywall.

Russ finally backed open the door, his left hand choking the doorknob, his right knocking back one last Bud. He flipped the empty to Chet, who handed it to Ginger, fished in his dungarees for his car keys; they're what he went back to get. Chet ducked out of the doorway, returned with the keys. The three of them laughed, said good night and Happy New Year one last time, and shut the door.

Russ took one step and fell flat on his ass.

Wayne looked at Hannah, the knowing look that can pass between brother and sister. She shrugged. Russ flashed them a rubber grin and waved, flapping his fingers like some goofy cartoon guy. Then he slid down the icy steps on his rump the way Hannah and Wayne used to bump down the stairs at the old house. Sarah's face granited up. The year wasn't but two hours old, and already she was in a fight with her husband.

Good thing Momma never got her driver's license, Hannah thought, or she'd take off without him.

Russ pussyfooted over the ice toward the car, a man tiptoeing through a den of timber rattlers. Gaining the Falcon, he sprawled on the hood and hugged it, his cheek flush to the frosted steel. Sarah reached over with an "unh" and banged on the horn. Russ shot up two-by-four straight—arms treading air—almost flopping backwards; Hannah and Wayne started to laugh, until Sarah turned and gave them that hawk-haunted Page look, passed on from generation to generation—a bitter, but necessary, heirloom. Chet glanced out the picture window.

Staring into the clear night sky, Russ grappled with the hood latch. He needed to get at the engine so he could fiddle with the starter. Falcon wouldn't turn over otherwise. They heard Russ's fingers thump against steel, heard the latch screek without giving. He slipped, smacking his knee on the bumper—"Sonuvabitch!!!" During it all, Sarah scrutinized her husband, her mouth small, tight, eyes razor slits.

In a voice colder than the night, Sarah said to Hannah: "Go help your father."

Russ, his fingers thick as farm sausages, fumbled the car keys, which clattered to the floor. Trying to scoop them up, he whacked his head on the steering wheel. Sarah reached down, straining over her pregnant stomach, and grabbed them without Russ noticing. Russ still searching, Sarah flung the keys against the driver's-side window.

Pumping the bejesus out of the gas pedal, Russ mashed the key into the ignition: The engine turned, wouldn't catch. Sarah sighed one of her thirteen-long-hard-years-of-being-married sighs. Russ pumped the gas some more, tried again; it caught, coughed, stalled. Beer in tow, Chet was at the picture window again, probably hoping like hell that he wouldn't have to come out in the cold to jump Russ with his new Jeep.

The Falcon, groaning like Russ with a Sunday-morning hangover, started on the third try, and he floored it for some ten seconds to keep the car going. They sat there for a good five minutes while the car warmed. Sarah stared out her window, giving her husband and his booze breath the back of her head.

Russ ground the car into reverse and backed up, squinting out the back window instead of using the rearview. The Falcon clipped a snow banking at the foot of the driveway and jerked crooked onto the Lamprey Road. Wayne looked at Hannah again; he'd never seen his father even come close to swiping anything with a car.

Hugging the yellow line, Russ drove at least twenty miles an hour under the speed limit. Sarah sat as far from him as she could, scrunched against her door. Wayne'd fallen asleep. Hannah didn't know how he could do that, fall asleep. The night fears, churning in her belly, had ahold of her already. The same night fears she got when it was after midnight and she heard the 'frigerator shudder on and off, could swear that someone kept sneaking by the kitchen window, and her parents were out too late—later than they said—and she worried on them, imagining the Falcon wrapped around a big old oak tree on some lonesome back road, and she was going to have to quit school, sign up for the welfare and take care of Wayne and the baby on the way even though she was only thirteen years old. The night fears that made her head pound and her palms grease up, that wedged a lump in her throat so she could hardly swallow. Night fears that nudged her toward throwing up and didn't get swept away until she swooned in that

sweet rush of fresh, late-night air when her mother—
red-eyed and flushed—banged open the back door,
trailed by her father, who tripped into the kitchen, grinning, his gray eyes blurry as he hissed open another beer
as she ran up to bed, hoping to fall asleep before the
yelling started.

The dashboard lights etched Russ's bloated face,
cheeks puffy, eyes heavy, jaw slack. Hannah'd never
been one of those kids who thought her old man was
perfect (or her mother, for that matter). She knew early
on that he drank too much, had a wicked temper, and
took a few too many days off from work—not enough
to get him fired, but enough to hold him back. But she'd
always trusted him. There was nothing she'd liked better
as a little girl than driving home late from visiting. She
and Wayne'd curl up on the back seat—woolly-bear
caterpillars—and fall asleep to the beat of the car, the
low voices coming from the front. With her father driving she'd felt like nothing in the world could hurt her;
she knew they'd get home safe and sound. Then, when
they crunched into their driveway, Russ would pick her
and Wayne up and gentle them over his shoulders,
where she'd smell his beery breath, feel his whiskers
scratch her cheek, listen to her mother rattle the keys in
the back door, and she knew that they were home. Safe.

But her father had scared Hannah that New Year's
morning, dredged up her night fears. It didn't take long
before her fingernails were gouging her palms, before
she had a headache from grinding her teeth. Sarah
wouldn't even look at Russ; it was the man of the

family's duty to drive, and if he wasn't doing it right, she wasn't going to watch. Abandoning her family, Sarah slunk low into her coat and drew her knees up to her stomach; Hannah'd come to expect that from her mother.

Russ weaved the Falcon down the Lamprey Road like it was the first time he'd ever driven. The car drifted to the right, to the left, straddled the yellow. Russ aimed the car—same as a pitcher who's lost his control aims the baseball—instead of driving it. His strong, stubby fingers sprawled limp on the steering wheel like dead worms as he hunched forward, squinted.

They crossed over Keegan's Bridge, where, one winter's night, Paul Keegan—the poor sonuvabitch—sliced his Ford pickup through the guardrail and got himself drowned in the Tucker River's black winter water. Hannah ticked off the milestones that lurked ahead, the whole morbid history of the Lamprey Road—its toll—crammed into her head:

Those left-right-left, roller-coaster turns just after the Piscataway Campground. Turns where Young Joe Gaudet flipped his Mustang and got crippled; Young Joe (being no little Joe) dressed out at a good three hundred pounds, and it took the fire department the better part of five hours to cut him out of that car.

Stevens' Junction, where a Boston & Main freight nailed a carload of high-school kids bombing home from Manor Beach late one warm spring night. The town cops parked that car out back of Stain Thistle's garage, and it seemed to Hannah that every kid in Granite got dragged there by their parents to take in that wreck; a gang of stupid, drunk kids turned into a lesson—cap *L*.

Great Hill, where, just the spring before, a school bus got turned sideways somehow in an April snowstorm and tipped over; no one got hurt bad, but it was all the town talked about for weeks, glossing the whys and wherefores and latching onto the grisly what-ifs.

It was so stuffy in the Falcon that Hannah yanked off her hat, unzipped her coat; sweat, like some nocturnal animal, crawled from her armpits, making her shiver. She stared at her father, who stared at the road, and grit her teeth so her ears rang. She felt as if the responsibility for getting the family home had somehow fallen on her. She kept thinking over and over—a prayer—"Get us home. Get us home. Please, get us home."

It was the best she could do as the Falcon fishtailed up Great Hill.

The traffic light at the intersection of Lamprey Road and Route 49 slid from yellow to red as the Falcon jerked to a stop, Hannah jamming her feet to the floor to keep from pitching forward. Russ flicked on the Falcon's left blinker out of habit. The traffic light turned green, but the Falcon didn't move. Russ peered up at the light as if he didn't understand. The light tripped through two more cycles.

"Dad?" Hannah said as the light greened again. "Daddy?"

He sighed, and turned slow into the intersection.

They crept down Route 49, tightroping the yellow

line, Russ panting. Hannah hoped a cop would drive by and pull them over. When she saw the sign for New Boston Road—their road—she tapped her father on the shoulder, pointed. He nodded.

The New Boston Road exit jug-handled off the highway. What they needed to do was bang a left at the bottom of the exit and cross back over Route 49. The new place they were renting sat about a mile down from the intersection.

Their old house stood across the road from the bottom of the exit. They had lived there six years, until their landlord, True Pease, had sold it out from under them the summer before. The guy who bought it planned to tear it down come spring and build a gas station; *a gas station*. Russ'd put a lot of work into that house, sweat and heart both. He'd dug a new cellar—by hand; torn out the plaster upstairs and Sheetrocked those rooms; rewired it; reroofed it; laid in new plumbing. Treated the place like his own because True Pease had promised he could buy it one day. But True Pease'd lied. On one muggy day in August they were told they had a month to move. So much for a man's word.

Its black, curtainless eyes staring at them, the house rose from the snow like a curse. No one lived there, or ever would again, but the driveway was plowed. Instead of turning left, toward home, Russ rolled across New Boston Road and into the driveway. Sarah woke, looked at him.

"Leak," he said. "Gotta take a leak."

As Russ lurched out of the car, already searching

for his fly, Sarah looked at Hannah—and she got out, too; she'd taken care of her father before, taken care of them all. Sarah, with a kind of relief, had seen early on that a vein of Nanna Page ran deep in her daughter.

She stood with her back to her father, listening to his insistent piss burn into the frozen snow. When he finished he leaned against the Falcon for a good long while, staring at the house the same way he must've thought about his life when he was sober; Hannah saw the animal longing in his face, a gut-craving for the man he knew he'd never be. A spasm of cold rippled through her and she shivered.

Though this was the house of her father's longing, Hannah was glad to be shut of True Pease's place. It was the house they'd stumbled into after they were forced to abandon Page's Village. A miscarriage-haunted house, whose rooms echoed with arguments sprung from dry wallets and empty purses, shuddered with sobs fed by aquifers of grief so deep and pure as to offer a kind of rapture. A house where Russ's drinking had threatened to drown the whole family; where Sarah'd retreated (become an invisible woman) and in that retreat nearly caused her family to fly apart; where Hannah got yanked from childhood at nine years old.

There are seasons, years, even decades, when one thinks back on them and all that can be remembered is bitter ash. For Hannah, her ninth year was such a time.

A fourth-grader, Hannah that year had missed ninety-seven out of one hundred eighty schooldays, yet she wasn't sick once; she couldn't afford the luxury of sickness that dark season. Sarah kept Hannah home those days, writing to her daughter's teacher (Miss Gold, same age as Sarah, drove a lipstick-red Corvette convertible) in a cramped, tortured scrawl: "I kept Hannah home from school to help me out around the house because I didn't feel good."

✖

Holding Sarah's worry-thin hands, Hannah guides her mother through the silence of seconds hours days, the flash floods of tears. She watches her father, mute and scared, smolder. Russ and Sarah need Hannah this, her ninth, year; she's a bridge, no matter how narrow and rickety.

Hannah supposes it's the miscarriage, yet another in this child-denying house, that breaks her mother. But she knows, too, that it was bound to happen sooner or later; her childhood is spiked with the signs and portents of this breakdown.

It isn't Sarah's shrieks that wake Hannah late that autumn night, but Wayne, crying, crawling into her bed.

"What's wrong with Mommy, Hannah?" Wayne bawls. "What's wrong?"

Hannah curls around him, strokes his hair; what she wants, needs, to say to Wayne she can't yet articulate. So she holds him, uses him as a hedge against her own fear.

Another howl, carrying the taint of pain, rage and despair. Muffled voices.

"Hannah!" cries Wayne. "Hannah!"

Their mother's screeching stops eventually, gives way to whispers, purposeful footsteps, the rush of running water. Hannah lulls Wayne into a shallow, chest-rattly sleep, worries over him. Waits.

She hears her father creaking up the stairs just as the first faint fissures of the coming day scar the eastern sky. She intercepts him outside her room.

"Sshh, Daddy," she says, "I just got Wayne back to sleep."

Cowed by his daughter's competence, Russ clears his throat, lowers his voice: "I got to take Mommy to the doctor's; she's sick. You get Wayne off to school. But I want you to stay home to help Mommy. Okay?"

"Okay, Daddy."

She listens to the windowpanes quiver as her parents slam shut the back door, their shoes scuffle in the dirt driveway, the click-chunk of the car doors. After they pull away, she creeps downstairs. Blood, still tacky, spatters the kitchen linoleum. Hannah heats water and scrubs the floor while Wayne sleeps.

Fall deepens; Hannah misses more school. The trees' brilliant children barely blaze as wind-driven rains douse, then discard the leafy fireworks before their time.

Sarah's past is her daughter's past, too, so Hannah, in a blood-knowing, understands what is what with her mother. Hannah hides the knives (and makes Russ do the same with his razor blades), won't let Sarah in the kitchen alone, sleeps only when her mother sleeps.

For Sarah, the sun shines too bright, the wind blows too hard and clean, the cheeky birds flickering at the seed-and-suet-stuffed milk cartons chirk too loud. Out of childhood habit, Sarah takes to licking window screens, savoring their dusty, salty taste, their musty smell. The unconscious actions that once bound her days—the sweeping and the cooking and the washing—are no longer enough. Sarah'd just as soon stand at a window, forehead pressed to the humid glass, in her rural solitary and watch the black rain, a raven's rain, slant down. Something's ruptured; Hannah's the suture.

Whether Hannah goes to school depends on Russ's rousing Sarah. If he can wake her and prop her at the kitchen table with her cup of Lipton tea, then he can guiltlessly go to work, convinced that the mere fact of his wife's consciousness means a normal day for his family. When she stays home, Hannah, now prey to sleepless, tooth-grinding nights, gets Wayne up and out, then climbs into her mother's bed, offering Sarah the consolation of her small warmth.

That was the best Hannah Britton could do as her family slipped toward the savage, white heart of winter.

❧

Russ finally gave up on his reverie, turned his back on True Pease's empty house, and Hannah led him to the car as if leading an old man from the grave of his wife.

They backed slow out of the driveway—something they'd done thousands of times before—but when they straightened out, a look shadowed Russ's face, the same one as when the real-estate man had told him that he and his family had to move.

"What took . . ." Sarah started to ask.

Russ floored it, tires squealing as the Falcon bolted through the red light.

And Sarah: "Honey! Honey!" As if those two words could fill thirteen years of black silences. Russ slammed on the brakes, only then realizing what he'd done. And there they sat, the Falcon catty-corner in the middle of New Boston Road, Russ pleading to Sarah as if his life depended on it:

"Keep talking, honey. Please, keep talking."

Sarah VI

The bramble-berries scrabble on the side of the road: Shoots ramble toward the crumbling tar, creep laterally in the sand, both attack and fend off the pushy puckerbrush. They twine, twine again, even again, snarled like long wet hair that's been slept on. But these low, mean plants bear beautiful sons and daughters, red and black berries hidden away in wombs of thorns and leaves. She scooches, peers at them, edges her hand toward the berries as if they could jump up and nip her.

Chapter Eleven

August 1985

A MONTH OF SI-
lence and anger limped by: Russ and Sarah couldn't
speak; they didn't hear from Wayne or Charlotte.

Sarah hadn't told Russ about the envelope, the ad-
dress, though she constantly picked at it the way a child
will worry over a Band-Aid. When Wayne and Charlotte had sold her granddaughter—that sentence sharp
and bitter, like one of her mother's kisses—Sarah had
sighed and given herself over to old friends: grief and
hate. Raised to be a victim, she'd learned to grieve, hate
and retreat. Not act. Nanna Page had brooked no actions but her own.

When it came to Wayne and Charlotte and Jessie, there'd been no question of calling in the police or the state or the social-work fools. A family matter, the family would take care of it. Even if that meant shrugging and doing nothing.

Nanna Page'd had no use for outsiders meddling with village life. When they did—it couldn't be helped sometimes—she would rage at her failure, then vanish into Cedar Swamp for days at a time. When Auntie Robena'd miscarried her only baby and about bled to death, Nanna'd grudgingly let Grandpa Elgar lope to the Marcouxs' to call the ambulance people; of course, Elgar—damned if he was going to let his daughter die to mollify his wife—had had to shut Nanna in the cellar first.

"They only come sniffing around when they think something's wrong," Nanna spit. "Where are they the rest of the time? They ought to hang the sons-ta-bitches. The whole damned peck of 'em."

What was it about her family, Sarah wondered. All of them, her included, still looking—praying!—to the house up the hill even though Nanna'd been dead and gone for twenty years and her house for more than ten. Why were they so scared of the past? Of one another? Of themselves? Nanna Page had saved them, it was true. But not a one of them had weathered the cure.

"Coming to work?"

Sarah kept on staring out her window, rocking the way a ninety-year-old woman propped on a porch rocks. Up before five, she hadn't moved from the rocker since.

"Damn it, Sarah! Look at me!"

She did.

"You coming to work?"

"I tossed and turned all night."

"Bud ain't going to put up with this much longer, you know. We're way behind on orders."

"Well, he can just go ahead and fire me then."

"Sarah."

"He can."

"What do you want me to say?"

"Whatever you want. You will, anyways."

"What's that supposed to mean?"

Sarah turned back to the window; time for Russ to go to work. But he wasn't moving toward the door.

"She's gone, Sarah," said Russ, trying to sand his voice smooth. "Jessie's gone."

Refusing him, she started rocking.

"What do you want from me?" he asked.

"Nothing."

"Want me to beat the shit out of Wayne? That make you feel better?"

"Don't know what I want no more."

"I'm sorry Jessie's gone, but I ain't the one sold her."

"You wouldn't understand."

"You don't think it don't eat my guts? Only I can't afford to mope around the house all day or live in that fucking rocking chair."

"We could've done something."

"What, Sarah? You tell me. What could we've done?"

"I don't know. Something."

"What could we do? Even if we knew where Jessie was, what could we do? Somebody paid good money for that baby. What're we going to do? March right up to somebody's front door and take that baby back? Huh? You tell me. You think about it. This shit's been going on for a month. I've had it up to here."

"Go to work. You'll be late."

Russ snatched his keys off the kitchen table and slammed out the door, rattling the windows.

(A mirror belonging to Nanna Page's mother lurked at Auntie Robena's, its mottled face, like parched leather, dissolving into silver-blue mystery swirls that seemed meant to decipher the mirrored's soul. Sarah had obsessed over that mirror in the past month. It seemed that, more than ever, her life, *her face*, too, was dissolving. Fighting with Russ, each thorned word, each dagger look, had ripped her pale flesh, diminished her, edged her toward black seas. Even before Russ had banged out the door, Sarah had imagined the weeks, months—even years!—coiling out before her as she nested in the bedroom's gloom, gnawing at her grief, nurturing her hate.)

Trembling, afraid even to look toward the bedroom, Sarah pulled on day-old jeans and a white tee shirt, scrawled a note to Russ, and set out on foot for Banks, New Hampshire.

Sarah didn't walk direct to Banks. Main streets and highways didn't sit right with her. She was, after all, a

Page. And there wasn't a Page alive who trusted the shortest distance between two points.

Scratching the backsides of both Granite and Lamprey, then looping on up into Banks, a haul of some twenty-five miles, she hewed to the back roads. Roads pocked, buckled and crumbling, taunted by willful grasses that'd bullied their way through the tar. Gnarled roads. Roads that, come midnight, were ceded to lovers and thieves.

Back roads, Page roads: sawmill screams; Merville's Muskrat Hideaway, a flatlander-infested campground where bare-chested Puerto Rican boys (trucked up from Boston) rake the gravel; rust-dappled house trailers propped on cracked cement blocks—ballicky-bare-assed kids roiling the dooryard dust as they roll around inside fifty-five-gallon steel drums; the groans of pick-ups shrugging the speed limit; splintered signs for hair-dressers, tool sharpeners and gerbils; Chick Conway's dump of fifteen million tires, which caught fire once— bringing on two weeks of night; the sticky-sweet smell of a half-empty bottle of Mr. Frostie root beer, honey-bees swarming the fizzy nectar; heat seeping through Sarah's sneakers, fine summer dust powdering her ankles; the old Route 101, which had once been the new 101, but had become the new Route 27, but everyone called it the old Lamprey Road because the new 101 had become the old 101 because a newer 101 had been finished the fall before; sandpits—back-road scar tissue; the gunpowder smell of firecrackers; bewhiskered widow ladies in faded, flower-print shifts adhering to creaky lawn chairs and gulping instant ice tea; the wet sweetness of blueberries; a snapping turtle, razor beak clacking, bulldozering across hot tar as soft as fresh-baked cookies; hidden, hulking in the woods, cancer-ridden cars the color of October leaves; and at Wilmot's Welding, Lamprey, Danny Wilmot's tin man, a scrap-metal Frankenstein's monster—welder's mask for a face—cobbled from rod iron, gap-toothed gears and copper wire.

Having hiked from the heat-haunted cool of early morning, through noon's red-eyed glare, and into the furnace of midafternoon, Sarah was grateful to dip into the sawdust-smelling shadows of Vining's Market and buy a tonic. She picked a Piney Pop—Piscataway Beverage's Flavor-of-the-Month—which carried the faintest whiff of pine pitch. Whenever she drank a Piney Pop, Sarah was reminded of certain Page's Village trees that, at summer's height, would ooze their thick, amber blood.

"The O'Connells, Rowe's Road," she whispered to herself, sagging onto the bench outside Vining's. She took a deep drink, tilting her head back so that the skin of her neck tightened, and slumped against the store. She pressed the rimed bottle to her forehead and closed her eyes, casting for a breeze. Wasn't any. Just the heat-whine piercing her inner ear.

Spitting stones, boiling dust, a green pickup skidded to a stop in front of the store. The shirtless driver, chest hair bleached by the sun, wore a roofer's tan smudged here and there by the deep green ink of faded tattoos.

Shoulders hung so, he dismounted from his hard-used Ford, adjusted his crotch, and swaggered toward the store.

He winked at Sarah: "Hot one, ain't it?"

He spoke in one of those gravel voices rasped raw by whiskey and butts. Sarah Britton, thirty-six-year-old grandmother, ducked her head and blushed as he swivel-hipped past. Once he was inside she allowed herself a small smile; she'd known assholes like him her whole life.

He strutted out lugging a case of Old Milwaukee beer, but still stopped long enough to give her the eye and ask: "Need a ride anywheres?"

Sarah looked up—his eyes were too blue, and she'd be damned if they didn't twinkle—and shook her head no.

Grinning the grin of a man who's already punished a six-pack since noontime, he shrugged: "Suit yourself."

Gears grinding, the pickup squealed and fishtailed out onto the road. Sarah killed her Piney Pop, sighed, and marched on Banks.

The O'Connells' house, a ranch bragging a brand-new picture window, was framed by a low split-rail fence that hadn't yet gone to gray. The driveway, the shiny blue-black of fresh-laid asphalt, was empty. Yellow-green grass seedlings stubbled the front lawn, which sloped toward the road; out back loomed chocolate-brown hills of new-dumped loam. A sign, in wood-burned script, hung above the garage door: "Gary &

Elaine O'Connell." Given that Rowe's Road wasn't much more than a glorified logging trail that looked as if it'd gotten paved over by accident once, there wasn't another house around for a good half-mile.

In the forgiving late-afternoon light, a woman younger than Sarah (but older than Charlotte) held Jessie in her lap. She nuzzled Jessie's neck, tickled her feet, sniffed her diaper, played "Peekaboo!," "Oh my!" and "So big!" Her every word, each gesture, aimed at pleasing the baby.

Hidden across the road in the wild woods, Sarah had been watching for almost an hour.

The woman—Sarah envied her the delight she took in her granddaughter—picked Jessie up and hugged her, rubbing her cheek against the baby's, the baby's fingers tangling in her hair. Sarah stared, unblinking.

A telephone rang. The woman looked at Jessie, toward the house, at Jessie, and then sat her in the playpen and ran inside.

Walking that day, Sarah had fought her panic at moving from the known to the familiar to the strange. The feeling had reminded her of wading in the lake as a child and being scared because she didn't know whether the next step was the one that would plunge her in over her head. That old fear clenched in her stomach.

Sarah rushed across the road, hurdled the fence, and snatched up Jessie, who buried her face in her chest. It was what Sarah'd imagined all day—this stealing back of her granddaughter—what had prodded her along. But as she stood there holding Jessie in the dying light, she realized she would be no happier with or without the baby. Oh, having Jessie in her arms had, for the moment, taken the edge off her grief, the same as cleaning house or making love did. But, in the end, there was no appeasing it. Her wounds were too deep, too old.

She kissed Jessie on the forehead, gentled her into the playpen, and vanished into the dark woods.

Midnight on Route 49 outside Banks: Sarah sat on the guardrail, courting the future and gutting the past. Granite, the remains of Page's Village, Russ—a bedroom that smelled of sweat and sadness—lay south down Route 49. North? She couldn't say.

Auntie Leah hadn't been able to leave; her mother hadn't been able to stay; and Nanna Page'd forged her own universe. Where did that leave her—Sarah Page, Sarah Huckins, Sarah Britton?

She looked both ways before crossing the empty highway. Walking north into the deepening night, she supposed that she was her mother's daughter, after all.

She almost smiled at the thought.

Interlude:

Ella Huckins, 19—

DREAM-DRUNK, heart thundering, Ella Huckins jerks up in bed, tussles with the curtains and, finally, snaps up the shade. She strains to look out the window, forehead pressed to the cool night glass, as if she expects her long-dead mother to be out there pacing the dooryard at two in the morning. She looks long and hard, full of bullheaded conviction even as the dream is flushed away. She tumbles from dream to a wakefulness suffused with relief, but nicked, too, by disappointment. Her heart slows, ragged breath smoothes.

Ella dreams Nanna Page most nights, hasn't been

able to get rid of the woman since that winter's dawn
she fled Page's Village and abandoned Sarah; even now,
years later and hundreds of miles away, Nanna's claws
are still in her. She wonders whether her sisters and
brothers, whom she hasn't seen since the day she left,
dream Nanna. Knowing them, none of them would ever
dare ask or want to be asked. To a Page, a direct question is as much a threat as a loaded gun.

Sighing, Ella reaches up and tugs down the shade,
snugging it to the windowsill, shuts the curtains, and
knuckles the small of her back. It's only as she eases
back into bed that she realizes her leg hurts something
wicked.

Thick, coarse veins of blue-purple and green-yellow
road-map Ella's legs. On her right calf, the veins tangle,
pass into a kind of venous switchyard, then merge into
a crab-looking knot of vein, gristle, and black-and-blue.
The Crab. That's what she calls it. And it's the Crab
that's grouching. A knurly beast sprung from a life
spent working on her feet: a pedal-pumping, machine-
wed factory girl at shoe shops, textile mills and the
like; a cigarette girl; grocery-store cashier; waitress;
department-store help. Women's work. Which is to
say, hard work. Low-paying, man-fending work. Shit
work.

Eyes shut, Ella listens to the Crab grumble, winces
at its bite, but luxuriates, too, in the ebb and flow of
pain, in the numbness scuttling up her leg. She knows
that this handling of pain—the way she's seen Christ-
crazy born-agains coddle copperheads—is a thing

Nanna would've done. Ella can't remember Nanna once confessing to hurt; there was a lot Nanna wouldn't confess to.

Oh, Nanna, thinks Ella, lulled by the dull rhythm of her ache, you raised sturdy women (and puny men), but what good has it done us who dream you every night? . . .

An hour later the pain, yanked a notch tighter, nudges Ella awake again. She clicks on the light.

The Crab hisses blood, staining the starch-stiff sheets a deep, almost black, red. Burst veins — like water pipes on a subzero night — and the first thing Ella wonders is what Nanna would do. For some seconds, she pines for Nanna, wishes that her mother were there to stanch the blood, kill the fear. Nanna could always be counted on when there was blood; blood spoke to her.

Ella supposes that she should do *something*. But watching the blood boil from her leg soothes her somehow. The longer she lets it bubble, the less moved she is to act. If it stops, it stops. If it doesn't, it doesn't. She almost smiles.

She hasn't seen a doctor since Sarah was born, since Sarah, whom Nanna forced her to bring into this world, in the newborn's rage to be free tore her up and about killed her. Left her barren. She hemorrhaged — "hemridged," the women of Page's Village noted with sage nods at the news — bearing Sarah through the birth canal on a river of blood; both of them, mother and child, bloody and screaming. If anyone had been stupid enough to cradle her new baby girl in Ella's arms that first week, Ella would have strangled Sarah and had done with it.

Light-headed, Ella floats back onto her pillow. There's a throbbing at the base of her skull, reminding her of the trip-hammer set off when you haven't eaten for a couple of days.

Ella knows that drumbeat. There'd been weeks at a time when she couldn't drag herself out of bed. Never mind eat. Or take care of Sarah. She hadn't been able to love her daughter, just as Nanna hadn't been able to love them, until she ran from her, left Sarah sleeping in that cold, dark shack. Did Nanna, in her furious weaving of silences, learn to love Ella, too, in her absence?

And she finds now that the thing she has hated most is, perhaps, the thing she must love best. Her years after Page's Village give in to the gristmill of small jobs, small rooms and small towns. Years punctuated only by her surrender to hard-bodied whiskey men, nameless men who made love as if they were laying bricks and in whose barrel chests she could hear the whispers of cancers in waiting. But Page's Village . . . Though she has put thirty years between her and her family, she's never truly escaped Page's Village. She's still that twelve-year-old girl hung up on barbwire. And this time, goddammit, Ella Huckins cries for that girl, thick, salty tears of redemption that pool at the corners of her mouth.

Short of breath, ears buzzing, Ella props herself on her elbows. The blood hasn't stopped—if anything, it's sieving worse—her leg is dead numb. The Crab has grown black, bigger; it pulses. Ella shudders, bowels clenching. (A taste of warmed Karo corn syrup oozes into her mouth; Nanna fed it to all of them when they were sick.) Another vein blows. Another.

Dizzy, she closes her eyes, sees herself turn the shack's doorknob—cold, even inside—hears the door stick before she sneaks once again into that long-ago frigid dawn. A scentless winter wind rakes her cheeks, waters her eyes, and she hunches to curl her warmth tighter; icicles, like frozen pickerel, leer from the eaves. Once more, she hears her boots squeak on packed snow. That is the song of her sin, her desertion. Black rubber boots squeaking down past Leah's place—a faint jangle of boot buckles—and up the hill (without looking back) to the waiting car, a black Cadillac wearing red-wall tires, and a man whose name she will never remember.

Part II

Chapter Twelve

October 1985

BUSHED, HOBBLING, stomach bitching, Wayne Britton skulked home to Granite. A shrunken ghost hunched against a midnight downpour, one of those relentless October rains that aims to flense your flesh and leave the bones for crow barter.

You can get the screws put to you wherever you live, Wayne'd figured. So he'd decided he'd rather have the people he'd grown up among do him, instead of strangers. That's why he'd come back.

He and Charlotte hadn't lasted a month after his old man'd thrown them out. They'd passed their days lashed to thorns of silence, spent their nights making hate:

They snarl at each other's naked shadows, Wayne fucking Charlotte up against a wall, her body slamming back and forth, back and forth as he bangs at her, Charlotte punctuating his face with knobby fists, tearing at his flesh with teeth and nails, driving at him with razor hips—in their fierce granite lovemaking—just as hard as he drives at her. Until, at last, they heap to the floor—sore, sweat-slick, empty—in a tortured tangle, aching for sleep.

Those last Charlotte nights had scared Wayne. And one chilly morning, when he realized that either of them was capable of killing the other, he left.

Though he couldn't see much more than squat blurs—water-stained pen-and-ink drawings—in the rain and dark, he stopped on Route 49 and took in Page's Village. Of all Granite, Page's Village, a place that he knew was somehow holy to his mother and her people, held the fiercest grip on him.

Born to its shadow, his earliest place memories were of the village . . . Nanna Page's house. He'd spent his childhood nursing on his mother's obsessive whispers, her tales of Page's Village; he and Hannah could see it in their mother's eyes, hear it in her voice, taste its presence, her urgency in telling these stories, these family myths. Sometimes, though he knew it wasn't so, he wondered whether he hadn't grown up in the village himself.

Nanna Page had died before he was born and the village had already started to give in to time's slow strangulation. But in Page's Village, Wayne knew, squirmed the secrets to his raw anger, to the marrow melancholy that had marked him, Hannah, his mother, and every Page he'd ever laid eyes on. But especially his mother. Especially Sarah.

Sometimes it seemed to Wayne that it was Hannah, just a year older, who had raised him, and that Hannah, by force of will and in true Page fashion, had raised herself and taken care of their mother when necessary. His old man had been a deep-voiced invisible man and, once in a while, a detached hand warming their asses for sins both real and imagined.

Russ was a good egg, a guy who worked hard, did without for his wife and kids, and whose sole vice, really, was the case of beer that greased his weekends. The poor bastard simply had married a woman who for days, even weeks, at a time wasn't all there. And who, even when she was, couldn't be trusted to be herself. Facing Page's Village, Wayne snubbed the rain and closed his eyes . . . remembering.

❧

It's a warm October afternoon, summer's last mad rush at immortality. The air smells of brittle, brown leaves, rotting tomato vines. The late bees, harvest bees, square-dance at the eaves. Sitting at the kitchen table, Sarah stares out the window toward Route 49. But she doesn't see the cars, or even hear them, as she absent-mindedly pirouettes the tip of a paring knife on the pale bellies of her wrists.

Hannah stands watch. Already, at age five, she recognizes in her mother faint stirrings in her own soul. Clutching his sister's skirt, Wayne hovers behind Hannah.

Pressing knife to skin—hard enough to hurt, not hard enough to cut—Sarah draws the blade across her wrist, the skin blanching to albino white at the knife's passing.

"Momma," Hannah says.

Sarah holds up the knife as if looking into a fogged mirror, tries to decipher her face in the blade's dull silver.

"Mommy?"

Hannah creeps toward her mother, who kisses the knife blade; Wayne buries himself in hallway shadows.

"Mommy!"

Still, she presses the blade to her lips.

"Mommy!"

Sarah sticks out her tongue and brings the knife point to the tip; blood seeps, a dark, red spring percolating to the surface.

Hannah knows that she's about to lose her mother. And that knowing, rather than freezing her or sending her scurrying for the bony arms of sadness, turns into a rage that suffuses her whole trembling body as she scoops up an ABC block, wings it, and cracks it off her mother's skull.

The knife clatters to the table even as the purple bruise, like a gravestone rubbing, blossoms on Sarah's forehead, even as she shrieks: "Hannah!"

Then Sarah looks at the knife, at her children, and starts crying—wild sobs wrenched free as if she were being devoured by some fierce, heart-eating beast. The children cry, too, Hannah moving to her mother, wrapping herself in her sorrows, Wayne rigid in the hall. Pulling Hannah to her chest, Sarah finger-combs her daughter's hair, whispers:

"I'm sorry, babies. Momma . . . I . . . Please don't tell Daddy."

Sarah is a woman who lives ninety-nine percent of her life under the skin, and she's incapable of telling her children that what she meant to do that remarkable October afternoon was to bundle all of them into the stock car, start it up, and leave the barn door shut. And that, in a sense, she had pulled the knife on herself to save her children from their mother. It would be years before Sarah could peel away the layers and look at that truth.

Wayne shook his head. Nanna Page's house was gone, their old place, too. Sacrificed when the state'd decided to widen Route 49 for the northbound tourist traffic. But memory won't be denied. Nothing is truly destroyed until all memory of it is erased, and the half-life of memory is long.

Wayne had come back to Granite meaning to light on his parents' doorstep. But the call of Page's Village, even as a corpse, was strong. He'd returned home steeled to do battle with Russ and Sarah, insist on his

place in the family. Instead, he found himself free-
wheeling down the hill to Page's Village, crashing
through sopping puckerbrush and thrashing through
the marsh, gone feral with no Pages left to tame it.

He nudged open the door to what had once been
Auntie Leah's place, tripped over the threshold in the
dark, fell, and succumbed to sleep where he'd landed,
home again, on the time-grooved floor.

Wayne woke to the cold tickle of gunmetal pressed to
his neck.

"Don't you go trying nothing funny, mister"—a
woman's voice. "This twenty-two'll kill more'n just
rats."

"Auntie? Auntie Leah? It's me—Wayne."

"Sarah's Wayne?"

"Yeah."

"Roll over."

Leah squinted at him and scowled. "It's you," she
said, though she didn't set the rifle down.

Stiff and damp from sleeping on the floor in wet
clothes, Wayne creaked as he sat up and said: "Hi,
Auntie."

"I thought you and that coozie of yours run off after
all that riggin' you pulled with that poor little baby."

"I come back."

"What for? To drive your folks crazier than they
already are?"

"Don't know," Wayne said to the floor.

"And what're you doing in here, anyways? You ain't got no business being in here."

Wayne had stumbled into Leah's shack expecting the barren filth that fifteen years of abandonment brings; instead, he'd lurched back toward childhood.

"It hasn't changed," he whispered, looking around for the first time. "It's the same's it always was."

"Some folks go to church. Some tramp around Cedar Swamp. I come here when the need moves me."

"You never give the place up. Even when you moved."

"Nope."

Wayne stood, brushing off the seat and knees of his dungarees. And slowly, like a kid sipping scalding cocoa after an afternoon's snow-shoveling, he took in the shack: the same cast-iron woodstove with the same chipped enamel pots and pans—white-speckled black— standing guard; the sooty kerosene lamps; the blue-and-white-checked curtains, the blue faded to the color of his mother's eyes; the fried-pepper-and-onion stink; wind wheezing through uncaulked cracks; Auntie Leah in uniform: untucked flannel shirt, dungarees, work-scored boots.

"Makes me feel five years old again, Auntie," Wayne said.

"I wish you was five again," she said.

"You don't think too much of me right now, do you, Auntie? Do you?"

They took each other's measure, the nineteen-year-old boy (barely a man) who thought he knew most everything, but didn't know nothing, and his fifty-one-year-old great-aunt, who pretended to know nothing, but who always made it her business to know more than she let on. She shook her head, as if viewing him in a coffin, and said:

"If it was up to me, Wayne Page Britton, I'd boot your sorry ass from one end of Sanborn County to the other, and then start in right over again. But it ain't up to me. You're Russ and Sarah's problem. You just best better be thankful that your Nanna Page ain't living. Then you'd have some serious worrying to warm your bed at night. I ain't going to act like I know all about your troubles. We all got troubles. Start the second that sperm jumps the egg in your momma's belly, and then just gets worser and worser from there. But you got to straighten out, Wayne. I been around Page men since I was a baby, and if you put 'em all together you still ain't got a whole man. Far's I can see, you ain't no better."

She couldn't tell whether he was listening. He'd pulled on his Page face, that closed-mouth, piss-you-off thicket of squints, twitches, frowns and sideways dog-glances that'd passed for communication for generations of Pages. God, he was such a Page! But, too, in the barbs and dead ends of his mask, she saw a hint of his mother's helplessness. That trace of Sarah's weakness trapped in Wayne's hard face shocked Leah toward a deeper understanding of her grandnephew, nudged her toward momentary forgiveness. She owed Sarah that much at least.

Leah sighed as she spoke: "But if it's any help, you can stay here in Auntie's place for a while. You just take care of it, maybe do some yardwork around here. Auntie can't keep up no more the way she used to. This place, Page's Village, is yours, too, Wayne. Belongs to all us Pages, no matter how mean, sneaky and ignorant. Maybe what you need's a good, stiff dose of it."

Wayne glanced around the shack as if he didn't quite trust it, the same way you mistrust that supposedly sunny mutt that growls. He knew his great-aunt was offering him more than a place to stay, that, in her own way, a request was being made. Though he didn't understand what was being asked, he was expected to accept.

"Thanks, Auntie," he said. "I'll do what I can."

After Leah left, Wayne lit a fire in the woodstove, wrestled off his damp clothes, and draped them over a couple of chairs that he set next to the stove. Satisfied they'd dry — he'd come home with only the clothes on his back and a crumpled finbuck in his wallet — he climbed into bed and slept till noon.

When he woke he lay there for a few minutes, fingers laced behind his head, savoring the ceiling's rough beams, the woodsmoke's bittersweet smell, the breeze soughing through the open window where the curtains curtsied.

He ate a breakfast of fried bologna and eggs, then walked out to the shed, ready to go to work.

Leah's shed was a low, trembly improvisation of a type Wayne knew well. Oil-stained, packed-dirt floor; paint-cracked storm windows stacked ten-deep; scores of baby-food jars jammed with screws, nails, nuts, washers and the like; cans of kerosene, rolls of tar paper, a tin of Three-In-One oil. He could tell from the shed that his aunt still wasn't a woman to flinch at hard work.

But there were surprises, too, among the practical tubes of caulking and the five-gallon pail of whitewash: a working wasps' nest, a papery gray football, wedged into the far corner; the yellowed envelope marked "Billy Page" that held a few snips of human hair; the black-and-white portrait of a good-looking woman with dark eyes and long, curly hair—"In case you ever forget what I look like, Love, Rachel," written in a hand as girlish as the woman's curls; a spider had spun a tiny jewel of a web in the lower right-hand corner of the frame.

Wayne squinted at the woman for a few seconds, thought: I wouldn't mind screwing that, shrugged, and took down the sickle. Its blade and handle had been oiled within the week.

Abandoned wood grays, splinters, punks up and, finally, rots with intent. Page's Village lay in that late, humid state:

Roofs—"rooves," Graniters said—had caved in, leaving jagged black wounds; windows were blinded by membranes of ten-year dust; paths, trails and roads washed out, weed-killed and woods-swallowed; the skitter, slither and scurry of mice, snakes and ants; a loamy, deep-woods smell of decay; a rust-gutted washboard slouched against sagging steps; a Cloverleaf Dairy milk bottle, dead flies carpeting the bottom, waiting in an outhouse; marsh oozing, trees threatening, the bramble-berries' skinny, green fingers wrapped around every neck.

Stooped, knees slightly bent, sickle loose in his hand, Wayne started by clearing a path between Leah's and where his grandmother Ella's shack had once stood, swinging the razor half-moon in quick, compact strokes, cutting down the brittle grasses on his forehand and backhand. When he reached the scorched circle that had once been Ella Huckins' house—charred timbers, like broken bones, sticking through the rubble—he blunted an urge to poke around; his mother had always warned him and Hannah against the place, and the edge to her voice had made them listen. Here, finally, was his chance.

Later. He had work to do.

Giving himself up to the back-and-forth, back-and-forth of his whirring blade, Wayne worked his way from Ella's up the rise and down to Fat Dot's—cheeks burning with the work, sweat creeking down his back—where he banged a right and hacked uphill, thorns and sickleweeds giving back as good as they got, back to Uncle Dead's shed. While Sarah'd had to warn Hannah and Wayne away from Ella's place, they'd known enough to steer clear of Uncle Dead's on their own.

The shed squatted mean and low, a troll turned out-building, in a gnawing tangle of rosebushes that'd traded in their blossoms for extra thorns. The building, even the windows, had been painted and repainted black; then someone had laid on gobs of dark red paint in thick, angry slashes. The windows'd been nailed shut along with the door, which also was padlocked. A tomb for a demon.

Wayne knew that Uncle Dead had raped one of his nieces, one of Sarah's first cousins, in that shed. And he knew that his mother'd always been lying when she'd said that none of them knew how he'd died. Wayne had always suspected that he could finally get to meet his dear, departed Uncle Dead—what was left of him, any-ways—if he was willing to bust into that shed. Then again, he had enough troubles with his living relations without riling the dead.

Taking in Billy's shed, Wayne realized how thirsty he was. He didn't really want to use the water pump, a rusted question mark, that stood there. But he didn't feel like hiking back to his aunt's either. He shrugged—little rust ain't going to kill me—and de-cided to give the pump a shot.

The water in the priming can was a stew of cobwebs, leaves and bugs, but Wayne poured it down the cylinder shaft anyway and started screeking the handle.

At first, there was just the dry, grease-starved whine as Wayne sawed the handle up and down. Then, as the pump drew air, a strained wheezing, like a deaf man trying to speak for the first time. And, finally, the pump spit, coughed and started puking chunks of rust and a trickle of water that eventually widened into an orange gush. Still pumping, Wayne drank his fill; the taste of rust stayed with him the rest of the day.

Working even faster now, Wayne scuttled up the hill from Fat Dot's toward where Nanna Page's house had once reigned.

As he cleared the road, arm muscles tightening as he passed by Robena's old place and slogged through the unshackled marsh, he imagined that, if he worked fast enough and hard enough, when he finished, Nanna's house would once again be glaring at Route 49. Standing guard over Page's Village.

The last fifty yards seemed to rise at a ninety-degree angle. Wayne's back and arm muscles spasmed and clenched, but he kept swinging the sickle. Choppier, though, like a slugger asked to lay down a bunt.

He'd always been a worker, had never been afraid of busting his ass. He took a small pleasure in that fact. Where some men liked to brag that they could drink anyone under the table, Wayne believed he could work any sonuvabitch into the ground.

He could barely lift his arms and couldn't stand straight the last ten yards, but he kept cutting, kept moving. It mattered to him, more than anything, right then to finish at the top of the hill. It was as if he thought that that day's work could somehow make up for what had happened that summer, show that Wayne Britton wasn't a total fuck-up.

Some three yards from the top, muscles quivering and ears ringing, Wayne's gut knotted. He threw up the water from Uncle Dead's pump, lacing it with a trace of his own blood.

When he finished vomiting, he passed out.

Russ got to Page's Village as the day's late, deep purples were about to bow and give way to the coming night. He pulled the Dart off Route 49 and crunched along the shoulder. Russ had run into Earl Duston at Buzzell's, both of them buying a six of cold ones, and Earl'd said he'd seen someone looked like Wayne clearing land over to Page's Village.

Whenever he thought of the village, Russ still imagined it as it had been, a thriving hive of (mostly) women and children ruled by Nanna Page, not as the ruin it had become. God, he had never been more afraid of anyone, before or since, than he had been of Nanna Page. She looked like she'd just as soon rip out your heart and chaw on it as give you the time of day. And she'd hated him for taking Sarah from her. In Nanna Page's eyes, Russ had stolen Sarah from her, stolen valuable property.

Russ found Wayne sleeping on the ground where he'd passed out—his son picked the damnedest places to snooze—and nudged him with his foot.

"Wayne? Son?"

Wayne groaned, rolled onto his back.

"Wayne?"

Squeezing his eyes shut, Wayne imagined his father

picking him up, slinging him over his shoulder, and lugging him back home where he belonged.

"Son, you're one sorry asshole."

Wayne sat up, back to his father, and hugged his knees as he admired his day's work, the paths dark scars on the village's lighter skin.

"Oh, I know what you're thinking," Russ said. "You're asking yourself whether that sonuvabitching father of yours is going to give you a pat on the ass for the job you did today. Just remember this: if doing the job ain't enough satisfaction in and of itself, don't do it."

Wayne gave his father a "what-the-fuck-do-you-know?" look.

"I was pissed at the world, too, when I was your age, Wayne. I was so mad. I had a wife and two kids, and I had no idea how it'd happened. I hated my job, hated my family and, most of all, I hated myself."

Wayne sighed, shivered.

"Don't you sigh at me, damn it! I'm trying to talk to you. Or are you like every other goddamned Page that ever lived? You too good to be talked to?"

"Dad," Wayne said, still looking at the village. "What do you want?"

He used the sentence the way you use a razor blade to scrape old paint from a windowpane.

"Fuck you, Wayne! Just fuck you! You come sneaking back into town and you can't even come and see your own family. And then you treat me like shit. You can just go fuck yourself!"

Russ peeled out, the Dart shrieking in the new night, spitting dirt and rocks at an unmoving Wayne.

When Russ pulled into the driveway—missing his wife, still mad at Wayne—he found Charlotte West waiting on his back steps.

Sarah VII

She attacks the kitchen linoleum, the dirt flying before
rasping straw bristles bent double. A cold light frosts
her eyes; her chin is set razor-sharp. She won't put up
with dirt, no g.d. way. Dirt and dust, mold and mildew,
the ring around the bathtub. These are things she understands, symptoms she can treat with just a little elbow
grease. Pieces of linoleum break free, a bristle snaps off.
Dust devils billow, swirl and snap at her ankles. Her
auntie says she clicks on the radio whenever she sweeps
and dances with her broom the way she never danced
with her husband. None of that nonsense for her. A
broom isn't a lover. It's a weapon.

Chapter Thirteen

✗

October 1985

NIBBLING AT A DAY-
old doughnut, Hannah sipped black instant, the kitch-
enette lit by a jack-o'-lantern's guttering candle; the
cottage reeked of scorched pumpkin, that October
smell of childhood. The jack, with its guitar-pick eyes
and jagged leer, made Hannah smile a small girl's
smile. Her mother had insisted on the pumpkin, had
gutted it, carved it, and candled it to life; the mother
of Hannah's girlhood had insisted on nothing.

Her mother. Hannah shook her head, after two
months still not quite believing that she and her
mother—*her pregnant mother!*—were roommates. But

when Sarah, helpless against the black waves breaking over her, had washed up on her doorstep late
that heat-thick night, there'd been no question but
that Hannah would take her in. Against all her will
and cunning, Hannah'd become the family's desig-
nated savior, the one sought, the one who never
said no. But the role didn't ennoble Hannah. It scared
her.

Cocooned in her quilt, Sarah slept on the pull-out
couch next to the picture window. Hannah couldn't tell
her rustle from the sputter of the jack-o'-lantern candle.
She had forgotten what a fine, small thing it was to listen
for the breathing of someone loved, like straining to hear
a freight train still miles away or distant fireworks at
dusk on Independence Day. Though surprised by it,
Hannah did not deny that she was grateful for the company of her mother.

Yet Sarah ... Sarah carried a whiff of the
past—Nanna Page's rule, bramble-berry scars, Uncle
Dead, Russ's stock car, silent tears—the way washing,
fresh-plucked from the clothesline, smells of the wind.
That faint scent, a distillation of Hannah's first eighteen
years and before, reopened wounds of the life Hannah
thought she'd fled. But here that life was. Back, and
sleeping on the couch.

Hannah checked the clock. She had to get going if
she wanted to find a parking place *and* make it to her
eight o'clock: newswriting with Murray. Still, she
stalled. Like the shy girl on the first day of first grade,
she didn't want to leave her mother. But, finally, she

rinsed her cup in the sink, snuffed the jack-o'-lantern, and snicked the door behind her.

Sarah woke missing Russ—his bulk, his animal heat— yet satisfied in her solitude. Absence, that negative space of the heart, gnawed at Sarah's days: her father, Chaney Huckins, remembered only as stubbled warmth, as a mangy scrap of tee shirt tucked in a dresser drawer; Ella, boot treads vanishing in the snow; Auntie Leah's fairy-tale Rachel; Heidi Meeks; Nanna Page; Baby Jessie; even Wayne. And now, though by choice, the man she'd been married to for twenty years. Absences, coarse, black threads binding her days; was a time when those absences strangled her.

Unwilling to give up the warmth of bed, she shut her eyes, listened to the wind-ruffled lake lick the dock, shush the shore.

Shingles slapping, storm windows rattly and cracked, cedar shakes scored and riven, the cottage cowered on a barren finger of granite that jabbed into the lake. A house used to flinching at the weather.

But the cottage suited Sarah. Small enough that she could gather it about herself—at most, five strides from back wall to front door—it spoke to her of the shacks where she'd come of age. Too, there were satisfying strokes of strangeness: years-worn wallpaper turned transparent; a cigarette-charred windowsill used by a previous tenant as an ashtray; a dead woman's dress (so the landlord claimed) dangling lonely in a coffin closet.

Unexpected touches straight out of her Page's Village childhood.

Still lake-hypnotized, Sarah rubbed the gentle slope of her pregnant stomach, weighed her sore but blooming breasts in the palms of her hands, kneaded swollen ankles. "The baby," she whispered. "I need this baby."

After a Shredded Wheat breakfast, Sarah, lured by the rowdy confluence of wind and water, took her Lipton tea down to the dock. Though the center of Choate's Junction was only a mile away, nothing to a walker like Sarah, she tended toward home. It was as if on that day when she'd searched out Baby Jessie, then spurned Russ, her past, she'd spent her reserves of courage and will; like a salmon surging upriver to spawn, she needed to rest in still waters before moving on.

She saw the coming winter in the lake's iron-gray water—Nanna had told tales of raw-nerved women who'd given themselves abortions in winter water that color—smelled it on the damp wind ravishing autumn's late leaves, those clingy faded beauties whose season had come and gone; Sarah'd always preferred her fall foliage a shade past peak.

Bristling with its signs and portents of the end of things—husks and seedpods and summer cabins wintered up—October was her dangerous season. Days when she was most likely to slip away. A time to swim quarries. To sharpen knives. How had she ever managed to make it whole to this particular dock?

Sarah, who sometimes thought of her marriage as

twenty years of October, shivered, touched her stomach.

It hadn't been complicated in the beginning. Russ, simply, had been the first boy to touch her. She'd grown up among people who recoiled at the least touch, as if another person's skin burned like to-the-bone acid. Had been raised by women who, in those desperate hours after midnight and before sunrise, clawed at their own eyes and turned razor blades on themselves. But Sarah, choked and wilting in their barbwire gardens of thorns, craved to be touched, believed she might have shriveled and died if she hadn't been able to escape to the contrary softness of Auntie Robena; Sarah sometimes wondered whether her cousin Jenny, just as starved, hadn't gone willingly to Uncle Dead's shed that day.

So, Russ touched her — still, she could feel his sweaty, grateful hands cradling her heavy breasts — and it was like the lake ice going out after a long, long winter. The sixteen-year-old girl she'd been couldn't tell you much about Russ Britton. But, God, she loved to take her clothes off for him, guide his callused fingers over her hungry body, jam her tits into his warm mouth. And that sixteen-year-old Sarah, so smooth and pale, toes wriggling and back arching, ached to fuck. Was greedy for Russ, as hot and thick as boiled Karo syrup, to pour into her as she locked him in her long, strong legs.

Sarah laughed, girlish and clear, amused and amazed by that brazen, insatiable girl who'd gone into hiding upon Hannah's birth. She had, of course, gotten pregnant; Sarah couldn't think of even one friend who hadn't been in the family way when she took her vows. The worst part'd been telling Nanna.

✖

Sarah paces the dust-smitten gloom of Nanna Page's kitchen. Though she has lived with her mother and Auntie Leah and Auntie Robena, this is the room in which she grew up. Where, amid woodsmoke, flour and chicken guts, Nanna taught her to cook, clean, sew and weave furious silences—to be a Page woman.

This kitchen is the original Page dwelling, the seed from which the rest of the house (and Page's Village) sprouted. Pages were born in that kitchen, Pages died there. Sarah, throat dry and palms wet, wonders how many times the tale she is about to tell has been told in this women-haunted kitchen; wonders whether Nanna had to tell it, too.

Upon hearing Sarah, Nanna creaks down the stairs; no one, save Nanna herself, knows yet of the cancer laying siege. Reaching bottom, she pauses, leans against the banister. Grimacing, she steals a deep hurtful breath, stiffens her back, and strides into the kitchen; there are, after all, illusions to sustain.

"Sarah," Nanna Page says.

"Hi, Nanna," croaks Sarah, who, on seeing her grandmother, feels more like a ten-year-old pitching in with the biscuits than Russ Britton's careless lover.

Lowering herself into the rocking chair next to the woodstove, Nanna doesn't take her bright, black eyes off Sarah, who blushes, already fighting the tears boiling behind her eyes. But Nanna won't let her off the hook, will not look away. It was Sarah who summoned her, after all.

Glaring at the Page-worn floor, Sarah doubles her fists into white-knuckled knots, grinds her teeth, refuses her tears — this, this is what it means to be a Page — and, trembling, says:

"I'm having a baby."

And Nanna: "I know."

I know. Seemed to Sarah that Nanna lived just to be able to say those two words: I know. There was no fooling Nanna; no lies believed (unless she had her reasons), no secrets safe. As Grandpa Elgar liked to say: "The old bitch can still pull the fastball."

✂

Now, a grandmother herself, Sarah didn't understand how her love had taken root in such unforgiving soil as Nanna Page. But she had loved her grandmother, that granite fortress of a woman, without reservation. Even as her relatives — aunts, uncles, cousins, all of them — steeped themselves in hate, fear and prickly submission, she loved her.

Conjuring Nanna Page in the fitful lake, Sarah suddenly shuddered, ambushed by a whisper of old October whispers: not even a full thought, really, a nudge; a feeble phantom urging her toward the water.

"No! Goddammit, no!"

Sarah dug hands and heels into the dock's splintery planks, fixed on their toothy grain, their bite; she had come too far to settle to the bottom of a lake whose name she hadn't bothered to learn.

Straining against the gentle, so gentle, tug, she shut her eyes, used Russ to smother the whisper: Though she'd put a good two months, necessary months, between her and her husband, Sarah couldn't escape Russ. Out of habit, she worried over him; wondered whether he was eating right . . . whether he had enough clean clothes . . . whether he was drinking too much.

Hannah had driven down to Granite the very next day after Sarah'd showed up to tell Russ what was what. He'd shrugged (when had Russ stopped struggling and started shrugging?), let Hannah take what Sarah needed; he neither said a word, nor lifted a finger. They hadn't heard back since.

He'd shrugged, Hannah said; Sarah couldn't get over that. Time was when Russ'd busted down doors for her.

Russ and Sarah aren't married yet, but Page's Village knows that Ella's girl is carrying Russ Britton's baby. That's when Grandpa Elgar lights into Sarah, hisses his poison.

"Russ Britton," he spits. "What do you want to go and marry him for? Ain't no damn good. Ain't no worker or nothing. You marry him, I give you six months. Tops. Six months. Soon's that baby pops, he's going to be long gone and hard to find. You think he's going to let a wife and a baby tie him down, you ain't as smart as I give you credit. I was you, I wouldn't trust that boy further'n I could wing him."

Elgar starts her crying, red blotches spreading on her cheeks like the marsh in spring, which tickles him no end. But he doesn't expect Sarah to run and tell Russ that her grandfather's been spouting off.

It's two in the morning, and Russ, clutching a dead Gansett Giant Imperial Quart, sways in Nanna Page's dooryard, just drunk-brave enough to do what he's about to do.

"Elgar! Elgar Page! I want to talk to you, cocksucker!" he roars, chopping the last word so it comes out "cot-sucka!"

Waiting, dizzy with the shouting, Russ drains the G.I.Q. dregs (more spit than beer) and flings the long-neck toward Route 49, where (it seems like a minute later) it shatters.

"Come on, you old sonuvabitching chickenshit! I'm waiting on you!"

An upstairs window, a black eye swollen with spring downpours, groans open. Filling the window, Nanna glowers at Russ, who's too loaded to be afraid; not even Nanna Page can bully a drunk.

"Elgar! You're one pussy bastard! Sure as shitting! One big, friggin' pussy!"

Nanna smiles; it does her heart good to hear the truth about Elgar being spoken by someone other than herself. "Russ," she says, her voice even, amplified in the darkness, "go home."

Russ, pawing at the dirt: "You tell your husband to

lay off Sarah! You tell him to leave her alone, stop feeding her his crock of shit."

"Sarah?"

"You tell him!"

Studying Russ, Nanna sees he's full of the drunk's righteous conviction. She looks back into her bedroom where Elgar pretends to sleep, then jerks the window closed.

"Goddammit all! Don't you go slamming no windows at me!"

Russ trips up the back steps—"Fuck!"—smacking his knee a good one, and starts whaling on the back door, windowpanes chattering.

"Open the door, damn it! Or I'll fucking knock it in!"

He lets up, the lull in a thundershower before it rains even harder, steps back, the screen door slapping shut. Panting, sweaty now, he bends over, forearms resting on knees; he doesn't see Sarah standing on Robena's doorstep at the bottom of the hill.

Point made, he's ready to go. But out of the corner of his eye, a flash of upstairs curtain, Elgar shrinking back.

"You chicken's prick," Russ mutters.

He tears the screen door off its hinges and punts open the back door, window glass chiming to the floor.

Rocking in the night kitchen, Nanna scares him this time. Russ jumps back and tumbles down the steps ass-over-bandbox.

Nanna stares down at him as if she's ready to pounce: "Russ, go home."

Meaning to make amends with the affronted back doors, Russ drops by Nanna's early the next morning, to find Elgar already on the job. Elgar won't look at him, but Nanna comes out to meet him; he's surprised it takes her so long to creep down the steps.

"I'll fix up those doors, if you want," Russ says.

"Elgar'll do it," Nanna says.

"I was real pissed off last night."

"He won't bother Sarah no more."

Two sentences. Nine words bearing the weight of the unsaid. Most people would've talked Russ's ear off for ten minutes — explaining. But when Nanna Page spoke, she let you hear the truth, not her voice delighting in itself. Russ nods at her words.

Nanna holds him with a barbed look of both anger and acceptance. "You treat her right," she says, her words spiked with the unspoken threat. "Take care of her."

※

Russ had done the best he could, thought Sarah, but the poor bastard just didn't know what he was getting into. She shook her head as if shredding a dream; Russ had helped her ride it out.

Walking back to the house, Sarah saw that her fingertips were bristling with blue-green slivers wrenched from the sorry heartwood of the rotting dock.

Striking a wooden match, the blue-tips Nanna'd favored so, Sarah held a sewing needle to the flame till its point blued with the heat. Careful not to dig too deep, Sarah slid the hot needle into the pad of her right thumb, stabbed a sliver, and wrestled it out. Skin raw and weeping, it took her the rest of the morning and into early afternoon to needle all the slivers out of her fingertips.

Supper seized most of the afternoon: beans set to simmering, the flame just so; each hot dog scrubbed long and hard before boiling; canned Boston brown bread, molasses-damp, opened and sliced as fine as lace; napkins folded triangle sharp; canned beets, as purple as a shivering newborn squowling at the cold, dry world.

And, finally, the jack-o'-lantern kindled — Sarah's twilight tears hissing in the flame — its maniac's grin perhaps the only thing standing between her and the bottom of the lake.

Sarah VIII

She's on her knees—bottom arched, weight on her left hand—scrubbing the kitchen floor. Her knees ache and her hands are red, scalded by the hot water; her grandmother scrubbed so fierce and poured water so hot that she blistered both the tops and palms of her hands when she washed the floor. As she scrapes the stiff brush back and forth, hair lank in her face, she forgets cleaning the crumbling linoleum—like the peeling, dried-out skin of the dying salamander she found out to Route 49—and daydreams about what else she does on her knees: ties the kids' shoes, sweeps under the beds, shoots marbles, sucks her husband, washes the legs of the kitchen chairs, cleans the oven, gets switched by her mother, picks bramble-berries, throws up, pokes the kids' ball out from under the car, lets her boy cousins burn her hands on the woodstove, prays.

Chapter Fourteen

✄

November
1985

CHARLOTTE WEST
—relentless, stubborn, a three-day blow dropping three
foot of snow—moved in. Russ hadn't the will to resist.

He ceded the upstairs to her, gratefully falling asleep
nights to the light footfalls, May rain, above him. She
cooked, cleaned, did the wash; he clung to his job up to
the chenille shop, looked toward Friday nights and his
weekend case from Buzzell's.

They circled each other, Russ and Charlotte. Wary.
As if the least dry touch might stir the spark needed to
kindle some ravening fire. With twenty years spent as
a Page-in-training, Russ, especially, kept his distance,

treating Charlotte like a ribby stray (found under the porch eating her kittens) whose trust must be earned.

Just as he'd seen those misery years of miscarriages mirrored in Sarah's eyes, so too, he saw the betrayal of Baby Jessie in Charlotte's. Noted how it quarried her face. Wondered whether she'd ever talk it, or give in and let the child's absence devour her.

Russ couldn't sleep; hadn't had many restful nights since Sarah'd run off to Hannah's. But instead of wrestling his sleeplessness, the way he'd fought everything once upon a time, he lay there in the dark and killed Lucky Strikes (Sarah'd forbidden bed smokes), and stared at the creaking ceiling. Charlotte was ironing; the scorched-cloth stink reminded him of the summers when he was first married and racing the Pontiac, the Crown Seven, down to the Pines and over to Hudson.

Mashing out the Lucky in the windowsill, he got up, dressed — knee-gnawed dungarees and flannel shirt — and went outside. The ground crunched and crumbled as he hurried toward the shed. He could see his breath.

The padlock chilled his hand as he keyed it. One winter, as a boy, he'd made the mistake of holding an outdoors lock in his mouth. His warm, wet tongue stuck to the cold steel, and Russ felt like he'd just chonked a pincushion. His old man, not even trying to hide his whiskey grin, unmarried flesh and steel by pouring hot water into Russ's mouth. There'd been no appreciable loss of tongue meat.

He flapped open the shed doors, broad as ravens' wings, and stepped into the Pontiac; hadn't had a driver's-side door for years. Gripping the steering wheel, he shivered.

It started on the first try—only car he'd ever owned that would—growling, but balky and sluggish in the November night—a rough Detroit beast rousted from hibernation.

As the Pontiac warmed, the old racing smells, dulled at first by the cold but freed by the engine's heat, swarmed Russ: the hot, heady reek of gasoline, oil, grease and burnt rubber. Smells that gave Russ solace, smells bearing the days when he was young, angry and racing. Over the years, as his hard-bodied rage had given way to adulthood's acquiescence, Russ had taken to prowling Granite's back roads in the Crown Seven on those nights when he couldn't sleep. Restless, stalking something lost. A thing he knew could never be regained.

He coaxed the shuddering stock into the dooryard, waited; she'd only stall if he pushed too hard too soon. Listening the way a new mother listens for her baby, Russ slowly, almost gently, revved the engine till he sweet-talked it into its natural ragged grumble.

Charlotte looked out an upstairs window, melted away; he wondered how long she'd been watching. He eased the car into first, rumbled to the bottom of the driveway. Looking left, then right, he was about to pull out when he hit the brakes and ran back to the house.

"Want to go for a ride?" he asked Charlotte.

She took a couple of more swipes at the shirt she was ironing, unplugged the iron, set it upright on the ironing board, and said: "Okay."

"Me, Dickie, Orrie . . . we all thought we was something when we were racing this car," Russ said to Charlotte. "We wore black tee shirts, black dungarees, smoked naked Luckies and drank like hell. Thought we was hot shits.

"Once mud season come, I'd get off work from the steel-drum factory, crank it home and get washed up, and have supper with Sarah and the kids. Then I'd go over to Orrie's and we'd work on this motherin' car till two, three in the morning. We were all about twenty. All of us married—and not a one of us real happy about it. All had kids, too. To be honest, I don't know how Sarah put up with it.

"But if I didn't have car racing back then, I don't know what I would've done. I could take working a shit job, and being married and tied down to a couple of kids and all, but only 'cause I could race. I tell ya, we raced everything: tar, dirt, ice; bombed around Cedar Swamp and the sandpits for the sheer hell of it. Nothing's better than racing when you're twenty years old and pissed off at the world."

Russ shunned the Plains and the highway, weaving the Crown Seven down broken-backed roads whose natives were as used to the Pontiac's savage, window-shimmying passage as they were to the woods-echoing rifle shots of hunters, and the yips and howls of dogs

running deer in winter. Headlights plucked years before, painted quarry-water black, the stock car was a
blind night-creature lumbering along Granite's secret-
freighted ways at no more than thirty, thirty-five miles
an hour; Chief of Police Leon George had told Russ
long ago that as long as he took it easy and kept the
stock off the main drags, then he'd look the other way.
Russ turned left onto Britton Road.

"See that house there?" Russ said. "That's where
they found Freddy Mallory all knifed up a few years
back. Never did find the guy did it.

"Freddy Mallory . . . Christ, I ain't thought of him
in years. Wouldn't give ya the sweat offa his balls, but
those watermelons he sold were something. You remember that? Remember Freddy Mallory?"

She nodded.

Russ waited, expecting, needing, something more
than a nod. How in hell are you supposed to talk with
people who hoard their words? Who act like a nod, a
sigh and a grimace are the basic parts of speech. Sarah'd
been like that, too. Same difference.

"Anyways," Russ said, "you're riding in a '37 Pontiac coupe. Six-cylinder flathead. Stock, except for the
automatic rear end we laid in because the ratio was a
little bit better.

"Paid twenty bucks for it—running. Saw it sitting
in this guy's dooryard one winter, bought it, brought it
home, stripped it out, plunked in a bucket seat, and got
it all welded up—the roll cage, gas tank and such.

"Boy, didn't we have fun. Lot of damn work, but we

weren't cheated; we got in our licks. I can remember getting stove up down to the Pines Speedway one Saturday night and bringing the car home and working on it till five-o'-fucking-clock in the morning. We weren't *too* drunk by the time the sun come up; six hours later we're dragging our sorry asses over to Hudson for the Sunday afternoon races.

"When we bought it, we worked on this sucker all winter, and then April come and our first night at the Pines. We had a coupla beers before we left, a coupla beers on the way, and a coupla more beers when we got there."

Russ paused, like he was taking time for a gulp of beer, went on: "You ever been to the races?" (Charlotte shook her head no.) "The thing that gets ya when you get close to the track is the thrill in your gut when you hear the bellerin' of the stocks warming up. I tell ya, when we pulled into the Pines that night, me, Orrie and Dickie were grinning at each other like three guys about to get laid for the first time."

Russ shook his head, smiling, remembering: "There's just something about the sound that always gets me, ya know. It starts way down in your crotch and doesn't let go till it's tickling your ears. You stand there, sopping up the smell of the hot rubber flayed from the tires, and your ears feel like someone's pouring in fresh candle wax.

"Dickie did most the driving, 'specially after I put her off the third turn one time at Hudson and about plowed under the outhouses; I never see people run so fast in my life.

"Anyways, that first night at the Pines Dickie starts turning laps. I still can see him, going around real slow, testing the car, getting a feel for the track. Coming off the turns, picking up a little more speed, a little more speed. Orrie and I are watching, shouting: 'Boy, that little mother's holding the track good!'

"Know what's the funniest thing? I can't, for the life of me, remember any of the races from that night. All I know is we took the car off the stock-car trailer. We tested it. We raced it. And at the end of the night, we put it back on the trailer and it was still in one piece. We were happy as hell. Went there in one piece, left in one piece."

Russ stopped at the top of Meeks Road, which dead-ended at Route 49; Page's Village lay a quarter-mile away. Russ made to turn back down Meeks, when Charlotte said: "Can you drive me up to where Dickie West's used to be?"

Russ looked at her; he couldn't've been more surprised if Wayne'd come by and give him the money he owed. It was the first time Charlotte had ever asked anything of Russ.

"Ain't more'n a half-mile," she added.

"Sure," Russ said. "But if Leon George catches me, my ass is grass and he's the one pushing the mower."

Years before, when the state'd widened Route 49, taking with it Nanna Page's place and the house Russ and Sarah'd lived in when they first got married (Hannah and Wayne still called it "The House They Tore Down"), the road crew hadn't even bothered to demolish Dickie West's place. The shack simply got bulldozed down the embankment. Got left to rot—caved in, front door gaping at the sky. Vines and creepers cracked its bones, the wood-eaters sucked out its guts, and its gray face crumbled at the soft nibbling of rain and snow.

"Can't hardly make it out," Charlotte said.

"Yut," Russ said.

They stood across from the Mahoneys', squinting down the banking into the night; the Pontiac grouched, waiting.

"They say he died hanging curtains," Charlotte said.

"How the hell would you know a thing like that? Christ, he died even before *I* was born."

"He was my old man's father. Always meant to take a look at his shack."

She rubbed her arms against the night and, satisfied, walked back to the stock, leaving Russ to ponder Dickie West's estate.

"We raced three, four summers," said Russ, seeking the solitude of back roads after the highway. "Damned if I can remember many of those races. The pits is what I remember best: engines purring, sputtering and gunning; guys, their greasy hairy guts showing, stretched out under their cars liked beached whales or something; tool chests big as summer camps.

"This one guy—drove a real nice pickup, one of

those custom-made jobs—had this great big tool chest
. . . supposedly. It was a tool chest, all right. That
suckin' thing was half-full of beer. Tools on top, brews
in the bottom. I'm telling you, Charlotte, wasn't a body
in them pits didn't like that guy. He was one hot shit.
Wish I had me one of those beers right now.

"Oh, I did some driving. Never in the feature races,
though. Dickie'd come up to me and say, 'Want this
heat?' And I'd pull on the helmet, snug the black ban-
danna over my mouth and nose—we couldn't afford a
fire suit or any of that shit—and I'd climb into the car
and take her out.

"Starts were always something. You got twelve,
fourteen of us—jostling, jockeying—jammed onto this
quarter-mile oval, two abreast, Kenny Small, the flag-
man, trying to keep us in line. Then we're coming out
of turn four one more time, and we know this is it,
Kenny's gonna give us the green. We're bearing down
on him now, like we mean to run the poor sonuvabitch
over. He's backpedaling in his black high-tops, waggling
those flags at us like he's a goddamn bullfighter or something; then he jumps straight up in the air, knees tucked
like a second baseman turning two, waving the green to
save his life. And we floor it—don't even see Kenny haul
ass out the way—all of us sucking dust and exhaust, ears
pop-pop-popping till you don't even think you have 'em
no more. For ten laps you're tasting and smelling heat
and rubber, keeping your eyes—all crusty and gritted
up—glued to the ass-end of the car in front of you, the
rest of the cars no more than black, red and gold flickers

as the lights lick at the shiny steel. Something. Really something.

"Christ! There wasn't no money or nothing involved, you know. We did it for the hell of it. Because it was the balls, the nuts."

Drunk on his own story, tasting the bitter backwash of his spent past, Russ fell silent, content to let the '37 Ponny speak for itself as they dove deeper into Granite, sounding the back roads, dark nameless roads, roads Charlotte had never suspected, much less seen. Even in the night, with no headlights, Russ knew them; he owned those roads. When he drove them, he imagined that they were the roads Sarah traveled when she'd be sitting *right there* in the next room but you couldn't find her. Yes, Sarah's roads, too.

"Why'd you quit?" Charlotte asked.

"Huh?"

"Racing. Why'd you stop?"

Russ took his foot off the gas and let the car coast to a stop in the middle of the road. When he spoke, his words had lost the nudge-you-in-the-ribs, storyteller tone he'd used all night with Charlotte. Instead, he fixed his eyes on her, a skinny noon shadow in the darkness, and explained in a voice low and spare; words and sentences as stripped as the Pontiac itself:

"It was the feature at Pines, thirty-five, forty bombers banging around the track. A spinout on the back straight. Dickie went high to go round. He got bumped. The throttle stuck. Jee-sus, he went flying down that back straight. Orrie and me knew he wasn't going to make the turn. We looked at each other and started running.

"He was airborne when he hit that stand of pitch pines; it was like a lightning strike. We heard what sounded like a shotgun. Saw fire.

"Howie Brown, in his number-sixty-four car, was leading that race. And I'll never forget this long as I live: He slammed on his brakes, scrabbled out, and ran down the banking to Dickie. Pulled him out the burning car.

"Dickie didn't get hurt too bad. Cracked ribs, legs burned some. Car was gone for the season, maybe for good. We kept talking about putting her back together that winter, but nothing ever come of it. It was getting too expensive to race, anyways, and, to be honest, I think Dickie lost his nerve in the crash. We, none of us, were ever as close again.

"Dickie and Orrie give me their shares in the car. I took it home. Spent the next five years piecing the Crown Seven together again. For what? I don't know."

He put the car in gear and turned her toward home. "Took the Thibeault brothers two wreckers to load her on the trailer that night," Russ said. "Orrie stayed over with Dickie at the hospital. I hauled the car home, got drunk, puked my guts out, then drank some more; think I stayed drunk three days, and Sarah wouldn't talk to me for three more after that."

Charlotte edged toward Russ and lay her head on his shoulder; he cradled her in his arm.

Chapter Fifteen

✳

November
1985

LEG WAGGING,
barbed chin cupped in his palm, Wayne sat hunched
on Uncle Dead's chopping block and contemplated his
great-uncle's shed.

That shed haunted him. Wherever he worked in the
village, he felt the shed at his back, listened for its whispers. In his daydreams, his nightmares, the hill steep-
ened, the shed, coiling and uncoiling, transformed into
a writhing castle blacker than deepest quarry water; its
thick, red scars as unbearable as fresh blood on first
snow. Still, Wayne longed for its ancient Page secrets
locked behind doors and windows nailed shut before he

was born. He obsessed over that shed, picked
at it, brooded—finally, let it consume him so his
cheeks burned, his ears buzzed and rang, his appetite
shriveled.

Since being run to ground in Page's Village, Wayne
had spent his days scavenging the musty, cobwebbed
past. Creeping through rooms of spongy floorboards
and three-legged chairs, of cloudy mirrors and walls
insulated with crumbling Sunday funnies, of bald
brooms and still-tacky fly-strips fly-fossil-speckled.
Rooms straining under dust so old and so heavy that it
shrugged at his passing and stayed put.

But neither the shacks—corpses, really—nor Auntie Leah's museum piece of a place spoke to Wayne of
Nanna Page, of the family myths Sarah had steeped
them in as children. But Uncle Dead's shed, black,
bound and forbidden, sang with possibilities.

Here was a place where a man, *his great-uncle*, had
raped and about killed his own niece. And who, himself, had vanished or been murdered, and no one had
ever willingly talked about him. As Wayne stared, the
shed's black skin seemed to darken, its red slashes
pulse raw and proud, the shed bristling with the rage of
being born a Page. It was an invitation Wayne couldn't
refuse.

Barren, thorned, snarling, the rosebushes—Page bushes—
grew thickest, grew meanest at the shed door. You want
in, boy? they taunted. Then you got to go through us.
Staring them down, Wayne thought of Grandpa Elgar.

He lashed at the toothy tangle with a rake, dug in, and tugged; when the rake head snapped off, Wayne staggered backwards and tripped over the chopping block. The hoe broke, too. And he couldn't get close enough to try to shovel the bushes up by their roots, not that he could have.

Panting, starting to sweat (even in the gray cold), thorn nips stinging, Wayne, for an instant, considered leaving well enough alone, forgetting about the god-damned shed. But he didn't. He couldn't. He hadn't been raised that way.

Throwing down the shovel, he grabbed the rose shears, lowered his head and moved in on the bushes the way a good boxer moves inside on a bigger fighter. Joined to a battle for which they'd been planted thirty years before, the rosebushes gave as good as they got, clawing, tearing, scratching, as Wayne, licking his own blood and sweat, cut them down limb by defiant limb.

The last vine bit him worst. Just as he was about to snip it, a raven lighted on the shed and shrieked: "Quaaa-orrk!!!" Wayne jerked away and up, a thorn snatching at the corner of his eye and ripping the soft flesh from there to the bridge of his nose. Fifteen minutes, and one blood-soaked handkerchief, later, he got back to work.

That raven, blue-black feathers oil sleek, settled on the shed peak and proceeded to bitch at Wayne as he took hacksaw to lock. Shrilling, trilling, drumming, the bird

wouldn't keep its beak shut. Bullying, scolding, com-
plaining—a beady-eyed foreman sporting a four-foot
wingspread.

"Aw, screw you," Wayne muttered. "Been putting
up with the likes of you my whole friggin' life."

The raven quorked at him, hopped sideways.

"Why don't you just shut the fuck up?"

"Quaaa-orrk! Qui-ill!!!"

Wayne squinted up at the bird; the raven cocked its
head sideways, studied Wayne.

"Caw!" Wayne rasped. "Caw! Caw! Caw!"

Raven stared.

Wayne flapped his arms, slapping his sides as he
did: "Caw! Caw! Fucking caw!"

Still staring.

"Caw! Caw! Caw!"—Wayne scampering in antic
circles, a kid playing airplane—"Caw! Caw!"

Black unblinking eyes; eyes that have seen it all;
Nanna Page eyes.

Wayne scooped up a rock, the raven already aloft,
and whung it, never thinking for *even* a second that he
might hit, never mind hurt, the bird.

The rock caved in the raven's skull, the sound echoing like the crack of a winter oak riven by frost.

The bird arched a couple of feet higher before tum-
bling into the grabby puckerbrush beyond the shed; its
jagged trail of inky blood seemed to hang in the air for
minutes after the bird's passing.

Head down, Wayne kicked the shed: "Shit."

———

After the sawing of the padlock in two—and the mangling of three hacksaw blades—came the squeal and groan of yanking one hundred nails out of the shed door. One hundred. Even. Twenty-five up top, twenty-five on the bottom, twenty-five each side; every nail driven straight, to the hilt.

The last nail pulled, Wayne retreated to the chopping block. The rosebushes' spiked arms and fingers, carpeting the ground, conjured Charlotte, of how they had snapped and ripped at each other; neither one strong enough alone to bear the burden of Baby Jessie. Women might drape themselves in flowers on their wedding day, he thought, but they're cloaked in thorns by the time it ends. He shrugged and stared at the shed door.

His arms ached (he'd be lame tomorrow), his sliced eye throbbed, the cold burrowed into his cuts and scratches, but he wanted to savor the freed door before he flung it open. Someone—Nanna Page? Auntie Leah? Uncle Dead himself?—had wanted that shed shut for good, and Wayne had defied them; he pleasured in that defiance, that small victory.

Taking a deep breath, he stood, brushed off his dungarees, and marched toward the closed door as if he were getting married or graduating from high school. Rose tentacles sprang up beneath his feet and jabbed.

He two-handed the door handle, virgin rust crumbling to red powder, and pulled; the same burred steel bit his palms that had tasted his mother's flesh on that day Billy Page raped Jenny Page. Heels planted so his toes pointed to the low clouds, Wayne grunted at the door, that broad, black wing slammed shut with intent a full generation before. Oh, he could've run back to Auntie Leah's for the Three-In-One oil or the WD-40 and sweet-talked the door open; he could even have taken a hammer to the rust-seized hinges. But Wayne wanted that door to give in to him. *Him!* He wanted to hear hinges shriek as Uncle Dead's darkness leached once more into Page's Village.

Body bent in a sideways vee, calves and hams screaming, back muscles snakes-in-the-sack rippling, Wayne kept tugging, straining, strong and steady, putting constant pressure on the door, on the past. He pulled: raw, blistered hands bleeding; blue arm veins, rivers etched on a pale map, bulging; breath hard and shallow. He pulled. Against his natural self, his Page-hood, his anger. He pulled.

And when it seemed he would break, that Nanna Page would grind yet more bones to meal, he wrenched a hateful moan from the hinges, a deep beginning-of-time groan that meant Wayne Britton had waked Uncle Dead's shed from its thirty-year slumber.

He kept on—gritting his teeth as rust-smitten steel grated against rust-smitten steel—the shed's black maw yawning wider, wider. But before Wayne could make the door describe its full opening arc, the top hinge snapped, spit screws like rotten teeth. Top half free now,

Wayne hefted the door and swung it so it one-hinge hung from the shed at a backwards, broken-winged angle.

Door subdued, he squinted into the dry, thirty-year night that had been the shed and saw a truck. An old truck. A truck wrapped—no, tucked—in a razor womb of barbwire.

He stamped his foot, like a schoolgirl cheated out of her turn at jump rope. Then he laughed.

"I'll be good and goddamned," he said. "Even Pages have a sense of humor."

Abandoning his tools to the dying light, Wayne dragged himself home. The truck could wait.

What Wayne liked best about Page's Village was the nights. After supper, sore and tired, he'd turn the kerosene lamp low, this side of sputtering, sprawl into Auntie Leah's rocking chair, close his eyes and start rocking, start remembering, trying to recapture those dreamy years of childhood before grammar school, when his world was bound by Route 49, by the dark woods of Cedar Swamp:

❦

Sarah leads Wayne and Hannah into the marsh, the punky gray walk-boards sinking as they slink through; the water is gooey with pollywogs; the marsh weeds—saw grasses, pussy willows, cat-o'-nine-tails—paw at them as they part dusty curtains of pollen. . . . Drowsing to the Red Sox on the radio (its guts glowing orange in the mosquitoey darkness), Russ slumps bare-chested on the back porch; he cracks another sweaty beer, lets Wayne soup up the warm foam; sweat, beer and cigarette smoke, these are the smells of manhood, the smells that soothe Wayne as he wriggles closer to his father and falls deep asleep. . . . Sarah rakes and rakes and rakes—gathering autumn's scaly crimsons and emeralds, fire-breathing oranges and golds, rusts and browns—and, before Wayne's and Hannah's eyes, transforms the unpromising pile of leaves into a leaf dragon; Sarah's dragon slumbers next to the clothesline, until one blustery morning, in a swirl and a rustle, the wind-seduced beast miraculously takes flight. . . . Using the hood from an old Buick as a sled, Sarah pushes Wayne and Hannah across the squeaky, hard-packed snow, past Grandpa Elgar's, past the barn, the chicken coops, and, just as the path dips to begin its long dive into Page's Village, she hops on, hugging her children and whooping as they—teary and red-cheeked—whiz past Auntie Robena's, the marsh, Fat Dot's, past everything until the path itself vanishes and they slingshot into midair, laughing, shrieking, the black hood of the Buick poised above a creamy blanket of virgin snow.

✖

In the rocking chair, Wayne fell asleep before the three of them came back down to earth.

Up out of the darkest swamp, Great-uncle Henry blinked at the full moon, shrank back at where the woods ended and Page's Village began. He had watched the boy all day, eyeballed him for weeks. A creature of thickets and hidey-holes, he whimpered, trembled with fear. But the call of the open shed was too much, and he scuttled across the sandpit, past his sister's burned-down shack, and toward Uncle Dead's shed.

Sarah IX

She's retreated to the porch, curled up in the musty overstuffed chair — it smells like the cellar — sipping tea sweetened with Pet condensed milk. The trees low in the breeze, and she's tempted by sleep. But just barely, almost beyond hearing, she hears the school bus moan as it turns onto her road. The children are almost home, and she allows herself a quick inward smile that flushes her the same as the early-morning sun; she worries herself sick that, one day, she won't want to see her children come home from school.

Chapter Sixteen

December 1985

"FLOORS SURE GOT tracked up with all that rain," said Sarah, swirling her spaghetti mop in the ammonia and scalding water. "Looks like we ain't washed 'em in a week."

"Sure rained," said Hannah, filling her bucket. "Christ! That ammonia's awful."

"How was school today?"

"All right," she answered, smiling to herself; Sarah'd been asking her that question since first grade.

They slopped their mops onto the bowed, wooden floor of Sawyer's Mill Grocery and, working side by side, scrubbed away the day's traffic. Hannah'd gotten them the job—minimum wage, 9:00 P.M. to 1:00 A.M., Monday through Friday. Though carrying the sweet weight of pregnancy, Sarah kept up with her daughter; made a point of it. She might only been making the minimum, but when Sarah slipped into her faded blue smock, her name stitched in red thread over her heart, she was ready to work, gladdened by making her own small way in the world.

"When's your appointment at the clinic, Momma?"

"Friday morning. You can still take me, right?"

"Yes, Momma."

"I could walk. Wouldn't mind. Probably do me some good."

"Mom, I'm giving you a ride. Okay?"

"Want some gum?"

"Sure."

Sarah gave her half a piece of spearmint; she'd been doling out half-pieces of gum since Hannah had teeth to chew; Page's Village was never far away.

Finished with the aisle, they took a break, tuned in to the grocery's late-night symphony: the clank and hiss of radiators, the blink and buzz of fluorescent lights, the scuttle of river rats—brazen, belly-scraping beasts kept in check only by Sawyer's yowling fleet of goon-cats.

"Boy, I remember some the rats we used to get down backa Page's Village," Sarah said. "Big as loaves of bread. Uncle Henry and Uncle Dead used to go around shooting 'em."

Listening to her mother, Hannah couldn't believe that this was the same woman who'd raised her, who'd

spent words as if they weren't minting any more. Understanding the healing power of stories, Russ had been the
talker; Sarah, tongue coiled tight as new rope, had
served black silences.

"Momma . . . what was it really like there . . . in
Page's Village?" Hannah asked. "Growing up . . . like
that."

Lips faulting into a nervous smile, Sarah blushed,
winked away tears: "It's hard to talk about all those
goings-on, Hannah. I know it matters to you. But . . .
it makes me feel funny talking about it."

"What was it like, Momma? Tell me."

Sarah's face blotched red and white.

"Tell."

Sarah cleared her throat, spoke a hair above a
whisper:

"We was so poor. But I miss it so, Hannah. And
when I think about it too much, all those things I miss
burn inside like acid.

"I miss Auntie Leah filling me with hot lemon juice
with honey and ginger when I have a cold, and feeding
me salads when I'm pregnant. I miss the stink of shitty
diapers. I miss my father, Chaney Huckins. Can't even
remember what he looked like no more, Hannah. All's
I can do is feel his barbwire whiskers on my cheek. Sniff
the Brylcreem in his hair.

"And I miss Uncle Allen. God, I miss him. I swear
Auntie Bena kilt him; love-starved him, then worked
him to gristle. When I stayed over Auntie Bena's, after
I got all scrubbed and put on my nightclothes, Uncle

Allen'd play his Hank Williams records and we'd all
gallivant around the shack doing the country waltz.

"One time, though, when him and Auntie'd had one
of their big spats—some nights they kept the whole
village up with their squalling—and she'd thrown him
out again, he lugged his Victrola, one of those old-time,
hand-crank record players, out to the front step and
played 'I'm So Lonesome I Could Cry' over and over,
wailing along with the record, till she let him back in
the house—at about three in the morning.

"We was all so sad, Hannah. Maybe it was worst
for Nanna because she had to bear it all. And it ain't
changed, Hannah. It ain't changed. Wayne and Charlotte giving Baby Jessie away like that. Ain't an hour
goes by I don't think about that baby. And look at me,
running off. Running away just like Ella did. It don't
change.

"And the awfullest part is when you know that the
sad, disgusted look on your face is the same one you
learned sitting at the kitchen table with your mother
when you was a little girl. That's the awfullest part."

So they mopped, mother and daughter, together
speaking the ancient, bent-backed tongue of women's
work, cleaning ladies (as Old Lady Sawyer called them)
splashing and sloshing up and down the aisles where,
during store hours, no one'd give them a second look.
Scouring the past; Hannah digging, probing, quarrying
family bones; and Sarah, having shed her former life,
trying to grow into the new. Talking and talking and
talking, until they'd killed another night's work.

Hannah sighed a Sarah sigh, a sigh seeping from the shadow corners of Page's Village. "I don't know, Momma," she said. "I don't know what to think anymore. Kids I go to school with don't understand Page's Village or why I work like a dog. And everyone back home thinks I've gone off to college and gotten too big for my britches. It's like someone's tied me to two horses and told them to run in opposite directions.

"And I get so mad. My old roommate, Pauline, was bitching the other day because her parents won't fly her out to Colorado over Christmas so she can ski. I wanted to slug her, she was acting so damned spoiled. Nanna Page would've switched her so she couldn't sit for a week."

Sarah laughed, making Hannah laugh, too.

"I don't mean to yack at you, Momma," Hannah said. "I know you got enough troubles without me pissing and moaning. But I just get so damned frustrated."

" 's okay," Sarah said.

"And I can't forget a thing. I'm just as mad today at that True Pease for selling the house on New Boston Road out from under us as I was back then. Maybe madder. When I think about what that did to you and Daddy. . . .

"Know what I was thinking about last night before I fell asleep? Fourth grade. *Fourth grade*. When you were sick and all that and kept me home all those days."

Sarah's eyes narrowed as if she were wincing, her voice shrank: "What about it?"

"Know what gets me about that year, Momma?"

Hannah said. "Know what really ticks me off? No one from the school ever came by to check up on me. I missed ninety-seven days of school that year. *Ninety-seven*. I was the friggin' phantom of the fourth grade. And not one peep from nobody. Know why they didn't check? Because of who we were; because of who we are. Because I was the daughter of Russ Britton and Sarah Huckins; the apple don't fall far from the tree, so why bother picking up that bruised, wormy piece of fruit?

"Even though I kept up my grades, Miss Gold, in her fucking red Corvette, just wrote me off as one of those things. Couldn't be bothered. Treated me like I was a Gonyer or a Hartford or a Degrote. She wrote me off. . . . I ain't never forgetting that. That whole school year, she scribbled just one sentence in my report card. One sentence. Want to hear it? I know it by heart."

Looking at Hannah, all Sarah could see was the rage of generations of Pages brought to bear in her daughter's face: "What did Miss Gold say, Hannah?"

" 'Hannah has missed a great deal of math instruction and this is reflected in her work.' That's it. One lousy sentence. Sixteen mealymouthed words. It would've been better if she'd written nothing; absolute silence I can understand; silence, at least, is honest.

"People look at us and think we don't count. They shake their heads and cluck their tongues or, worst of all, don't even see us. *Don't even see the white niggers*. Remember when I got my picture in the paper for being valedictorian, and Dad run into Happy Wiggin at Buzzell's? And that bastard Happy asked Dad where in hell his daughter got all her brains. Remember? Daddy should've decked him. People think they can just walk all over us."

"Hannah, you're going to make yourself sick, you're so mad."

"Why shouldn't I? Should I be like you, Momma? Keep it all bottled up inside till I have a breakdown, or explode? Till I want to kill myself? Or run away?"

"Hannah!"

"What about it, Momma? You talk about sitting at the kitchen table with your mother. What about when I had to watch you sitting there with that knife, while you were thinking about killing yourself? What about that? Huh? Sure as hell beat going to kindergarten."

"I weren't going to kill myself."

"You didn't even know we were there, Momma!"

"I weren't."

"Damn it, Momma! Tell me the truth! You wrapped Daddy, wrapped us, wrapped everything in your sorrows, and you were going to shove them down our throats till we gagged on them. You were going to kill yourself, till I smacked you in the head with that building block."

"You don't know everything, Hannah. Just because you finished high school and go to college . . ."

"Say it, Momma! Say it!"

"Don't know half of it."

"Say it! Make me understand!"

Hannah grabbed her mother's wrists, bore down on her: "You owe me, Momma!"

Sarah flinched at Hannah's truth . . . spoke as if trying the combination of a new lock: "I was going to smother us to death in Daddy's stock car in the barn. That's why I took out the knife."

Hannah and Sarah clung to each other, and cried tears so hot and so strong that they could have used them to clean the floors of Sawyer's Mill Grocery Store.

Sarah drinking a pint of milk, Hannah smoking a cigarette, the two of them sat on the floor, slumped against a wall—quitting time. Sarah, feeling the baby kick, smiled at its small insistence, its demand already to be reckoned with.

At Sarah's beckoning, Hannah flushed her cheek to her mother's stomach, listened to the faint, stubborn message from her sibling-to-be.

Chapter Seventeen

December 1985

THE TRUCK-SHACK-ling barbwire snipped into six-inch strips and stacked. The rosebush remains bundled into bristling sheaves. The shed door's sheared hinge fixed. Tools cleaned, oiled and set just so on the chopping block. That's how Wayne found Uncle Dead's shed the morning after he'd liberated it. And though he wasn't cold, he shivered.

"What the . . ." he managed before his jaw unhinged and his eyes widened as if they needed to draw more light to make sure that what he saw was so. "Can't be."

Swiping away his tools, he plopped hard onto the

chopping block and stared. Stared the way someone will at the news of a friend's getting killed in a car crash, or at finding out his wife's cheating. Stared with the wind knocked out of him.

He wondered whether he hadn't worked in his sleep. Whether his obsession hadn't flooded his dreams and carried him back up the hill to work the night shift at Uncle Dead's. Shaking his head, he tried to figure out what he'd gotten himself into this time. It was only after he'd been sitting there a while that Wayne realized how bizarre the truck was:

Uncle Dead's truck, swapped to his brother Henry in the summer of '57, was a black Frankenstein's monster of a truck. A homemade, V-8 crazy quilt—a grinning Dodge grill here, a bug-eyed Chevy headlamp there—patched together in defiance of time and Detroit. A contrary monument to Page perversity and spot-welding. But that still didn't explain what'd happened in that shed the night before.

The longer he stared at the truck, the more it felt right to Wayne. It made sense that a truck a Page had a hand in building would be such a half-assed mutt; it struck him that it was the kind of truck he might've cobbled together himself, given the chance. He wondered what his mother knew about it.

At that thought, Wayne heard humming coming from the shed; someone droning "The Wreck of Old Ninety-Seven."

"Aw, Jesus," said Wayne, legs rubbering.

Even so, Wayne's weak knees couldn't rein his Page

blood, and he found himself being drawn into the wood-smelling shed. The humming, flat, muted, kept on.

"Who the hell's here?" he shouted, the shed swallowing his words.

The humming stopped short, like a leaky faucet tightened that necessary notch, and Wayne flinched into the old, dry darkness. He was scared, yes. But he didn't even think about turning back, scampering to Auntie Leah's. The questions conjured by Uncle Dead's shed were too many and too deep for him to chicken out.

"THEY GAVE HIM HIS ORDERS IN MONROE, VIRGINIA!" sang Henry Page as he jack-in-the-boxed up and out of the truck bed, while Wayne jumped out of his skin and staggered backwards. Wayne's face and ears flushed, his whole body prickling with the sudden heat of shock; he thought he might puke.

"*Good morn-ing*, Sarah's boy!" Henry gibbered. "Ya prob'ly don't remember me from a piss-hole in the snow, but I'm your Great-uncle Henry. I seen ya taken a shine to my truck . . . Wayne. Is Wayne, right? I do try to keep up on relations and all. Though the swamp does keep me running."

Uncle Henry? Henry Page? Wayne'd figured him dead, gone to swamp. No one'd sighted him in years. Not even Auntie Leah or Auntie Robena. He wouldn't't've been more surprised if one of the shacks had nudged him and started whispering in Nanna Page's voice.

"So. You want her, Wayne? I paid me a pret-ty penny to get ahold of her. A pret-ty pen-ny. But I'll give her to ya, Wayne, you being blood and such. No strings.

Want her? She's yours. You're the one set her free, after all. Fair's fair.

"And I'll tell ya, son, real confidential, she goes like a raped ape."

Wayne said, "You the one cut up the barbwire and everything last night?"

"Least I could do. Least I could do. I wouldn'ta dared broke into this shed. Nanna put a curse on it, ya know. Ma's been dead twenty years, but that don't mean nothing. Ya learn things, serious shit, out in that cedar swamp of mine. She might've shut her eyes, spit her last breath, and been buried, but I don't believe for a minute that Ma's dead."

As they walked into the new day, Henry blinked, ducked his head, then planted himself on the chopping block; Wayne stood, staring at his great-uncle.

Henry Page's long, dank years of exile—first banished by Nanna, then by his own nature—had warped him into a true swamp creature: a shambling root system, gnarly bulb of a head bobbing on a skinny stalk of neck, hung with speckled skin of potato-pale parchment. Ravined face wild with old-growth beard, cornflower-blue eyes countersunk in sockets deep as artesian wells, jittery hands just itching to throttle some small, unfortunate mammal. He smelled of permanent sweat, fried bass and heartwoods decay. The swamp rattled in his chest.

Shootlike fingers tracing the oak block's blood scars, Henry said: "Me and your Uncle Dead, one time we stole this goat from over the Mahoneys' field and

chopped its head off right here. Then we cooked that
tough old bastard up in a big ol' bonfire and ate on him
till there was nothing left but bone, guts and gristle; dog
pickings. Then we proceeded to puke our brains out
for the next three days 'cause we'd let the blood
get into that goat meat. What a coupla numb fucks
we was."

Henry spoke too loud—a man used to gabbing to
himself for years at a time—and would only look at
Wayne sideways.

"So," Henry said. "You wanna fix up that truck or
what? You sure enough went through hell to get at her.
You as beat up and lame as you look? Christ, son, you
look like you've been fucking barbwire; liking it, too, I
bet. Saw ya skull that friggin' bird yesterday. That's one
sonuvabitching arm ya got on ya, boy. So what're you
doing? Huh? Huh?"

Seemed to Wayne that his great-uncle was quorking
at him the way that dead raven had. Was trying to make
like he was some kind of irresistible force from up out
the swamp. But Wayne was pretty damn good at being
stubborn, and his uncle had ticked off the mule in him.
Wayne wasn't thick. He knew Henry wanted to see that
truck fixed up and running. And Henry couldn't do it
alone.

"What do ya say, nephew?"

"Uncle Henry . . ."

"Yeah."

"Shut the fuck up."

Anger clouded Wayne's face, making Henry think

of brother Billy; seemed most the time they'd spent together Billy was cursing him out over one thing or another.

"Tell ya what, Wayne. I'll leave, come back later. Let
you think on it. How's that? Ain't no rush or nothin'."

Wayne nodded, didn't even watch Henry slink down
the hill toward Cedar Swamp.

Wayne couldn't keep his eyes off the truck. Knowing
Uncle Dead built it made him look at it long and hard.
He admired the twisted Page energy trapped in that
truck: the tips of bumpers sharpened to spearpoints,
hexagonal chicken wire stretched over window holes, a
shotgun mounted on the driver's-side hood. Not for
Uncle Dead the gentle steel curves of his time; but,
instead, razor angles and rasped planes; steel cut,
chopped and bent; steel corrupted, mangled and tortured; steel that, finally, yielded to reflect the spiky soul
of its master. Billy, in the end, had sculpted a truck that
at its most innocent was meant to bite and scratch; at
its worst, to impale and slurp blood. A truck bristling
with Page rage. And Wayne understood.

He went to the truck then. Polished the right front
fender with his handkerchief. Sniffed and licked the
thick, black paint, hand-layered by Uncle Dead in
ridged, madman swirls. Xylophoned his fingers up and
down the leering chrome grill. He found the yellowed,
four-times-folded leaf of paper wedged between grill
and fender; a piece of paper that only could've been
discovered by someone standing too close to that truck.

Browned edges powdered as Wayne opened it; fissures grinned along the folds. The letter, dated August 28, 1957, was written in a plain, no-nonsense hand— blocky, draft-horse letters printed with Shaker severity:

> **Dear Fool**
> **Thats what you are if youre reading this letter. Your standing in a dead mans shed. And leaning on a dead mans truck. You aint got no business here. So get. Leave this shed be. Let the truck sit and rot. Theres blood in this shed. Blood on this truck. Blood on my hands. No good ever come of this place. No good ever will. You whoever you are should just get the hell out and nail that door shut behind you. I didn't bang in those hundred nails for my health.**
>
> **NANNA PAGE**

Drunk on the whiff of ancient Page secrets, Wayne read the letter through three times before he refolded it and tucked it in his breast pocket. Though he'd never known her, it seemed to Wayne that Nanna's voice had crackled in his ear as he read; he'd have to show the letter to his mother sometime.

Still, Nanna Page's warning didn't blunt his hunger for Uncle Dead's truck; he'd have to be simple to pay any attention to a dead woman's scribble—even if she was his great-grandmother.

He opened the truck and found a decomposed copperhead curled on the front seat.

(Any schoolkid ever entered Granite's town library, the Thomas W. Cole Library, couldn't help but recognize copperhead bones. Once you grunted open the heavy oak doors—fairy-tale doors, swiped maybe from some ogre's castle keep—there it was, suspended from the ceiling in its clear, plastic case, jaws yawning, fangs bared, then three whippy feet of backbone and tail: "The last known copperhead (*Ancistrodon contortrix*) seen in GRANITE, New Hampshire," read the typed three-by-five card taped on the case. "Trapped in the Old Cedar Swamp by Florrie Page in 1937." Wayne and Hannah used to wonder how many Graniters gave up on books because they couldn't take that copperhead reading over their shoulders as it drooped from the library ceiling.)

The scaly flecks and flakes of copper red dusting the driver's seat, as if the snake'd somehow rusted to death, told Wayne that the copperhead had been alive when Nanna shut it in the truck. So much for 1937. And Wayne was willing to bet that Florrie Page and Nanna were blood (another question to ask his mother) and that Uncle Henry, right then and there in 1985, knew where to turn up a copperhead or three.

"What a fucking family," said Wayne, slamming shut the door.

"First thing is we got to get the bitch started, then we can worry 'bout everything else," Henry said to Wayne. "This is what we need: gas'line, grease, a oil filter, ten-weight oil and forty-weight oil, new batt'ry, tire pump, siphon hose, book of matches, and a nail file. We'll use my brother's tools; I seen his toolbox in the back."

Wayne heard the possessiveness that poisoned Henry's voice, knew that in his great-uncle's sly imaginings his long-denied truck already was socked away in the swamp, knew that he was only abiding Wayne's company and the memory-laden barrens of Page's Village so he could lay hands on what Uncle Dead owed him.

So, Uncle Henry bossing and nagging, Wayne got down to work.

He back-wriggled under the truck and popped the oil plug (hoping he didn't strip the threads), the oil taking its sweet, sludgy time to give in to gravity and drain; dropped in the new battery and sanded the blue-green corrosion off the leads; siphoned the old gasoline, tasting but a sip before spitting it out, and spilled in the new; swapped oil filters; unscrewed the distributor cap and separated the points, running a matchbook striker in between to clean them; pumped the tires; scraped rust and gunk from the spark plugs with the nail file; pulled the hubs and checked the brakes (still good); greased and oiled the hell out of everything else; and, finally, poured gasoline into the carburetor to prime it.

Gazing at the grease-shiny engine, Wayne and Henry stood there for a minute or so, as if they expected the truck to start itself. Oiled and greased himself,

Wayne looked like something just crawled out of the tail pipe.

"This is it, Wayne," Henry said. "Go ahead. Try her."

Wayne slid into the truck and looked to his uncle through the chicken wire. His fingers tingled when he touched the steering wheel.

"Now once she catches, I'm gonna pour in this ten-weight so we can loosen up the valves. You just keep on revving the shit out of that engine. This stuff pours like water. Go 'head."

Taking a deep breath, Wayne turned the key: a half-growl, the smell of gasoline, sparks crackling and arcing at the battery.

"Stop!"

Henry tightened the battery leads and spit on the carburetor: "She always was one temper-mental touch-hole," he said. "Now try her again. And pump the gas a couple times, Bill."

Henry didn't even hear himself call Wayne Billy; far as he was concerned, it may as well've been 1957. Wayne noted it, cringed then shrugged, and tried the truck again. Kicked over, but wouldn't catch.

"Whore's moanin', but she won't come," Henry complained. "Give her another go. Careful you don't flood her, though. Then we'd really be up shit's creek."

Wayne turned the key slow this time, listened to it click in the ignition, heard the gas pedal squeak as he pumped. The truck coughed, sputtered, shuddered, backfired . . . and kept going.

"Rev it!" shouted Henry as he fed it oil. "Rev the shit right out of it!"

Wayne floored it, the truck bucking and rocking, clouds of black smoke billowing out from under it and into the cab as it burned off some thirty years of captivity.

The smoke ambushed Wayne, swarming thick and foul into his mouth, nose and eyes. "Jesus Christ!" he gasped, diving from the truck and rolling across the shed floor and out into the crisp December air; Henry kept pouring oil.

Listening to the truck idle, Wayne and Henry sat on the chopping block.

"Sounds pretty," Henry said.

"Guess," Wayne said.

"Your Uncle Dead always let her run rough."

"Thought I was going to fucking choke to death. All that smoke blowing in there like that."

"Always happens you start up any car or truck's been sitting."

"Thanks for letting me know."

"She sure is something. Took Billy a long time to get her just right. Was a time I would've given my left nut to own that truck. Billy never let me touch her, though, the selfish little prick. Never. Not once."

"Uh-huh."

"Fucking brother of mine never let me do nothing. Never let me have nothing; not even Ma."

Wayne stood up, walked away from his uncle. He

had enough troubles of his own without getting bogged down in Henry Page's swamp of woe.

"He shoulda just give me that truck, after all I done for him," Henry said. " 'stead, he made me trade him for it—the sonuvabitch. He deserved ev'ry bad thing happened to him."

Wayne slipped into the shed. He jabbed his leg on one of the truck's bumpers, blood staining his dungarees, ignored it.

Henry didn't notice that Wayne was gone: "He always was Ma's favorite. Was always Billy this and Billy that. Well, she found out, didn't she, 'bout her Billy boy. Darling little Billy boy. If they'da had their way, I wouldn'ta got nothing in this life. Woulda kept getting it up the yee-yaw till the *A*-fuckin' day I died. Way Ma used to look at me with those wickit eyes of hers. She wouldn'ta cared if I'd gone and killed myself. And our old man was 'bout as useful as tits on a bull. Elgar fed me, fed all of us, to her, and she just chawed us up and spit us out like we was nothin' "

Wayne put the truck in gear—clutch loose, shift balky—and rolled out of the shed; seemed to him the truck should be blinking in the harsh December light. He tried the horn—broken; so he goosed the gas, goaded the truck into a semiroar.

Looking up from his one-man town meeting, Henry saw the truck out of the shed and Wayne behind the wheel. His face exploded to red through purple, then into all the raging colors of a winter sunset.

"What the fuck're you doing?" he cried, the rootlike

cords of his neck rigid. "Fuck're you doing? That's my truck, you little asshole! My truck!"

Henry grabbed a tire iron and started whaling on the truck, wild looping blows battering steel defeated years before; Wayne's bones shivered at the vibration.

"Aw, come on, Uncle Henry. Quit it. Cut it out. Come on."

Wayne backed up, but Henry kept banging—clang! clang! clang!—so Wayne nudged the truck forward, tried to crowd his uncle.

"Cut the shit, Uncle Henry!"

But Henry wouldn't budge; he'd spent too many decades in the swamp to let himself be badgered thirty years later by another Page.

"Pound sand!" Henry shouted. "Suck dick!"

Uncle Dead's truck lunged—Wayne swore up and down to himself that he had nothing to do with it—knocking Uncle Henry down. Henry smacked the back of his head on the chopping block, his blood spreading evenly over the thirsty oak, runneling into the scars and divots that marked the wizened wood.

By the time Wayne killed the truck and ran to his great-uncle, Henry Page, who hadn't dared venture from his swamp since his mother passed away, was dead.

Wayne stretched out on the ridged December earth, his legs dangling over the quarry lip. The quarry of his mother's grief. Where he'd almost died. He could still feel Sarah's frigid hand clamp his small wrist, feel her sudden strength surge into his body as she tossed him over her head, threw him to safety. The eastern sky brightened from charcoal gray to felt gray as Wayne sucked in the head-clearing December morning, urged the frozen ground to knead his knotted back.

Despite his deceased payload, Wayne had enjoyed rising before daybreak and threading his way through the dark woods that had haunted his childhood. He still didn't quite know what to make of Uncle Henry's sudden appearance, and equally sudden death; it's hard to feel real bad at the dying of someone you thought was already dead.

Wayne dragged Uncle Henry, cement blocks tied to his ankles and chest, to the edge of the quarry and pushed him over. Henry broke through the thin skin of ice and sank into the black quarry water. Wayne supposed he should feel something like regret at Henry's passing, but all he truly felt was that he was finishing a job begun even before he was born.

Uncle Dead's truck seemed to run more smooth on the drive back to Page's Village. Hanging from the rearview mirror, Nanna Page's copperhead skeleton swayed back and forth, the bones chattering and clacking, chattering and clacking.

Sarah X

She kneads the hamburger, the too-red meat oozing through her slick fingers. She squishes it with intent, molds it, pats it the way she would a newborn's bottom, and finally balances it in her hand, holding it up to the ceiling—an offering. The frying pan hisses with grease, the steaming water for the macaroni-and-cheese begins to boil.

Chapter Eighteen

Christmas
1985

RUSS WOKE AT FIVE
on Christmas morning and, for a few woozy minutes,
wrestled the demons of wakefulness. Losing, he
shrugged. Hands threaded behind his head, he stared at
the ceiling, chased the Christmases of his childhood.
Goose pimples pebbled his arms; he wriggled closer to
Charlotte's warmth.

Magic-shorn and more dreaded than hoped for, the
Christmases that pile up after you're ten years old don't
much matter; it was those pure, it's-never-going-to-get-
here Christmases that came before that Russ pursued
down the Pickpocket Road of his past (that skinny,

frost-heave-buckled patch of tar where he'd grown up not-quite-poor); Christmases that seemed traced from the corny *Saturday Evening Post* covers he used to resort to at Charlie the Barber's when the comic books ran out.

Christmases of: hollow glass bulbs straining toward the floor; water candles bubbling; Ovaltine, chocolate-chip cookies and carrots left out on the kitchen table for Santa Claus and his reindeer; Elvis Presley moaning "Blue Christmas" on the gray-and-white Sylvania record player; his old man spending his week's pay the day before to make the family's Christmas; the Lionel train and Lincoln Logs set up beneath the sticky, prickly, pine-smelling tree; cranberry and popcorn garlands; first snow soft as angel down; crawling under the house with his old man to thaw frozen pipes with candles; chilly night rides to ogle the town's riot of Christmas lights; and his earliest memory—standing in a crib, snow scratching at the window, and a new, slobbering puppy licking his face.

Russ peeked under the window shade, disappointed at the bare ground. He wanted snow that Christmas Day, wanted his children under his roof, his wife in his bed; they were the sum of his past twenty years, and he refused to give them up so easy. Not on Christmas, anyway.

But then he laughed at himself, mean and scornful, disgusted that a man his age, after all these years, should pine most after the things he knows he can't have, should warm himself at the sentimental fire of nostalgia; amid change, he never had; give him a six-pack and a Hank Williams record and he'd be bawling before the night was out. Pressing closer to Charlotte, he draped an arm over her, cradled a breast. Tried to fall back asleep.

But even as he held Charlotte, held the unlikely woman willing to bind the unraveling threads of his days, he imagined his favorite photograph of his wife:

Sarah's five years old in the scallop-edged snapshot, straddling a fresh-killed deer her uncles Billy and Henry have draped splay-leggèd over two sawhorses. It's Christmastime, though the bloodstained earth is bare of snow; Grandpa Elgar's evergreen wreaths slouch from the barn. It's Sarah's expression in this picture that has always moved Russ. Even at five, the wistful ghost of resignation haunts her face. She wants to please the photographer, but she can't quite bring herself to look direct into the camera, can't pull the trigger on a smile. And when Russ thinks about his wife, remembers the ache in her eyes, he can't get that small kerchiefed girl out of his head. Only five years old. Already in retreat.

"Y'aren't going to make it snow, no matter how hard you stare out that window."

"Seemed we always had snow for Christmas when I was a kid," Russ said to Charlotte, who had just woken up.

"Well"—she yawned, not covering her mouth—"Merry Christmas."

"Merry Christmas."

Russ rolled away from the window, kissed Charlotte—her thin lips still tasted new and strange to him—and clicked on the radio. WBZ out of Boston: "Jingle Bell Rock."

"Song's almost good as a blizzard, huh, Russ?" Charlotte teased. "Maybe they'll play 'I Saw Mommy Kissing Santa Claus' next."

"Brings back some memories."

Charlotte snorted: "You Brittons and your memories. I swear the lot of ya'd sit around in the damned dark all day long and moon over the past, given half a chance."

"Past is all we got," Russ said. "Weeds of the past're always choking the here and now."

Charlotte shook her head: "Maybe."

"Kind of Christmases you have when you was a little girl?"

She laughed, smiled at Russ; if nothing else, in Russ's care some of Charlotte's harsh angles had begun to give in, relax toward soft curves; Wayne had sharpened those same angles.

"You got to know, don't you?" she said. "You got to know every damned little thing. 'cause you can't place me yet. You don't know where I fit."

"I like to hear folks' stories," he said. "That's all. I like to hear how they plane smooth the past."

"The past? I don't believe in no past. I'd sooner believe in Santa Claus. If I'd've believed in the past, we wouldn't be laying here talking right now."

"You're the one wanted to look at Dickie West's that night."

"That was different."

"But . . ."

"I ain't talking no past. Ain't no future in it."

"There ain't no love without the past."

"What the hell's that supposed to mean?"

"Just what I said: There ain't no love without the past. My mother used to say that. And I believe it."

"Well, you know what, Russ? I don't believe in love, neither. Know what I believe in? Friction . . . sparks . . . in rubbing my bush up and down your chest. That's what I believe in."

Lean, hungry and needful, Charlotte pounced on him, bit his neck, kissed him as if their lips were hammer and anvil, sank her nails till they drew blood, rasped at him with her hard body.

Russ, his unquenchable loneliness flattered by her desire, yielded; simply kneaded her bony back and bottom with his strong hands, waiting, as she moved on him. And when *she* was ready, the hunger—her own deep, panting hunger—kindling her body, she found Russ with her hand and yanked him to, then collapsed on him, surrendering, the way a suicide tumbles from a quarry cliff.

———

As they lay there, spent, Russ still quivering inside her (a faint rumor), Charlotte whispered humid in his ear: "That's what I believe in, Russ."

She kissed him on the cheek—a dainty, mistletoe peck—the way one might a new baby or an old grammy, and lay her head between his chin and shoulder. "Blue Christmas" sobbed on the radio.

Chapter Nineteen

January 1986

RESURRECTED BEneath the midnight shroud of a new moon, Uncle Dead's truck blindly (cock-knockin' headlights'd never worked) picked its way down from the shed, creaked past Auntie Leah's black-eyed windows, and groaned up the hill to Route 49, where it paused—making sure the highway was dead—before darting across the road and into the trees like some startled night beast, a coon, say, or a skunk. Sniffing out a lapsed logging trail, the truck wound its way parasite-deep into the dark winter woods; skeleton trees slashed at its steel skin with bare claws. The truck knew these woods, had never forgotten them. Guts scraping the earth, years ago it had stolen away hundreds, if not thousands, of cords of firewood, had hauled the burlap-secreted carcasses of deer killed out of season. No man paints a truck black unless he has larceny in his heart.

The truck lurched to a stop where the woods suddenly scrawnied up and gave way to the crumbling butt-end of a sandpit. Standing there, suspended between trees and gravel, were some dozen fifty-five-gallon steel drums. Menacing, expectant, elbowing each other, the drums reminded Wayne of the leather-jacketed hives that, come summer, swarmed certain corners of Manor Beach.

Truck idling, Wayne swung out of the cab and swigged a breath, forcing the January night deep into his lungs; the flood of cold made his temples ache.

If he had any sense, he knew, he'd shrug off those steel drums, climb back in Dead's truck, and get on home. Yet, the simple fact of the drums waiting there, criminal and seething with God-knows-what poisons, thrilled him. They were a dare, like cannonballing into quarry water or barrel-assing past Chief of Police Leon George's at two in the morning. Smothered by a childhood blanketed in caution and reticence, Wayne couldn't resist a dare. Besides, he owned the truck for the job. What better truck for midnight dumping than Uncle Dead's?

Slow . . . deliberate, like a man laying out his clothes who's made up his mind to leave his wife, Wayne tugged on the goggles Stain Thistle'd given him, then the rubber gloves and plastic apron, each slick and stiff with the cold. Flexing his stiff fingers first, Wayne tilted one of the steel drums, heard the thick, mysterious slush slosh, felt its weight shift. He let go, the drum falling back with a liquid thud.

Looking for work—something steady, but not *too* steady—Wayne'd gone to Stain Thistle's garage the week before. When he'd walked into Stain's office, Stain's hungry eyes'd lit up, and Wayne'd found five raspy-new sawbucks scratching his palms before anyone had spoken word one.

Fatherless at birth (motherless, too, some claimed) and disfigured by a raging red birthmark that masked most of his sly face, Stain Thistle drove leather-reeking Cadillacs, was working on his fourth wife in ten years, and had his nimble fingers stuck at least knuckle-deep (if not up to the armpit) in most any money-making pie in town; screwing young and old alike, the rich and the poor, he wouldn't turn thirty for another two years. Real estate, hunting dogs, used cars, construction, limo services, campgrounds, video stores—you name it—if there was a buck in it, so was Stain Thistle.

Though the least of his enterprises, Stain still chose to do business out of the garage. Same garage he'd finagled away from Vernon Collins, his first and only boss, by first finagling (then marrying) Vernon's desperate daughter. The garage'd been his first success; so why chance his luck? When Wayne'd hunched into his office, Stain'd been trying to figure out how best to accommodate certain of his Massachusetts associates, who wanted to dispose of some "sensitive semi-solid waste" in neighborly New Hampshire.

"Fifty more where that come from, Wayne-o," Stain says, after he teases him with the first fifty. "Can you get hold of a truck?"

Wayne nods his head yes, not even hearing Stain's words so much as listening to the rhythm of his sentences; some folks seek salvation by speaking in the spasming tongues of God, but Stain Thistle sought his in the beguiling cadences of cash.

"Now, this is the deal," says Stain. . . .

And that was why Wayne, freezing his balls off, found himself in the January woods wrestling with fifty-five-gallon steel drums at one in the morning; once Stain had set the hook, Wayne hadn't stood a chance.

Wayne grabbed a drum, set it on edge, and rolled it toward the grumbling truck.

Wayne didn't try not to think about what he was doing, he just *didn't* think about it; the way water doesn't think about the drowned, fire the burned. He was getting paid to do a job, and he'd do it; that's all that mattered. Pure Page-ness: You either did a thing, or you didn't; no point in hemming and hawing it to death.

So Wayne—not thinking, just doing—weaseled through the woods, slunk back over Route 49, and crawled down the hill into Page's Village; with each bump, each chuckholed change of direction, the steel drums clinged and clanged, jostling like so many gallons of poisoned milk.

Instead of turning left by Auntie Leah's and heading up to the shed, he drove straight, down toward Uncle Dead country. At the backest edge of Page's Village, where the land sloped away tricky and spongy, lay a natural deadfall: a ten-foot drop thick with tree corpses and puckerbrush remains. It was this spot, in Cedar Swamp's shadow, Wayne had thought of when Stain'd made his offer.

When he got down close, Wayne turned the truck around and backed it to the lip of the deadfall. Not even bothering with the goggles and such this time, he scrambled into the truck bed, walking on the drum-tops to reach the tailgate and unhook it.

Then he dropped the drums of poison, as cold and slippery as his heart, one by one into the crackling brush.

Wayne and Uncle Dead's truck were wintering together. He'd moved into the shed after Uncle Henry died and hadn't had the heart to kick the truck out after all the trouble he'd gone through to get at it. He'd gotten the shed's potbelly stove working, and had scrounged a cot, a saltine-thin mattress and a kerosene lamp from Auntie Leah's. That was all he thought he needed. He knew how to get by: He'd gouged holes in belts to make them last; he'd bound shoe and slapping sole together with twine to get the extra wear; he'd lived plenty of places without running water and knew what it was to build head-pounding days around one small meal; he'd worn dungarees whose knees were stiff with the scar tissue of patching, repatching, and patching yet again. He was a Page; he could do without (and make it a virtue, goddammit). He might not be a Woods or a Mallory or a Tucker, or part of any other *fine* family of Granite, but he was worthy of Page's Village, worthy of Uncle Dead's shed.

But busting open Dead's tomb of a shed had settled nothing. The questions raised by the shed had, instead, driven him up the hill. Though it was a snow-barren winter of clear, crisp days, the air inside the shed seemed thick as good stew to Wayne, barely breathable some days. Redolent of woodsmoke, bock beer and blood—those things that texture the past—like an old hunting camp.

He lay on the cot in the dark, truck's engine still ticking as it cooled, stove embers murmuring in the hard, old-man consonants of spit and crackle. It shocked him how easy it had been to steal through the woods, load the drums and dump them. He supposed he should find another burying place—one of the quarries, maybe—but he had to admit it'd been satisfying to dump those drums down back; there was something about Page's Village that brought out the junkyard prick in him, made him glad to strike out at it. Maybe it was what it did to Uncle Henry. Or how it had crippled his mother. Or that it had driven Nanna, Uncle Dead, and who knows who else, to such extremes. He could almost taste Uncle Dead's reasons for raping Jenny Page, his niece, his half-sister. But the thought didn't scare

Wayne; instead, it made him feel a little closer to each of his great-uncles.

Page's Village may have been dead for most of their lives, but even he and Hannah were frantic in its web, just as their children would be; its long, dry slivers were sunk too deep not to scar another generation. It was Page's Village had carved on their mother, and it was their mother who had lathed them. Russ had never been a consideration.

Just thinking Hannah's name made Wayne ache for his sister. His anchor in the family, she was the one who had protected him and raised him, even as she cared for Sarah. Hannah, sensing the awful possibilities, had made sure that Wayne mattered. He knew that his mother loved him in her sad, sighing-eyed way, but it was Hannah whose love had been tangible.

❧

Trembling, Wayne and Hannah huddle in the back of Russ's pickup late one October night as the truck back-fires toward home. Russ is in between cars again, the money-guzzling Ford Fairlane (which you could only drive in second, anyway) having thrown a rod and keeled over. So, there being next to no room in the cab, Wayne and Hannah are exiled to the grease-stained bed of the truck.

A cold night wind, tasting of metal, breaks over them, bores to the bone. Their eyes tear, cheeks burn, and hands ache. They cower, newborn mice discovered in a barn corner, and hug each other, Hannah instinctively snugging Wayne to her chest and bearing most of the wind.

"Hannah," Wayne whines. "I'm cold."

She hugs him tighter, rests her chin on top of his head: "Sshh. I know. We'll be home soon. Already in Lamprey."

Hunching his shoulders, he tries to shrink into his sister's warmth. She smells of burning leaves, bubble gum, Ivory soap. "Hannah . . ."

Wriggling off her jacket, she wraps it around Wayne, draws him into her bony nest of ribs, arms and legs. Goose pimples mottling her bare skin, she shudders; the sleeves of her white tee shirt flap and snap.

Hannah tented around him, he falls asleep, dreams of the great, kiting wings of one of his mother's leaf dragons. She clings to him, his small, throbbing warmth. Her helpless baby brother. Her second heart.

⚭

Dreaming himself dreaming—and Uncle Dead's truck whispering its poisons—Wayne Britton, midnight-dumper, finally succumbed to sleep.

Sarah XI

The kitchen sink is crammed with dirty dishes: A strainer sinks into the white bubbles bearding the steaming water; knives, spatulas and spoons poke through the soap like periscopes; plates smeared with ketchup and mustard and bean juice list to one side; plastic glasses bob on the surface, fill, drift to the bottom. Her hands (they prickle in the hot water) are submerged; bubbles creep up her bare arms. But she has turned from the dishes to look at the beat-up Sylvania, the radio she and her husband bought the week they were married by Justice of the Peace Merland Bake and only her husband's mother and her drunk of a boyfriend would stand up for them. The radio is on fire, yellow and orange flames licking out the back. Even so, it still sputters out the weather—she lives for the weather—even as the plastic melts, even as chemical-smelling smoke, coils from the Sylvania, the *S* still hanging upside down.

Chapter Twenty

February 1986

SPURRED BY THE DIS-tant thunder of baying hounds, Hannah thrashes through quarry woods: stumbling over and around deep stone scars ooz-ing mica; slashing across sparkly, moss-thick craters; splash-ing into mute pools of night. With thorns and thistles lunging and lashing, she staggers across a ravaged, grooved granite-scape of rust-seized work machines (infernal steel all tooth and claw) and imploded shacks, sheds and shanties. She hears the dogs surge closer, imagines them breaking over her in one snarl-ing, snapping wave, their rank, humid breath prickling her bare neck. Legs dead, chest heaving, she lurches into the cool dark of a shack just as the dogs, reined in one hand by Nanna

Page, crest the rise. Bristling, straining, the animals bear human faces: Auntie Leah, Fat Dot, Grandma Ella, Jenny Page . . . Sarah. Nanna, tall and bleak, casts a shadow, an eclipse, that inks the woods. In the weepy half-light, she surveys the blasted hollow; though hidden, Hannah feels as if her great-grandmother stares unerringly into her treacherous heart.

"ACCEPT YOUR FATE!" Nanna commands in a voice to shame the thunder.

Unable to resist, Hannah sighs and moves toward the voice, but a naked shadow — Uncle Dead! — darts from another shack and makes for the trees. Nanna cocks a crooked finger, and the shadow is gnawed by flames. Ash funneling into the sky, the shadow crumples to earth, throbs like hot coals. But the air smells of wet leaves, cleansed, as after a hard rain.

Borne by dream logic, Hannah suddenly finds herself quivering at the lip of Sarah's quarry, that gaping, obscene mouth that nearly devoured her mother, her brother. The water's thick . . . still, the color of Nanna Page's eyes. Hannah looks back at Nanna (a one-last-look look) who beckons with gnarled finger; a finger as twisted and mangled as the fates of Page's Village.

Hannah jumps, knifes into the water, and is sucked down without a ripple. Her hair parachuting, she sinks, hears the knitting of ice up above, feels her blood gravy up, her heart slow. Hugging herself, she closes her eyes, savors the pleasant weight of water pressing on her shoulders. Prepares to speak the ancient tongue of the water-thinks-it's-stone.

Sinking. Giving in. Drowning.

✂

A quilt of ice grew on the inside windows of Hannah's cottage; more ice skinned the toilet-bowl water. The night-driven wind—that ice-clawed maniac roaring down from the Arctic—snatched at the doors and windows, shook them as if they were unruly children. Keeping the mother's watch outside Hannah's room, Sarah ladled water onto the smoldering wood that bordered the floor furnace; wood and steel hissing and steaming at the intrusion. Sarah hated that damned furnace, trusted it about as far as she could throw it. But when she'd gotten home from work, Hannah still hibernating beneath her bundle of blankets, the kitchen stove wasn't throwing enough heat, and the place'd seemed colder than the meat locker at Sawyer's Grocery. Desperate to blunt the cottage's icy edge (she pictured her baby frozen solid and blue in her womb), she'd grudgingly fired up the furnace; she would shut it before bed.

Was a floor furnace killed Missy Parker and her two kids some fifteen years before, and Sarah could never look at any floor furnace without seeing sweet Missy. Granite Fire Chief Tommy Tucker III had said at the time that the fire had started when diapers being dried over the floor furnace had kindled. She'd gone to school with Missy Parker, who'd always been a levelheaded, no-nonsense girl, and it made Sarah shudder to think that Missy, strong, reliable Missy, had made a mistake that ended up killing her and her children. But, of course, there was more than one way to kill a family . . . deaths slower than others.

Pillow-propped, Sarah stretched out on the floor, her pregnant stomach a motherly hummock bulging from her midsection; cold air whispered through floorboard cracks. Closing her eyes, she listened for Hannah, homed in on the steady rise and fall of her daughter's chest, the bellows of sleep.

Hannah. Oh, Hannah. Sarah had seen the signs, yet had denied them: the subterranean river of sadness in her gray eyes; her words fewer, flatter, but bitter with rage; bone-deep sighs wrought of an unquenchable longing that had made Sarah flinch in recognition. It had been coming, all right, just as sure as the first seeds of winter are sown amid Labor Day's cookouts. As the months had fallen away in their domino predetermination, it had seemed to Sarah that the stronger she got, the weaker Hannah became. Perhaps Hannah, in seeing Sarah shed the past and take responsibility for the present, had realized she could shrug old obligations, could, herself, finally collapse. Break down at her mother's feet.

When it came, it came quiet. No hysterics. No rooting out of hair, or dancing knives. Just a dose of Page acquiescence: tents folded up and vanished overnight. Hannah simply had gone to bed one night the week before, and hadn't gotten up since. That first morning, thinking Hannah had overslept, Sarah had tried to wake her, not yet knowing that Hannah had thrown herself into the quarry dark.

✕

"Hannah," calls Sarah, her words turning to vapor as she speaks. "Hannah."

Grunts, mumbles, the underwater sputter of those half-asleep.

"You'll be late for school."

"Not go. Sleep."

"Hannah?"

The blankets shift: "L'me 'lone."

Sarah broods on the bloody history that binds mothers and daughters. Of young flesh first marinated in blood, then coaxed (forced?) to yield, the further ripping and tearing; oh, the rending never ends, does it? Yes, women, privy to the secrets of stanching, were born to bleed. But *that's* physical history, mere menstruation, capitulation and childbirth. There's a darker history, the history passed on in silences and stares; sobbed over guttering candles. The history that murders newborn babies, that carves its hieroglyphics on soft wrists, that lands women in strange, hurtful beds. That sends them, hearts ablaze, screaming for the quarries.

Just as the door was closed on her so many times, Sarah closes the door on Hannah—a mother's loving snick; now is not the time for talking, plenty of time for that later. Now is the time for Hannah to sound the depths. Sarah heats water, brings strong tea to her. They sit quiet in Hannah's darkness, sip the bitter tea sweetened with Pet condensed milk; Sarah absentmindedly finger-combs her daughter's thick, snarly hair until both of them fall asleep.

❧

That was how the first, tear-stained week had gone as Sarah did her damnedest to keep her daughter from breaking apart on the shoals of depression. Hannah would do nothing for herself except trudge to the bathroom. Sarah fed her, bathed her and dressed her, leaving her only to walk the two miles to their job at Sawyer's Mill Grocery where, seven and a half months pregnant, she did the work of two women; Nanna Page, she reminded herself, had done the work of a hundred. And not just women, neither.

Knowing there were no answers, Sarah asked no questions; questions were life's black flies. She did what she did best. She waited, lounged in the languid lap of time, and soothed Hannah as best she could. She regretted the demons she'd passed on to her daughter, and which, earlier, had been passed on to her, but she refused to give in to the insistent wheedling of guilt. Nanna had despised guilt, and when she'd sniffed it in others, she'd always used it to her advantage; guilt as leverage. She shook her head, wistful at the thought of her grandmother.

Sarah clicked off the furnace, which shimmied and groaned in its dying, and ladled more water onto the charred wood—as smooth and hot as a feverish baby. She swore to herself that she'd never use it again. She'd rather shiver and wear ten sweaters than rile Missy Parker's ghost one more time, or worry over house-wood trying to turn on itself and become fire and ash. She wondered whether it wasn't time to leave Choate's Junction; she'd meant all along for the baby to be born in Granite.

The cottage shuddered, seemed to shift on its foundation, as brute gusts of wind worked it over; Sarah winced, suddenly unsure of the house's ruggedness. She fingernailed ice off the picture window, the glass trembling beneath her fingers, and saw that not a one of the dozen or so bob-houses out on the lake remained standing; so much for ice-fishing. Another gust wailed down the lake, scooped up one of the flattened fishing shacks, and sent it bouncing a good hundred yards—a milk carton tossed from a speeding car. Sarah grinned; she never had been able to resist a good, rowdy wind.

Checking the furnace and the floor one more time, Sarah pulled on her coat and hunched into the wind-crazy night: treetops blown flat as the ears of a growling dog; the star-pricked sky clear and navy blue; the frozen lake a prairie of ice.

She hesitated at the dock. Oh, she knew the lake (still didn't know its damn name) was froze solid. Had been since December. But she and that water, froze or not, had a history; she hadn't forgotten that gray day in October, didn't discount the possibility of that lake creaking open its lockjawed maw and swallowing her up like Jonah's whale. But the wind, the unshackling wind, seduced her. And it was the wind she gave herself to when she sidled onto the lake.

The wind thrummed in her bones, set blood music

rushing in her ears. Ballasted by her unborn baby, Sarah took a couple of dainty, running steps and slid, surprised by the ice's stubble-roughness. She shuffle-stepped, jumped (barely leaving the ice), and tried to land on her right foot, but managed only to stumble, almost fall. Drawing the night deep into her lungs, she remembered the ice storm the night Nanna died, the forbidding blackness of quarry ice, how the wind had always made her feel drunk.

Snubbing the cold, Sarah unzipped her coat and planted her backside to the wind. Stretching her arms out straight, she unfurled the coat like a new butterfly's sticky wings and waited. Nothing happened at first, as her coat flapped and snapped in the whipping wind. But then—a slow train pulling out of the station—she began to move, shooed by the wind. Picking up speed, bumping over the ice, she started laughing, pure animal shrieks of joy lost to the night in the howl of the wind.

✕

Wrapped in depression's caul, Hannah hasn't moved for days. She is as still and silent as the winter water, the timeless granite. As a Page plotting revenge. So still, she cannot tell where her body ends, where the water begins. She imagines dissolving, molecule by molecule, becoming the water, consciousness afloat in the liquid night until that, too, melts in surrender. Maybe then, she will hear the ancient stone talk. She listens faithfully for the granite, has listened all along. She knows that when the granite speaks, it will sound like Nanna Page.

There were, well, *certain* things that Professor Constance Woods did or thought, *certain* things she believed in, that, depending on her mood, depending on which Constance Woods woke up on a particular morning, felt like either betrayal or survival. Not that she could so readily articulate what was being betrayed or saved.

For instance, even though she'd burrowed well into her fifties, was a full professor of linguistics up to the state university, and was decades removed (removed, yes, but not free) from her Gonyer upbringing, she still thought of Brazil nuts as "nigger toes," though she hadn't uttered the two words since before high school. The phrase both delighted her in its colloquial clarity, yet terrified and shamed her in its racist precision. As an adult, she'd never dared buy Brazil nuts, afraid that somehow at the point of purchase she'd start ranting, shrieking: "Nigger toes! Nigger toes! Look at me! I'm buying me some of those good nigger toes!"

Certain things: She still stopped to eavesdrop on ravens quorking and scolding; still pronounced Michigan as if it had a *j* in the middle — Mijigan; reused waxed paper till it shredded; liked stock-car races and pork chops fried crispy, brittle and tasteless; every dusk she paced her dooryard (yes, she still said dooryard), sniffing, sorting and sifting the confluences of cloud, light and wind.

That was why she happened to be driving over to Sawyer's Mill Grocery. She'd stood out back that very night and smelled the snow in the air: the warmish breeze wet and heavy, the cold-locked earth offering a little give, a snow ring haloing an Impressionist moon. Their dry winter, she knew, would soon be over, and she'd decided to stock up on staples before snow flew; there was no escaping being a baby of the Great Depression.

As the first few snowflakes licked at the windshield and waltzed in the headlights, Constance saw a woman, her hooded head down and her broad shoulders bunched, shuffling up Hartvale Avenue. A pregnant woman! In fact, a pregnant woman a good seven months along, dragging herself God-knows-where; a woman looking so pained and pathetic, she could've been a Gonyer. (Constance's mother, who never saw her fiftieth birthday, suddenly is there with her, chopping wood, lugging water, wringing chickens' necks, always pregnant, always weighed down by her blooming belly, by what she called "love's ball and chain.")

Slowing, Constance rolled down her window, the new snow confetti-ing into her face, and called out: "Do you need a ride?"

The woman scraped to a stop, squinching at Constance. "I know you?" she asked.

"I'm not sure," Constance answered truthfully.

"Me neither."

The woman shrugged, crossed to Constance's car anyway; she *did* need to get off her feet, and the driver seemed nice enough, if not familiar. Constance stretched across the front seat to open the door, and when the woman ducked her head to slide into the car, Constance gasped and cried out: "Sarah Huckins!"

"Mrs. Woods!"

The snow fell harder, Constance Woods and Sarah Britton suspended in one of those combustible moments that occur outside time, where the onrushing past rear-ends the stalled present. Where, suddenly, night and snow and thirty-two years fall away, and once again it's a summer's day on the Plains in 1953. The day these two women could have become something like mother and daughter. A day when everything could have changed.

"My God, Mrs. Woods . . ."

"Sarah Huckins." Her words carrying the weight of thirty-two years. Two words, four syllables, a woman's birth name, emblem of old grievances, stale sorrows.

"Mrs. Woods."

"Well, Sarah, get in." (All the while, thinking, as if it had happened last week: I should never have taken her back to Page's Village. Never.)

Sarah grunted into the car, but couldn't arc the seat belt over her stomach.

"Here, let me loosen that," Constance said.

" 's okay," Sarah said. "Store ain't far."

"What're you doing in Choate's Junction?" they both asked at the same time, then laughed—clear and fast, spring brooks twining in deep woods.

Sarah said: "Live here. On the lake."

"I live here, too. Almost ten years now."

"You don't live on the Plains no more?"

"Not since Davis—my husband—died. I had no stomach for the Plains after he passed away. I'd sooner live with my old man, my father, than alone in Davis Woods's house. So I deeded the place to our two sons. Little bastards've been fighting over it ever since."

"Uh-huh."

"I never figured you for one to leave Granite, Sarah."

"Me neither."

The snow plunging faster, thicker, Constance turned in to Sawyer's nearly empty parking lot. "What were you doing, walking out in this weather?" she asked.

"Going to work," Sarah said. "Me and my daughter work here. But she's sick, and I don't drive."

"Tonight? You're working tonight? They're predicting a blizzard."

"I don't work, we don't get paid."

"But what about your husband? What about what's-his-face—Russ Britton?"

"It's a long story, Mrs. Woods."

Constance stared at the windshield, the snow piling up like lint under the guest-room bed; twelve inches by morning—easy. Maybe fifteen.

"I really got to get going, Mrs. Woods," Sarah said. "My boss is expecting me."

"Sarah," said Constance, remembering the little girl Ella Huckins nearly had abandoned at her front door those many years ago, "I don't want you to take this wrong . . . but I'd really like to give you a hand tonight."

✖

It is the silence of blood swamping through your veins, of the stolid thud of an icy heart, of the dolphin squeak of water molecules expanding and contracting. But the silence in this dream wearies Hannah with its insistence. She begins to talk. Not even words at first, but rhythms and sounds and throat fragments spewing from her rusty-hinged mouth until the trickle of words, then the sentences and the paragraphs gush, like a water pump that hasn't been used in years:

"Born, raised and bruised in Granite, New Hampshire, I came of age among Depression-haunted people, Page's Villagers who called lunch dinner, ate woodchuck for pleasure, and considered a telephone a luxury. Something other people had, and besides, phones only let other people stick their nose in your business, anyways, and shouldn't Auntie Robena get electric and a flush toilet on her place before someone puts on airs and goes and puts in a telephone? We didn't even have toy phones. No point in getting our hopes up.

"So when my folks needed to make a phone call when I was a kid, I was the one — being the oldest — who had to take the long trudge to the neighbors, knock humble on the screen door, and mumble 'May we use your phone?' to my girl Keds.

"Seems to me that those musty, cat-infested houses (considerate beggars, we rotated the inconvenience) always were ruled by squat, sweating grammies, whose doughy double and triple chins were barbed by stiff old-lady whiskers. Their phones stank of b.o., sour milk and fried liver and were situated — always — under curling fly-strips studded with tiny crunchy carcasses.

"Gut clenching, mouth cottoning, I'd stand there gawking at the phone till I got asked: 'Want me to dial?' Then I'd fork over the damp paper scrap, the number scrawled in smudged pencil. When I was finished, I'd flee—the screen door whanging shut behind me—sprinting home, my family duty fulfilled. Till next time.

"Oh, to be honest, except for the forced marches to the neighbors, it didn't bother me much that we didn't have a phone. Didn't even think about it. Our phonelessness made our lives fuller, riper with incident and surprise. And believe me, we needed all the incident and surprise we could get our paws on.

"We wrote letters to friends and relations (well, me and Wayne wrote letters). Folks would drop by unannounced to say hello, kill a few hours, and we did the same; there was no more exciting sound to me and my brother than the tentative crunch of strange tires in the driveway. Bill collectors had to rap on our door and look us in the eye to state their business—none of this hiding behind the telephone.

"I remember one summer's afternoon of entertainment provided by a white-maned picture-Bible salesman, who paced up and down our dirt driveway, the dust caking on his light blue suit and his fancy white shoes; I'd never seen a grown man wear white shoes before. He was trying to sell my too-polite mother on the virtues of his 'FULL-COLOR, PITCHER-BIBLES! THE WORD OF THE LORD GOD IN LIVING COLOR!' He misread Sarah's polite shyness for interest, and it took my father to drive him off. And, let me tell you, didn't Russ enjoy that.

"Without a phone, trips to the town dump and to the grocery and to the junkyard (heaps Daddy drove, we spent a fair piece *scouring for parts) served a greater purpose than the errands themselves. We sought news of the world, our small chunk, anyways, and that's where we found it. Gossip pooled in places back then.*

"Don't know why I'm going on and on about us not having no phone. Weren't no big deal, really. Ends up just being something to talk about. Everything ends up being just something to talk about, obsess over, till you're sick with it: Daddy almost killing us all that New Year's Eve; our retard cousins, Elvis Presley Lopez and Ricky Nelson Lopez; how having to sell Nanna's furniture to that antique-dealing bitch from Lamprey nearly killed your mother; the rats and the outhouses and the kittens drowned in the bathtub; the maniac great-grandmother, the vanished grandmother, and the suicidal mother; you and Wayne touching each other once, just one time, hairless, amazed by the impossible smoothness of brother and sister, blood on blood.

"And you wonder how in hell you got out alive. Why are you the one who gets to leave? Why are you the one smarter than the rest? Why are you the one who's going to leave and maybe never come back?"

Hannah stops. Realizes that's all there is; that there will be no speaking-in-granite—not this time, anyway. Her fingers and toes, those wormy exiles, burn and tingle. The weights of depression unbind, fall away, and Hannah rises, accelerating as she nears the surface, until, finally, she's hurtling toward the sunlight and torpedos through the ice, hair thrown back and body arched, gasping, laughing, crying, screaming, skin turning from blue to white. Reborn! Free!

Sarah XII

She slips back into the shadow-light, legs tented, the last spasms of lovemaking still rippling inside. (Already her husband, dripping on the floor, has padded from the bedroom.) Nipples tall, encircled by the dark sea of joy that washes over her pale breasts, caught in the hard light spilling in from the kitchen. Wet, she touches herself.

Chapter Twenty-One

⚜

March 1986

HUNCHED, AS IF SUS-
pended in prayer, Wayne sat at Uncle Dead's work-
smooth tool-bench and sorted baseball cards, those
pasteboard gospels of boyhood. Buzzell's'd gotten in its
first shipment of the year, and he'd treated himself to a
thirty-six-pack box (sixteen cards and one stale, pink
tongue of gum per pack) along with his dietary staples:
Moxie, Cheerios, and Kraft macaroni and cheese.

Plucking a pack from the box, he slid his dirt-tipped
thumbnail along its wax-sealed seam, fussily unfolding
the wrapper as if changing a newborn's diaper. Plunking
the bubble gum on top of its own tottering, tooth-rotting

tower, he then, chonking on a jawbreaking wad the size of a chipmunk's head, dealt the cards by team, by division; he'd obsess them into alphabetical order later: Phil Niekro—Yankees, Kurt Bevacqua—Padres, Ed Jurak—Red Sox ("All right!"), Don Baylor—Yankees, Vern Ruhle—Indians, Charles Hudson—Phillies, Pete Rose—Reds, Andre Robertson—Yankees ("What's with all these friggin' Yankees?") and so on, until each pack was plundered, each of the 576 cards gentled into its place.

He'd forgotten how much he loved the slick, almost wet, feel of each wax-coated pack, the gum dust glazing the slippery cards, that baseball-season reek of pulp paper and Bazooka Joe.

Was a time when it seemed life couldn't have gone on without pulp paper. The pulp of cereal boxes and comic books and science-fiction magazines and Ace paperbacks (already yellowing in the drugstore book rack). Since he'd moved up to Uncle Dead's, he'd spent a good part of his days getting reacquainted with pulp—mashed, splintery lowlife of the paper world; had, without knowing, reached back for that keenness of childhood, that twelve-year-old's sense of wonder, that had deserted him somewhere between adolescence and adulthood.

Reading, burrowing, submerged in Uncle Dead's light-starved shed, Wayne devoured comic books—the Uncanny X-Men, the Incredible Hulk, and the Mighty Thor were his favorites—sometimes twenty and twenty-five at a sitting. And, better yet, he'd rediscovered fantasy and science-fiction magazines. He'd scared up a cobwebbed stash from the 1940s and 1950s stuffed in one of Dead's cabinets: spine-snapped, dog-eared copies of *Astounding* and *Galaxy*, *Fantastic* and *Unknown*, *If* and *Amazing*. Their browned, crumbling pages bursting with marvels and magic; stories by Heinlein and Van Vogt, Leiber and Sturgeon, Bradbury and Asimov . . . stories that, in a few flimsy pages, created undreamed-of worlds that never were and never would be, yet seemed more real, more plausible, than his own world of dark, shrinking rooms and not just diminished expectations, but no expectations.

After he put away his cards, stacking them in flush bricks next to his chronologically parked fleet of Matchbox and Hot Wheels cars, Wayne stretched out on the cot and scrutinized the raw-beamed ceiling. He couldn't tell you the day, the time, or even the month. He left the shack less and less: gangly, loping walks to Stain Thistle's garage and Buzzell's, midnight runs in the truck. Thought a lot about his great-uncles, Henry and Dead, though. Some nights, when he couldn't sleep, when the only light in the shed coiled from the glow of woodstove embers trapped in the truck's black paint, he imagined Henry and Dead appearing to him, taking form within the very walls. The whorled grain of the rough, slivered wood crackling, shifting and swirling, chipping and shaving, sculpting itself into the faces of his dead uncles, their stiff, wood-quilled lips quivering in pain and longing, but Wayne can't understand; all he hears is a sawmill whine, the shriek of riven wood.

A car door slammed down below. Wayne started, a ratcheting in his heart. A second door slammed, a solid American "chunk." He ran to the window; Auntie Leah always walked when she came by.

Sarah, Hannah and Auntie Leah idled in his aunt's dooryard, Hannah's shitbox Ford wagon floor-to-roofed with boxes; and even from up on the knoll, Wayne saw that his mother was pregnant, her body the shape of a summer squash. He gave them the eye, hawk-watched them like an old-fashioned Page paranoid. Christ! He hadn't seen his mother since the day Russ kicked him and Charlotte out of the house (hadn't seen Russ since his old man cursed him out that first day back in town), and he hadn't seen Hannah since before. But he hadn't even wondered about them, and that particular fact pleased him.

Gripping the rail, Sarah stumped up the steps and into the shack, while Hannah and Auntie Leah unloaded the car.

"What's this shit?" he sputtered to himself. " 's Hannah moving in? Can't no one leave me alone? That's all I friggin' need, Hannah living down the hill. Why don't she just move back in with Mom and Dad and leave me to hell alone?

"Damn it! Damn it! Damn it!"

With each box lugged inside, the more ticked Wayne got. They were stealing from him, his solitude and his silences, playing him for some damned Page man-fool. What was it with Page bitches, anyway?

Barefoot, flaunting black tee and cut-off dungarees

before the late winter cold, he banged open the shed door and stared down the hill, his arms folded too tight to his body—pinioned wings.

Leah tugged at Hannah's sleeve, pointed at Wayne. Her brother stood taller and skinnier than she remembered; in the watery midday sun, he looked like his own shadow.

Hannah waved, hollered, "Hi, Wayne!" and started for Uncle Dead's shed.

Wayne picked up a rock and whung it. Hannah skipped out of the way and retreated. Another sailed over the shack, while another hooked right, into the marsh.

"You cut that riggin' out right now, Wayne Britton!" Auntie Leah shouted. "What d'you think you are? A Seabrooker?!"

But the rocks kept coming—a wild, granite rain—thudding off Leah's shack and Hannah's Ford. The women fell back to the far side of the shack.

"That little bastard cracks my windshield, I'll murder him," Hannah said. "What's gotten into him, anyways?"

"He ain't been right since he moved up the hill," Leah said. "Can't barely get him to speak civil. Wished I never let him stay here . . . Look at him, running 'round like a chicken with its head chopped off."

"Well, one thing hasn't changed since we was kids. He still couldn't hit the broad side of a barn if his life depended on it."

"All's it takes is one lucky one."

The screen door screeked open, a long, elastic whine . . . pure childhood music to Hannah.

"What's all that racket?" Sarah asked.

"Momma . . ."

A rock ripped through the screen. Sarah heard it whistle past her face—"Oh!"—and she plumped to the steps.

Wayne stopped, arms jangling at his sides, rocks dropping from his loose hands. Nourished too long on fear and sorrow, he ached to walk down to them, to surrender his carefully cultivated garden of thorns and silence; but it was such a satisfactory garden in its dark, quiet way. He stood there for a few moments, a pitcher waiting for his manager to take him out of the game, then pivoted on his bare heel and sought the sad, bony arms of the shed.

So, Sarah thought, I've come back to Granite. *All the way back*. To Auntie's shack, to the marshy womb. To the rule and ruin of Nanna Page.

Wrapped in a quilt, she rocked next to the stove. The shack smelled of woodsmoke and nail polish—she and Hannah had painted each other's fingers and toes Pinprick Red before Hannah'd gone to bed—the polish's alcohol bite cutting through the musky woodsmoke. Sarah and Auntie Leah had painted each other, a rite of their barefoot summers. Summers of windows and doors flung wide, of barren heat-lightning convulsing on the horizon, of sleepless, sheet-soaked nights spent sprawled on the front steps, stalking midnight's secret breezes. Sarah shook her head, moved by the spirit of memory. She'd thought it gone forever, Page's Village. Had never imagined that her aunt had preserved the shack, the past, so faithfully: the grease-slick pots and pans; the mangy rugs and fraying curtains; the cracked windowpane over the sink; the faintest scent—to Sarah, the one, true smell of cleanliness—of Lysol and Lestoil; the north-sloping floor on which marbles rolled so well. She smiled, content that her baby would be born here, that Hannah had promised to stay until then.

Barely rocking, she drowsed, awakened only by the grunt of Uncle Dead's truck being wrenched into gear. How many years had it been since she'd heard that hateful, metal-on-metal shriek? Flinched at the passing of Uncle Dead's goddamned snapping truck? Dead had chased them in that truck—children, dogs, chickens—jouncing and squealing through the village, his stubbled, caved-in face set in what she recognized later (after Jenny) as a rapist's glutton grin. She refused to get up and watch the truck pass; hearing it was enough. She damned well knew what it looked like, and she didn't need to watch her son shame himself for a few bucks. Auntie Leah had told her about Wayne. Had let her know (without quite putting it into words) that Wayne, the truck and the whole deal was Sarah's problem to solve; she probably even would've lent Sarah the twenty-two—if she'd asked.

———

Wayne sharpened Dead's truck. Honed it beyond reason. Hadn't even cooled from the night's run, still ticked like a cartoon bomb, but he couldn't leave it be, fell on it: filing and grinding and keening, steel shavings corkscrewing to the floor in burred heaps. Scuttling from one razor edge to another, testing with fingertip and tongue, Wayne capered before his great-uncle's reawakened monster as if he were some kind of small-town, down-on-his-luck mad scientist and this the late show. And when Wayne finished, when his tools had been cleaned, oiled and put away so, he walked back to the truck, flirted with it before jabbing his index finger on the spearpoint of the front bumper. Holding his finger over the hood, he let one . . . two . . . three blooddrops plop onto the black steel, rubbing them in as if he were polishing the truck.

Sarah hadn't gotten within spitting distance of Uncle Dead's shed since the day she went to fetch her bicycle and found him mauling cousin Jenny. As she labored up Dead's hill, whispering back and forth with the ribby girl she'd been, she remembered how the muck sucked at her bare feet, the wasp warning her away from the shed, her uncle's awful slit-throat grin, the blood clotted on his penis. She supposed she had saved Jenny that day (whatever'd happened to Jenny? to all of them?) but she never imagined that, some thirty years later, Uncle Dead, killed nine years before Wayne was born, and his poison would somehow have leached into her son.

Legs achy, back aiming to buckle, she gained the
top of the knoll out of breath and lighted on Dead's
chopping block. She had climbed the hill meaning to
talk some sense into her son; she knew it would do no
good, but as Wayne's mother she was obliged to try.
But as she sat there, staring at that damn shed, she
shivered, suddenly chilled by the past, by what had gone
on in that shed. Sarah knew she could no more rap on
that shed, close her hand once again around that toothy
door handle, than bring Nanna back from the dead. She
refused to disturb Uncle Dead one more time, not with
a baby swimming in her belly.

Besides, Sarah had watched Nanna seal that shed,
nail shut the windows and doors, gob on the red and
black paint, plant the thornbushes. And Nanna's will,
Nanna's magic, still veined Page's Village; Sarah
wouldn't deny her—not in that place, anyways. Especially not there.

If Wayne wanted to see his mother, he knew where
to find her. Sarah sighed and walked back down the
hill.

"Full moon tonight, Wayne-o," Stain Thistle said. "That
okay?"

"Be tit," Wayne said.

"How those logging trails holding up, anyways? You
ain't gonna get stuck or nothing are you?"

"Most the snow's melt, but ground ain't unlocked
yet. Trails drive okay. I'll be all right."

"You've been doing good, Wayne."

"Thanks."

"What would you think of a raise?"

"Be fine," said Wayne, who'd never gotten a raise in his life; he'd been docked and screwed out of his pay plenty, but a raise?

"Starting with tonight's run you'll be getting another twenty-five bucks."

Wayne nodded.

"You been wearing all that protective shit and stuff, right?" Stain asked. "I don't want you getting sick and all on me."

"Yup," Wayne lied.

"Good worker's hard to find nowadays."

The phone rang, twice as loud as need be—"Yeah, Thistle"—and Wayne was dismissed.

"Momma, we gotta do something. I seen Wayne coming out of that Stain Thistle's garage again today."

Hannah'd just come home from work; Russ'd gotten her in up to the chenille shop (hadn't told her about Charlotte, though).

"We can't just sit around and keep letting him dump that shit and poison down back," said Hannah, lighting a Virginia Slim. "We ought to call the cops on him."

"Ain't calling no goddamned police," said Sarah, wrinkling her nose at the cigarette. "This is family. Ain't none their business."

"Well, what're we gonna do, Momma?"

"I'll take care of it."

Hannah had been all set to argue with her mother,

but, ambushed by the granite in Sarah's words, she fell silent: She'd never heard such strength and conviction in Sarah's voice before. It made her both proud and wary.

"I'm going out," said Sarah, pulling on her coat. "Don't know when I'll get back. There's some leftover beef stew in the icebox."

Hannah remembered the last time her mother'd decided to take a walk: "Where're you going, Momma? I'll give you a ride. I'm going up to the university anyway."

"Rather walk. Pregnant woman needs all the exercise she can get."

Where had this sudden forcefulness come from, Hannah wondered. Sarah's healing had been gradual back in Choate's Junction; it had been a struggle even to find the old balance. But, somehow, the alignment of Hannah's own breakdown, the coming baby, and the move back to Granite had stirred Sarah, pushed her, maybe, toward being the woman she had been meant to be. For the first time since Hannah could remember, Sarah acted as if she was the mother and Hannah the daughter. Sarah didn't *need* her anymore, Hannah realized; she was free.

"Be careful," Hannah said.

"Don't worry," Sarah said.

Wasn't but two miles to Russ's house, *her house*, and Sarah was grateful to be tramping the back roads in the fresh March chill, that treacherous time of year when the air trembles with spring, but the ground's still froze;

when a seventy-degree blessing can be dogged by a blizzard; and, when all is said and done, there's still the hip-deep mud and the suffocating cloudlets of black flies to be reckoned with.

She'd fled Russ (more her old life than Russ; poor Russ'd simply been standing in the doorway as she'd barreled through on her way out of town) on foot; she liked the idea of coming back walking. She couldn't say what remained of her marriage. Hadn't thought much about it. Russ, yes. Her marriage, no. Her marriage to Russ had offered the woman she'd been consolation; what it offered now, she didn't know. Today, she meant to ask Russ a favor. After that . . . ?

She paused at the "Slow — Children" sign, a sentinel whose day had come and gone, which stood watch in the elbow of the sharp curve that swept cars past the house; their days and nights had been punctuated by the rubber squeals of cars misjudging that curve. The school-bus-yellow sign, with its ball-chasing boy standing out in stark relief, nearly got Sarah crying. The sign spoke to her of loss. There were no more children to protect, merely phantoms of childhoods spent, never to be recovered. The rowdy Gregory brood, down toward the mill, had grown up and gone away; same with the Linenthal kids; good kids, all of them. Her children, too. But the sign, repainted by the town every year the first week of June, remained; she would've felt better if the sign, its duty fulfilled, had been left to rust or had been nailed flat by one of those curve-screeching cars it had been put up to slow. How many of those signs guarded now-childless enclaves, reminding those left behind of their loss?

"Slow — Children," Sarah whispered. "Should say: 'No — Children.'"

Warm, yellow light spilled from the house and into the twilight like fresh-planed wood shavings. Sarah smiled. There was nothing more inviting than a well-lit house at dusk on a chilly night; and damn if she didn't smell biscuits baking.

"Russ must be getting adventurous," she said.

Not noticing that Russ's car was gone, she scuffled into the driveway, prickling at the prospect of seeing her house again, of seeing her husband. She didn't know whether to knock before walking in. It was *her* house, after all, but she had been away. . . . She knocked lightly, as if she didn't mean it, the curtained window hardly rattling. Charlotte answered the door.

The two women, unflinching, stared. First the faces (Charlotte's had softened since the summer before; Sarah's had razored up), then the stomachs. Charlotte was pregnant, too; judging by the look on Charlotte's face, Russ had more than biscuits in the oven.

Sarah sighed, but almost amused, surprised there were no tears to stanch. Just what had she been thinking that day she lit out for Banks in search of Baby Jessie? Finders keepers, she thought, losers weepers.

Clearing her throat of all the questions she really wanted to ask, Sarah said: "Is Russ home?"

"He ain't here," Charlotte answered.

"I come to ask him a favor"—blocking the doorway, Charlotte gave no sign she meant to move—"but I can ask you. I want to borrow the Crown Seven. The stock car."

Charlotte squinched her eyes as if she didn't recognize her, the skin between her eyebrows bunching like the top folds of a curtain.

"I'm still his wife, Charlotte. No matter what all else has happened, I'm still married to Russ Britton."

Letting Sarah wait on the step, Charlotte went into the bedroom as if it were hers and returned with the key. "Shed's open," she said.

"Thanks, Charlotte. . . . Those biscuits sure smell good."

Fidgeting, a little girl who has to go pee, Charlotte nodded; but Sarah wasn't finished.

Snaring Charlotte's eyes, Sarah spoke, her words as sharp as Uncle Dead's truck: "I miss that baby something fierce, Charlotte. Something fierce. And I know you do, too. Don't try to tell me no different. And when I found that baby, and knew I didn't have it in me to steal her back, I saw no point in coming home, in coming back to Granite. Saw no point in nothing at all."

Charlotte shook her head, moved her lips, but the words stuck in her throat; the first few tears, morning dew hanging from barbwire, slipped free.

"You tell Russ I was here."

Charlotte watching, Sarah disappeared into the shed's dusk and slid into the Crown Seven, thankful that it no longer had a door. It started on the first try, a dry rumble, and she let it warm, the Pontiac's familiar racing smells making her ache some for the man Russ had been when they first married.

About to pull out of the driveway and into the moon-shocked night, she saw Russ's Dart slow, the flicker of its right directional. But when Russ Britton saw it was Sarah driving the Crown Seven, he swerved around the stock and back onto the road, stepping on it. But even then, savage gusts pounding in her chest as her husband ran from her, Sarah still refused to cry, refused to seek the refuge of water.

The full moon, hard and glittery as Nanna Page's eyes, ruled the night-blue sky. Wayne smirked at its cold menace, its pale rays slicing through the winter-raped woods and jigging on the truck's shiny black paint. The death-brimmed steel drums muttering in the back, he imagined hauling his load to the center of town, cracking the bungs on each drum, and then cruising up and down the Plains, letting his liquid skull-and-crossbones ooze where it might, March coming in like a fucking rabid lion for those cock-knockin', center-of-town colonials.

"Wouldn't those highfalutin' pricks be in for a shock?" he said. "And wouldn't they figure out in a fuckin' hurry who d'it. Keep dumping down backa Page's Village, no one'd stop me in a hundred friggin' years."

Giving the copperhead skeleton a backhand cuff, he laughed; these midnight runs were *so damn easy.* Free money. Right out of Stain Thistle's big-ass pockets.

Shedding the woods he slowed, creaked to Route 49 before bolting across and into the village. He was about halfway down the hill before he saw that the road was blocked where it forked at Auntie Leah's place: "Aw shit!"

The truck shuddered to a stop at the Crown Seven, sitting crossways in the road, and Wayne got out in true amazement. He hadn't thought of the Crown Seven in years.

"Hi, Wayne."

He flinched, saw his mother walking down from Auntie Leah's. "You put this here?" he asked. "You?"

"That's right, Wayne."

"Christ, Ma. I could've got killed or something I didn't see that thing."

"Night bright as this, Wayne, you would've needed to be blind or numb not to see it."

Arms folded against the cold, Sarah leaned on the stock car. Wayne stood in front of the truck.

"What you got in the truck, Wayne?" Sarah asked.

Wayne shrugged.

" 's all you can do? Shrug?"

He shrugged again, thinking it would've been better to get caught by the town cops than by his mother.

"Don't you know nothing?" Sarah said. "Don't you understand anything?"

"Come on, Ma," he said. "Don't go getting all upset and stuff. The baby."

"You break into Uncle Dead's shed, knowing damn

well it was Nanna Page shut it up. You get that hateful truck running. And then you start dumping poison down back. What's wrong with you?"

"Weren't that much, Ma."

"Weren't that much? Don't you know what this place is? Don't you know what it means to us? This is ours. This is Page's Village. Our people have been here since the 1600s. This is Nanna Page and every other Page that come before her and after her. It's me and it's you. This is all we got. This is it. And you go shitting on it, like some wild animal."

"Lot of good it's done us."

"Don't you get huffy with me. Don't you dare."

"What'm I supposed to do, Ma? I'm getting paid good money do this job."

"You're something, Wayne. Really something. A baby seller, a midnight dumper, and Nanna knows what all else."

"Lay off, Ma."

After all those years of being the sweet, quiet victim, it felt so good, so right, to draw blood that Sarah seemed to forget it was her own son she was preying on; like Nanna, she sniffed his weakness and went for the throat. A woman owed.

"Just how much money did you get for that poor little baby, Wayne? Pretty penny, I bet."

"Shut up!"

"How much!"

"*Leave me alone!*"

Wayne slammed the stock of the truck-mounted

shotgun (*that Uncle Dead was a prick, wasn't he?*) and there was an explosion and smoke and his ears were ringing. He thought he heard his mother scream.

"Ma! Ma! Aw Christ, Ma!"

Tears streaming, Wayne stumbled against the truck, sliced his calf.

"Ma! Where are you, Ma!"

"I'm all right, Wayne," said Sarah, getting up from behind the stock car.

His mother's voice, calm, even, sensible, brought Wayne up short. "Oh Christ, Ma. I thought I'd killed you or something."

I thought you had, too, Sarah thought before she said, "Scared me is all."

"I'm sorry, Ma. Don't know how many times I screwed with that gun. All's it ever did was dry-fire. Thought it was broke."

Still making excuses, she thought. Always making excuses, her son. She said: "Wayne, we got to talk. There's a lot going on you need to know about."

He nodded, sniffling.

"Hannah's out. Visiting up to the university. Why don't you just follow me to Auntie's."

" 'kay, Ma."

Sarah grunted into the stock car, started it, and guided it up to the shack. Seething in Uncle Dead's truck, Wayne hadn't made a move. He'd just told his mother he'd follow her, but he'd given his word to Stain Thistle, too; the money and the steel drums gnawed at him.

"Fuck it," he said, gunning the truck toward Cedar Swamp.

Wheeling the Crown Seven around, Sarah, her face gone granite, gave chase.

Uncle Dead's truck and the Pontiac roared through the moon-silvered night woods. Rare, dark beasts ripped from the past, reborn to duel in this one last race, urged on only by the witchy moon.

Growling, snapping, the Crown Seven dogged Dead's truck, but Wayne refused to give in, wouldn't let his mother, *his pregnant mother*, pass or ease him into the puckerbrush. Couldn't say why he was running, but right then it seemed more important than life itself that he ditch his mother and dump his load. He supposed that the smartest thing he could do was pull over, leave the truck and steel drums to rot in hell, and hitch a ride with his mother: "Fuck that shit."

Pregnant stomach wedged between steering wheel and bucket seat, Sarah knew exactly why she chased Wayne. She wanted him, for once, to be held accountable, to face up to what he'd done. And maybe, just maybe, she was helling like a madwoman through the quarry woods to seek her own redemption; when it came to her children, her family, she cringed at how much had been sacrificed on the altar of her depression; if Wayne could be saved (again), she would do it.

As they sizzled through the woods, bumping and shuddering, she did wish she were chasing anything but Dead's truck. Seemed to her that it represented all the brutal wrongs of her childhood that had haunted her into adulthood. Wayne jammed on the brakes, Sarah slaloming to keep from rear-ending him, then sped off. Sarah whacked her head on the roof, and the steering wheel knocked the wind out of her; she suddenly wondered how many women had gone into labor while driving a stock car.

Righting the stock, she remembered the wind-frenzied November day she'd saved Wayne from the quarry, had, in snatching him from the black water, saved her own life, too; she realized they were near that quarry, her quarry. Moonlight licked steel up ahead, and Sarah floored it.

Looking back over his shoulder, Wayne saw the Crown Seven, strong and relentless, once again bearing down; his mother wasn't taking no for an answer.

"Shit," Wayne muttered, disgusted with himself. This was turning into a classic Wayne Britton screw-up: collared in the woods, while carting hazardous waste, *by his mother*. "You asshole," he said to himself. He figured that the only way he was going to get out of this was by wracking up the Crown Seven (without, he hoped, hurting his mother).

He jumped the brakes again, but this time the stock skidded into the barbwire leer of Dead's truck—"Hey!" Wayne shouted—the Pontiac's grill snagging on a couple of the meat hooks hanging from the tailgate, convulsing the two vehicles into an old-fashioned Dee-troit waltz. Still, the stock humping the truck, Wayne wouldn't stop; instead, he sped up. Trying to untangle, Sarah braked, tapped the gas; braked, tapped.

Sarah's quarry, that black, weeping sore of her childhood, now lay a quarter-mile away. Straight shot. Sarah knew. Wayne knew, too—he'd dumped more than Great-uncle Henry there. Shamed or no, Wayne decided to quit playing games. He let off the gas just as Sarah braked and tapped one more time.

The Crown Seven didn't respond when she took her foot off the gas. And the stock car, accelerating, rode Uncle Dead's truck toward Sarah's quarry. The Crown's throttle had stuck, gas pedal flush to the floor, just as it had some twenty years before.

Stomach keeping her from bending down and pulling on the accelerator with her hands, Sarah jabbed and pried with her feet, finally kicking hell out of it like some grammar-school girl in a schoolyard brawl. Wouldn't budge. (*All she could see was four-year-old Wayne poised at the quarry brink, her desperate hand grabbing for him.*) "Oh, God, no!" Sarah pleaded.

Steel screeched, sparks spewed, rubber shredded, steel drums bounced out of the truck and spilled open; something, somewhere, was on fire.

"What the fuck!" said Wayne, hitting the brakes, trying to get free. Still, the stock bullied the truck, which'd ended up being all fang and no balls. But, drawing on all his imagined cunning and weasel-wisdom, Wayne took a deep breath and tightened his grip on the steering wheel; damned if he was going to give up that truck, not after all he went through to get it.

The quarry yawed, an ancient, black mouth in the night woods. The Crown Seven bellowed. Uncle Dead's truck screamed bloody murder.

Was a time Sarah had craved that black water, had ached for it the way she'd once ached for Russ; it had flowed in her veins, coursed through the heart-rivers of Page's Village. Black water, relentless, deep and cold and turned to stone, in which only Nanna Page could wade safe. And, still, it whispered to her, nudged her toward deep silences. . . . Sarah banged on the brakes one more time, not that it did much good, and rolled from the Crown Seven onto the unforgiving March earth, her arms and body curled tight around her blooming belly.

As Sarah braked, Wayne had wrenched Uncle Dead's truck hard left, spinning sideways and free of the stock car. The truck gasped and quivered at the quarry lip, and when Wayne rammed it into gear, it coughed and stalled.

The Crown Seven, driverless, shrieking like a burning woman, kept coming, freight-trained the truck, a textbook T-bone, the Pontiac mauling Dead's legacy as both car and truck, grappling, plummeted into the hissing black water.

Wayne Britton never had a chance.

Epilogue

✿

Sarah:
July 1991

RAIN — FIRM-HAND-
shake rain—fell with dusk. Steady and sizzling, spat-
tering the leaves, drumming its fingers on the roof. A
rebuke to the day's breath-stealing heat.

Inhaling the damp perfume of the cleansing shower,
that summer-sweet smell of contentment, Sarah rested
in Nanna Page's rocker at the screen door of Auntie
Leah's place; Sarah's place now, actually, her aunt having sold her town shack (as she called it) and built down
back of Page's Village; but Sarah would always think
of it as her aunt's. The pure moan of a train whistle,
amplified in the rain, rose over Cedar Swamp and

blanketed the village; the Boston & Maine clacking north, wheels thrumming—steel rain. Up above, on Route 49, the Friday-night tourist traffic hissed by, surging north through Granite. Sarah chewed on a piece of pine gum; it tasted of childhood's bitterness.

Holding hands as sisters will, Sarah's five-year-old, Page, and Charlotte's Winona sat on the floor, thrilling to the color plates buried like ancient treasure in Hannah's ratty, one-volume encyclopedia; Sarah still remembered the day Grandpa Elgar scavenged it from the town dump, remembered the hateful afternoon it became Hannah's. She smiled at the thought of Hannah and glanced at the letter, read a good half-dozen times, that lay on the kitchen table; Hannah was coming home to visit in two weeks.

"Nanna!" Winona said to Sarah. "Look at these pictures! There's all kinds of bugs and things, and a bunch of sting-bees! *Sting-bees!*"

Russ and Charlotte had gone up to the White Mountains for the weekend, and Sarah had agreed to watch their girls, Page's half-sisters, Winona and Baby Nan. Did the sisters good to spend time together.

"I like the planets best," Page said. "Just like big-sister Hannah. Right, Momma? Right?"

"I miss Hannah lots, Nanna," Winona said. "When she coming home again?"

"Just two weeks, 'nona," Sarah said. "Two weeks."

It made Sarah flush whenever Winona called her Nanna. It was a name to live up to. And Sarah, who was once and for all a Page (having shed her Britton and Huckins names like dead skin), wasn't convinced she was equal to it.

At bedtime, Sarah told the girls the story of how Nanna Page went berrying in the marsh once upon a time, and ended up with a snake in her mitts and a baby snapper muckled ahold of her boot; the girls were fast asleep by the time the turtle and the boot together tested the limits of gravity.

Sarah Page—Nanna Page—slips into the rain-lush night, floats down the puddled, time-hollowed steps, and lifts her face to the wet, the tears of the past returned to earth, seining for whatever small truths may catch in her modest nets: *Wayne . . . Baby Jessie . . . cousin Jenny . . . Ella Huckins . . . Heidi Meeks . . . Chaney Huckins . . .*

The baby cries, a squalling counterpoint to the gentling storm. Sarah strides into the shack and scoops up Charlotte's Nan, not yet four months old.

She cradles the squowling baby to her chest as they settle into the rocker, Nanna Page's enduring oak lap, and rock down the generations.